THE EX EFFECT

DANA HAWKINS

Storm
PUBLISHING

Ebook ISBN: 978-1-83700-057-9
Paperback ISBN: 978-1-83700-059-3

Cover design by Rachel Lawston
Cover illustration © Rachel Lawston

Published by Storm Publishing.
For further information, visit:
www.stormpublishing.co

ALSO BY DANA HAWKINS

Not in the Plan

In Walked Trouble

So Not My Type

Any Girl But You

I Will Always Love You (Maybe)

To My Forever. You are my happily ever after.

ONE
MORGAN

"Everything was *tight*."

If a more perfect review headline existed, I wasn't sure what it would be. Maybe everything was "pristine"? Or, a personal favorite, "perfect." I reread the review on my cell, savoring the callouts to "Morgan Rose's structure, attention to detail, and clearly defined schedule." That last comment was an endorphin-filled arrow striking me directly in the heart. Schedules had always been my best friend, providing the calm and comfort I craved but didn't receive from others. Warmth filled me, starting at my toes and landing directly in my soul, and I swear if I didn't just plan this woman's wedding, I might drop on one knee and propose myself.

I tapped off the phone and tossed it in my purse. I took a few moments to breathe in and out, begging my brain to give me just one tiny moment of reprieve before I started down my daily "what if" thought track.

In the wedding-planner business, reviews are everything. It only takes one disgruntled Bridezilla to tank a business. And ever since Dreams Wedding and Event Planning Services moved into the neighboring town of Duluth, Minnesota, three years ago—undercutting prices and offering things like a full staff, a beautiful showroom, with cucumber-infused water and miniature Belgian chocolates upon entry (*yes, of course, I scoped out the place*)—I needed every positive review I could get.

Although I couldn't admit it to anyone quite yet, because I barely accepted it myself, my business dangled by a thread. Dreams had done the same as a few chain restaurants and a big department store—stormed into our community and elbowed out the ma-and-pa shops that our town thrived on. Including mine. For years, spring and summer was my busy season. I was booked almost every weekend from May through September. But this season, none. Not a single wedding besides Olivia's.

Right now, I had just enough money saved to pull me through until the fall, and then I was done. My business absolutely could not survive on the scraps. And if that happened, I'd have to choke down the last of my pride and join my family's home-improvement business—which I wanted to do about as much as a Pap smear.

The thought of closing the doors on my business after a decade of blood, sweat, and tears (*literally*, although, except for the unfortunate Henderson wedding, the blood was normally minor), and sacrificing my personal life for success, made me want to throw up into my favorite Jimmy Choo pumps. Which was exactly why last week I did the unthinkable—I accepted a client with an impossible deadline: ninety days.

Now, ninety days would be tricky, but not impossible, for a destination wedding or a small backyard affair. But this bride, Olivia, wanted the quintessential traditional wedding with multi-tiered cake, several hundred people, a full wedding party, and made a joke about trying to book Miley Cyrus for the reception. At least, I hoped it was a joke, but at this point, I really wasn't sure.

Thankfully, I loved a challenge. Next to immaculate spreadsheets and the joys of punctuality, challenges were damn near delightful. But *this*? Ninety days was nearly impossible. Every venue, DJ, caterer, officiant, and photographer would be booked by now. After the anxiety of the timeline had rendered me silent during our consultation—a rarity—Olivia quickly slipped in two magical phrases. One, "I heard you were the best." *Swoon.* And two, "I'll, of course, pay a rush fee."

And... sold.

Truthfully, though, she could've asked for the graduating ballerina class at Juilliard, and I would have done just about anything to make it work. Olivia's wedding was a life preserver for my company, and I'd grip on to this gift. If I couldn't make her wedding work, I would close up shop. End of story.

I tugged on my peacoat, checked the large wood-framed mirror next to the front door, and frowned. The last hair stylist took a half inch too much off my perfectly respectable inverted chin-length bob, and I verged dangerously on having the Karen-cut. But, because every interaction was a potential client, I'd swallowed back my fury and spent the last week straightening my blonde locks within an inch of their life to create more length.

The front porch step creaked under my wedge ankle books. "Oof." The spring northern Minnesota air was crisper than yesterday and a trace of the fresh mineral scent from Lake Superior wafted to my nose. I snugged my collar, hopped into the car, and typed out the address to a venue thirty minutes outside of Duluth.

I waved to a neighbor walking their husky and turned down the street to drive near Lake Superior. Even though I'd lived in Spring Harbors my entire life, when I saw the tranquil, expansive water, my insides instantly settled.

This last week, I learned a few key details about Olivia. At first, I couldn't understand the rush for her to get married in three months. Then she explained her stepfather had recently been diagnosed with a terminal illness, and it was important to her that he walked her down the aisle. Also, she was a medical student at the University of Minnesota Duluth with limited time, had wealthy parents who were footing the bill, and zero creative vision of what she wanted for her wedding. "Just give me something to react to and I'll decide."

Thankfully, Olivia had surprised me with one life-saving detail: Her fiancé, Tommy, had access to a photographer, some friend of the family—Frankie Lee—who was available on short notice to take their wedding pictures. *Thank God*, I'd thought. With this short leeway, the only people available would be a high school senior dabbling with a cheap camera and no concept of lighting. Last week, I'd messaged Frankie to see if he wanted to scope out a venue with me and was pleasantly surprised when he agreed.

After rolling to a stop sign, I typed a quick message to Frankie.

MORGAN:

Hi, just making sure we're still meeting in an hour at Woodlands?

FRANKIE:

Yep

MORGAN:

Great. I'll wait outside for you, and we can go in together. Looking forward to meeting you!

FRANKIE:

Cool

Whatever. This dude was clearly not one for conversation, but would it kill him to be a smidge friendlier? Ultimately, as long as he wasn't a complete misogynistic jerk, I could work with him. These last few days, I'd had roughly two seconds to check out some photos on his website, and they were *stunning*. Landscapes, architecture, and lots of older homes.

The website did not, however, include any wedding photos, at least not that I had seen, which created a Lake Superior-size red flag. I pushed through the nerves and indulged in my extremely valuable poker chip: I didn't recommend him. If funky angles, terrible shadows, or edits went sideways—the heat was off me.

Thirty minutes later, I shook out my cramping hands from unknowingly holding the steering wheel too tight. *Breathe.* This place *had* to work. Finding a venue three months before a wedding was damn near impossible. I'd given it a go, of course, and discovered that every single location within a two-hour drive was booked. Yesterday, I went to the second-to-last place on the list—a church basement fifty miles south of Duluth. I should've known that the place would be disastrous after the church secretary not only said they had availability in August, but also waived the requirement that the couple had to be a church member to use its facilities. I was in and out of that place in under ten minutes.

Woodlands was only available because the place recently changed owners, and the new owner wanted to host events. They hadn't been planning on opening until Christmas, but I'd slap on whatever smile, charm, and elbow grease was needed to make the space work.

My car bumped over the deep pits on the gravel road leading up to the venue. Trees and foliage surrounded me, the unkempt grass spilled onto the path. I pushed my car into park and blew out a low whistle. The place was... *okay.* At very, very best. It looked like a million other former supper clubs turned into diners spread across the Midwest. Cracked wood siding, a low ceiling, windows that needed a solid cleaning, and a flickering diner sign that was a shade too neon.

But, with the right decorations and lighting, I could make this place damn near charming. Possibly. *Hopefully.* Large potted plants, greenery, and strings of white lights could transform almost any area.

The car shook as I cut my engine, and I refrained from making the sign of the cross in gratitude. I was overdue taking it into the shop, but every time I went there, I was out a thousand dollars. This baby was inching toward a hundred and fifty thousand miles, and the last thing I needed was to drop a bunch of cash that I didn't have.

Outside, the brisk air prickled my neck. I wrapped my scarf tighter and surveyed the space. The property was large enough, with a massive gravel parking lot, an abundance of No Smoking signs, a wooden fence, and a few scattered, cracked wood picnic benches nestled among the trees. The constriction in my chest loosened.

I peeked at my watch and as quickly as the tension had softened, it now hardened again. Ten minutes ahead of time was standard, and this Frankie guy was not here. My foot involuntarily tapped against the earth. Two minutes passed, then three. *Unbelievable.* I drummed my fingers on my crossed arms. At the four-minute mark, I marched into the restaurant with a huff.

The door weighed as much as a linebacker, and I heaved it open with two hands. The small entryway had a rubber mat over linoleum, low ceilings, and an odd hodgepodge of artwork that gave off the distinct vibe that the owner went to various garage sales and grabbed anything with a wooden frame. Horses, bears drinking pop, a beach scene, two hot-air balloons, and one really large creepy, crying clown with smudged makeup. *Yikes.* Brown round tables held napkins, ketchup, and mustard in a carrying tray, with stiff metal chairs shoved up to the edge.

The distinct smell of fryer grease and disinfectant from a freshly mopped floor reached my nose. Other than a few women at a table laughing, the place was empty. And eerily quiet. No music, no clanking dishes from customers, nothing.

I stepped to the hostess stand and waited. And waited some more.

The hostess's legs dangled from a bar stool as she swiped through her phone. She either didn't notice or didn't care that I had entered, and I wasn't sure which one was worse. My dad used to say I had a long list of good traits—smart, organized, driven. Patience was *not* on the list. Five agonizing seconds passed when I cleared my throat. "Excuse me." *Ugh*. My tone. I hated the way I sounded, but every second mattered and at this rate this wedding would be a complete disaster if they didn't hurry the hell up. I breathed out through my nose and softened my jaw. "I have an appointment with the manager."

"All right." The hostess peeled herself from her screen and dropped her legs to the floor. "I'll let her know, but it'll be a few minutes. You can wait here or outside, or wherever."

After she shuffled into the back room, I stepped back outside. A wretched, god-awful sound like a muffler fell off an old car boomed so loud through the open land that it shook the fragile diner windows. Dust swooshed through the air like a tornado as the Harley driver pulled into a spot and killed the engine.

Jesus Christ, this guy. Really? *Obnoxious*. I'd always hated motorcycles. They were loud, dangerous, and most likely part of some nefarious criminal organization. Although, I could admit that stereotype probably stemmed from my odd fascination with the biker show *Sons of Anarchy*.

Was this person really wearing chaps? Actual chaps. The last time I saw that was when I had the extreme misfortune of attending a friend's bachelorette party where we went to a male strip club in Minneapolis and tossed dollars to men in thongs. Sure, I'm gay as hell, but I could not fathom why these women screamed and cheered at men dangling their junk and gyrating on the floor. *Gross*.

I shielded my eyes against the sun. Was this Frankie? The guy hopped off his motorcycle and—

Oops. Facing me was slim hips, strong forearms, broad shoulders, and boobs. Definite, full boobs. Okay, not a guy, or, at least, not male presenting. And damn it, I knew better than to assume gender. Or anything, for that matter. Sure, I may look like the local PTA mom with my cute puffy-sleeved bow shirts and on-point makeup, but people asking if I have a husband annoys the crap out of me.

The person hung their helmet on the bike bar and ran a finger through their dark fringe. They tugged off their riding gloves, shoved them in their back pocket, and stepped toward me.

My breath froze.

No. No... this can't be right. I blinked at the image. The unmistakable dark chocolate-brown eyes now had soft laugh lines creasing from the sides. The once overly plucked black brows were now full, natural, and thick. Formerly round cheeks still had deep, devastating dimples, but the shape had shifted, the cheekbones more prominent, sharper, and higher. The lashes were still so long they nearly reached her eyebrows. The long dark hair often swept into a ponytail for soccer practice was now short and cropped on the sides.

Flashes of *that* night, the last time we spoke, pixelated through my mind. High school graduation gowns. Tears streaming down cheeks. Nasty words flung, more cries, and stomps. And my heart shattering.

Fifteen years flew by in a snap.

"Katey?" I finally spit out.

"I go by Frankie now." Katey—Frankie—tugged on the cuffs of her brown leather coat.

What in the actual hell was happening right now? I was in a weird dream. That was the only explanation. In ten seconds, alarm number one, followed by alarm number two, would blare and I'd jolt from the bed. *"You're* Frankie Lee? The photographer?"

When Katey—Frankie—left all those years ago, she was chasing the dream of being a photographer in New York City. And she did it, at least as far as I knew. After four years of loving her, and a lifetime prior of being best friends, Frankie left me and didn't turn back. Not once, not even a call, like I meant *nothing*.

Frankie stood before me, her eyes holding that same devilish glint that had captivated me years ago, the same one that had broken my heart when she abandoned me.

"Sure am." Frankie lifted her head in a quick nod. "Good to see you again, Morgan. Been, what... fourteen, fifteen years?"

I could feel my nostrils flare. The ticking of my heart moved from my chest to my ears, and I needed to rip off my scarf before I overheated. I slammed my arms across my chest and blurted the first thing that came to my mind: "Not long enough."

TWO
FRANKIE

Yes, I knew Morgan was the wedding coordinator for the son of a family friend, Tommy, and his fiancée, Olivia. Was it a dick move to not give her any sort of heads-up on who I was on our text message exchanges? Probably. The situation was going to be awkward as hell, regardless. At least this way I could have some control, before I most likely lost it for the next few months. Besides, much as I'd suspected, it was delicious seeing Morgan's surprised, then extremely irritated, face.

But, *Christ*, Morgan had aged well. She looked almost identical to when she was a senior, besides swapping the long, curly, blonde hair for a sleek, straight bob. I was taller, but now Morgan's platforms made her nearly eye to eye with me. The crispness of her sharp, Caribbean-blue eyes somehow was deeper, more vibrant, more nuanced than I remembered, layered with specks of turquoise and cobalt.

"What in the hell are you doing here?" Morgan dropped her hands to her curvy, full hips.

One thing that clearly hadn't changed—Morgan's salty attitude.

"*Pumpkin.*" I grinned and shoved the motorcycle keys in my pocket. "Is that any way to treat an old friend?"

A heated, red flare shot straight to Morgan's cheeks, which was the exact reaction I was hoping for. After how she treated me all those years ago, the last thing I needed to do was to make any of this easier on her.

"We are *not* friends," Morgan hissed.

Damn. Wow. Ain't no grudge like a Morgan Rose grudge. No matter, though. I was only here through the summer and not one moment longer. My life was back in New York, and my dream dangled so close I could smell it. I could handle Morgan's bullshit until after Tommy was married, then go back to living my cozy life in lower Manhattan. "I thought Olivia sent you the info. I just assumed you knew I was Frankie."

Morgan dug a heel into the ground. "How the hell could I have possibly assumed you were *Frankie?* The last time we spoke, you were eighteen-year-old Katey Lee."

Fair point. Not that I'd say that and give Morgan the satisfaction. Morgan had not earned the right to hear my story of how in my early twenties I went on a deep exploration to find my authentic self, which included shaving my head and changing my name.

The way Morgan left that night at graduation, breaking my heart and tossing me like I was trash, had scarred me. Sure, the scar had faded over the years, lightened with other loves and life experiences, but it never fully healed. In a moment, Morgan showed me she thought the same as everyone else—I was an unfocused fuckup.

Now, seeing Morgan's face again, something tugged in my chest. Yeah, sure, I social media stalked her a little throughout the years. But the pictures Morgan posted were minimal, mostly of venues or updates on her business. No shots of her shooting tequila from a balcony. No fun beach photos. No spouse, partner, or significant other. Not that I cared. At all.

Morgan dropped her hands and waved to the door. "Well, we better get inside since you're late."

Just like old times. *Cool.* Morgan clearly still held that obsession for being early and loved to rub it in my face that my life didn't revolve around clocks. I was surprised she hadn't lightened up over the years, but her ultra-rigid spine was a dead giveaway.

I kicked a small rock out of the way with my riding boots and checked my watch. "I'm literally right on time."

"Which is late." Morgan spun on her heels and stomped to the door.

This should be fun. I held the door for her, and she breezed past without even a simple thank-you, trailed by a vanilla rose scent. Apparently, other things also did not change. That scent snapped me back fifteen years to the first time I was closest to that fragrance... shivering outside under the stars, not from the cold, but from doing things I'd only talked about. I quickly blinked away the memories. Nothing good could possibly come from reliving any of that time.

The venue was fine enough, I supposed, but it probably wouldn't work. Over the years, I'd met Olivia only a handful of times, on the rare occasions when I succumbed to the time-honored Lee family tradition of piling on the guilt until I caved and flew into town for a holiday. During those times, I'd sneak away from the inevitable family drama and visit with Tommy's mom, a neighbor, a woman who'd always treated me with more respect than my own mom. A few of those times Olivia had been there with expensive wine bottles and cashmere sweaters. All signs indicated her tastes were more extravagant than what this place could handle without a complete remodel.

Morgan marched up to the hostess stand. "Hi. Still waiting for the manager."

Yikes. The words were friendly enough, but the delivery was like lemon juice on a stab wound. Thankfully, the hostess looked more bored than offended. She shoved her phone in her back pocket and pointed to a table. "Just grab a table wherever. Want something to drink?"

"Water's fine." Morgan crossed the room to a corner booth without glancing back at me. She dropped her purse with a heavier *thunk* than was needed and pulled out her phone.

Whatever. I wasn't sure why I was slightly disappointed. Sure, it had been years since we'd seen each other, and yes, that last moment was pretty terrible, but I really thought Morgan would say something after the shock of seeing me wore off.

I slid into the booth and pulled out my phone but forced myself to not check emails. For the last two weeks, I'd been refreshing like a maniac, even though they told me no news would arrive for at least six to eight weeks.

But still... maybe one little refresh wouldn't hurt.

As soon as I clicked it, the dopamine jolt flew up then plummeted with no new messages besides a notification for a health insurance auto-payment. I had to stop the obsessive clicking, but after landing an interview and a request for a portfolio submission from *Birch & Willow* magazine, I couldn't stop.

Professional photographers had different dreams. Some wanted to work at *Vogue.* Some, *National Geographic.* Some, *Architectural Digest. Birch & Willow* combined all these worlds. A highly respected lifestyle magazine that was both gritty and bougie, focusing on uncovering the hidden beauty in America. Forgotten homes, a woman weaving a masterpiece blanket by hand with her homemade loom, abandoned lighthouses, historical grain belts, and remodeled buildings from the industrial revolution. This was what I was destined to do. Everything in my life—eating ramen noodles for a year, bulldozing past my parents' "tough love" message that I'd never make it, taking every shit job available to afford rent and a decent camera in those early years—led to this moment.

I let my gaze flicker back to Morgan, who was typing with

her thumbs at a seriously impressive rate. Her pale skin was still lovely, one of those rarities who never broke out like the rest of the pimple-laden teen girls. Although the shape changed a bit, her face still held that round heart form and pouty mouth, making Morgan look younger than she was.

So many silent minutes later—minus the single table of cackling women in the corner—Morgan almost popped a neck tendon searching for the manager. She cocked her head at me. "Can you *please* stop bouncing your legs under the table."

God, she's the worst. I stopped, but not before I "accidentally" kicked the table hard enough to make the condiments rattle and some of Morgan's water tip onto the surface.

"Such a child," Morgan muttered and plucked a few napkins from the container.

Morgan glared at me, then finally sighed. "So did you move back to town or something?"

"Hell no." I didn't mean to say those words *so* harshly, but it was the truth. This town was great, beautiful, even. The full four seasons, Lake Superior, the endless lush greenery. The type of town where if your car broke down, the five people trailing you would help, no more than a three-degree separation existed from everyone, and full conversations took place in the grocery store line.

But this place also capped big dreams. Since I was little, I always knew I'd get out. It was more than escaping my toxic parents or giving the middle finger to teachers who said I was too obnoxious and couldn't sit still. The town simply wasn't big enough to hold me or my future. When I left right after graduation, I had one goal—move to New York and become a famous photographer. The desire for fame had dulled by my mid-twenties, and I settled for being lucky enough to pay for a halfway decent apartment I shared with my sister on my salary, while doing something I loved.

I took a sip of water. "I'm just back for a few months to take care of some family things." And the second I wrapped that up, I was hopping on a one-way flight, never to return.

Loud laughter from the table of women in the corner erupted. Morgan peeked over her shoulder, looked at her watch, and frowned. "You still in New York?"

I trailed a finger on the condensation on the glass. "Yep. Quinn and I have a place in Manhattan."

A hint of a grin formed on Morgan's face. "You're living with your little sister, huh? What's she doing out there?"

A better question would be what was Quinn *not* doing out there. Active social life, active work life, active everything. Ever since she was little, my younger sister seemed to be fueled by buckets of caffeine and a lithium battery. "She works on Wall Street if you can believe it."

"No way. Huh," she said. "Spunky little Quinn with her braces and freckles works on Wall Street? She's forever stunted in my brain as a bratty fourteen-year-old. I can't even picture her in a business suit."

"Well, she technically works on Wall Street, but probably not the way you think. She's the executive assistant of some bigwig. And she's still annoying." Quinn had both changed and not changed over all these years. Growing up, our grandma Peaches had called Quinn a jalapeño popper—crunchy, spicy, but inside she had some sweetness. Which was pretty much a perfect description. "What's your brother up to these days?"

Morgan shrugged. "Sam's the same. Works for Mom and Dad. Too many kids to count. Still arrogant, but I love him." Morgan checked her watch again and sucked in her lips.

I finally peeked at my watch. We'd been waiting for well over ten minutes now, and Morgan's face looked like it verged on blowing a gasket. She was gnawing away at the inside of her cheek, and I could hear her foot tapping under the table. Waiting like this was annoying, but what other option did we have? But red fanned from Morgan's neck and up her cheeks and if I didn't keep talking, I'd probably have to perform CPR. "So... wedding planning? How did you get into that?"

Morgan twisted the silver bangles on her wrist. "After college, I worked at a contracting firm in Duluth as a project coordinator. Since I had the lowest seniority, they'd put me in charge of coordinating office parties. I liked it, so they moved me to planning some community and client events. And then when Sam got married—"

"Wait—Sam?" I lifted a brow. "Who did he marry?"

Morgan cocked her head. "Who do you think?"

No way. "Lisa? They've been together since like freshman year, right?"

"Seventh grade."

I remembered Sam from when we were kids. He was a year younger and a nice-enough guy to banter with about the games. When Quinn and Morgan glazed over after two minutes of talking about anything with a ball, I usually defaulted to Sam. But it was hard for me to think of Sam as a married father, and not a backwards-baseball-hat-wearing, smart-mouthed jock.

Morgan finished the last of her water and wiped up the water mark on the table with a napkin. "They're still nauseatingly happy, too. Got three blonde-haired, blue-eyed babies. They look like a freaking toothpaste commercial."

I smiled and shifted in my seat. Sitting for any length of time always wreaked havoc on my system. Pretty soon, I'd need to burn the energy building in my limbs. "What about your parents? They still have the contracting company?"

"Yes, but it's elevated a bit. Contracting, remodeling, landscaping, the whole thing. They have a full staff, an office downtown, everything." Morgan peeled off her jacket and laid it in her lap. "They even bought Lutgen's Nursery."

"That place? Damn. They'd been in business forever." Mr. and Mrs. Rose were some of the hardest-working people I'd ever seen. Sure, my parents were not exactly known for hard work—

or stability, for that matter—but even so, Morgan's folks were King and Queen Hustle. "Good for them."

Morgan's fingers tapped against the table, and she turned, presumably looking for the hostess, who was AWOL along with the owner. She leaned back against the pleather booth and crossed her arms. "So, you said you're back home helping family?"

"Yeah, um." I cleared my throat. "Peaches died, so I'm getting her place ready to sell." Selling the place with so many good memories—warm cookies on Saturdays, chasing Quinn around the yard, watching goats eat mounds of grass—twisted my stomach.

Morgan inhaled a sharp breath. "Peaches? I'm... I'm so sorry."

I shrugged. It wasn't the right movement to convey my feelings, but throwing myself into my ex-girlfriend's arms so I could have a good solid sob wasn't the right move, either. My grandma, "Peaches," was a true force of nature. A five-foot-tall, strong, fiercely independent, and brutally honest German woman who took as much shit as she handed out. Peaches had loved hard, fought hard, and cussed so much, even I blushed. At ninety-two years old, it wasn't shocking that she passed. But it still hurt like hell not having her in the world.

"She was an amazing woman," Morgan said.

"Yeah, she was." Peaches had always liked Morgan. She called her an old soul with a "firecracker spirit" and said Morgan reminded her of herself. I never knew if that was a compliment or insult, as Morgan's stubbornness rivaled Peaches's.

"If her house hasn't changed, packing up is gonna take some time."

"It's even *worse.*" I fiddled with the sugar packets on the table. "Do you remember the basement cellar with all the fruit she canned in the eighties? Still there. Hundreds of jars of pickles, fruit, beans... sadly, no moonshine, though."

"Probably a blessing in disguise there was no moonshine. That cellar scared the crap out of me. Pretty sure the ghost we released still haunts me." Morgan tucked a lock of hair behind her ear. "Are your parents helping?"

I huffed through my nose. Morgan clearly did not remember my parents. "Nah. They are... busy." I'd asked them, but they said they had too many projects and didn't have time to "sift through all of that shit." Projects meant them tinkering around in a shed, holding down the job of the month, or bellying up to the bar. The second I asked, I had instantly regretted it. "They did say I should hand over any valuables, though." I chuckled, although it wasn't really funny.

Part of me couldn't blame my parents. In a final f-you act of rebellion toward her son and daughter-in-law, Peaches refused to buckle under the pressure my dad pushed on her, and she left the house to Quinn and me. Sure, Peaches had declared a million times while living that she'd always leave the home to us, but there was some obvious lingering saltiness that Peaches didn't change her mind at the end.

"She used to make the best rhubarb pie." Morgan closed her eyes. "With homemade ice cream, right?"

And... she smiles. Sure, not a full-on, mega-watt Julia Roberts or anything, but softly, enough to make me remember Morgan did not always walk around with a Mall of America-size chip on her shoulder.

"Oh, I forgot about the homemade ice cream." Such a lie. Why did I even say that? I didn't forget about the ice cream. I rarely forgot *anything* about my past; my memory was both a gift and a curse. Funny how I'd often walk into a room and forget what I needed or leave the house without my phone, but my mind gripped on to situational memories, replaying the good and bad in vibrant details.

Back during those childhood summers, Morgan and I would stop by almost daily for a scoop. Did Morgan have the same flash of memory as me? The first kiss that happened over home-made vanilla ice cream in Peaches's backyard. We were fourteen years old, sitting on the rickety wooden swinging bench on the back porch, and had Katy Perry blasting through an iPod. If I closed my eyes, I could still see the floating cottonwood and feel the flutters when Morgan gave me a shaky kiss on the mouth.

Laughter from the table of women made Morgan stiffen. "I need to find the hostess. We were supposed to meet the manager almost thirty minutes ago. This is absolutely ridiculous, not to mention highly unprofessional."

And... she's back. The softness swapped with the same uptight, rigid, uncomfortable woman I remembered. "Maybe she's caught up with something."

Morgan pushed herself from the booth. "We don't have time for this. Every second wasted sitting here is a second that I need for a million other things."

Wasted? God, she sucked. I just opened up about my grandma passing, and Morgan thought it was a waste of her time? I was seriously regretting telling Tommy I'd take this job.

Morgan's heavy wedges clicked against the floor as she marched over to the hostess stand. A moment passed when she crossed her arms and frowned.

Definitely not a good sign. "What did she say?" I asked as she returned.

"She thanked me for my patience and said the owner knows I'm here with a thumb up my ass and will be with me shortly." Her face fumed red. I probably should not be taking quite the amount of pleasure in this that I was. "Obviously, she didn't say the thumb part, but still. If we didn't need this place so bad, I'd hightail it out of here without a second glance."

I crossed my legs under the booth. "Because the manager is busy? Don't you think that's a little extreme?"

Morgan's eyes narrowed. "Extreme? How many weddings have you planned? Punctuality is *everything*. If they can't be on time for a simple meet and greet, how can I trust them to host an entire wedding?"

Even though Morgan had a point, I wanted to scratch off my ears with the condescending tone. I refused to let on that I agreed. In a snap, I was back in high school getting scolded by my high school girlfriend for not finishing a term paper on time. I lifted my chin in a quick nod. "Gotcha."

"Whatever."

Really? "What does *that* mean?"

Morgan sucked in her cheeks. "I know keeping promises is not your forte, but this is business, and we don't have that type of luxury."

Well, that went downhill fast. The words stung hard and fast like a slap. Not due to whatever history Morgan referred to, but because of my last two years in New York. "Are you actually serious right now?" I pushed back into the booth and crossed my arms. "You're not talking about some stupid high school romance, are you?"

Morgan's eyes turned a dark, angry blue.

What we had wasn't a stupid high school romance, and I knew that damn well. It was years of friendship that morphed into four years of building dreams and an intense first love, which took me years to get over. But I'd *never* let Morgan know she once held that kind of power.

Morgan's mouth dropped. "How—"

The laughter from the other table reached a fever pitch and cut through whatever Morgan was going to say. Probably for the best as I was a pacifist at heart, but if pushed too far, I'd snap and probably say some shit I'd regret. It had been years since I was in an organized sport, but the competition and fighting spirit floated just beneath the surface, ready to pounce like a panther on its prey.

A chair squeaked as a woman with a black blazer and frizzy blonde hair stepped to the table. "Morgan? Hi, I'm Jane, the owner."

Oh shit. Hate shifted from me to this woman. It took a solid few seconds for Morgan's pursed lips to flatten. Like a supervillain shape-shifter, she adjusted her expression, stood, and shook the woman's hand. Even though I didn't know everything about planning a wedding, I knew at this late of a stage in the planning process, Morgan needed this venue more than the owner needed Morgan's business.

"Follow me," the woman, Jane, said as she stepped back from the table. "I'll show you the grounds and answer any questions."

Morgan turned to follow the owner without another look at me. *Rude.* I scooted myself from the table and double-stepped to catch up.

Outside, we walked past a crooked, rotted fence with a dangling No Smoking sign. Jane removed a pack of cigarettes from her jacket pocket and tapped it against her palm.

Double no. If memory served, Morgan hated rule breakers almost as much as tardiness. I vaguely remember an argument between us when I begged her to live a little and skip class, and she freaked out at me at my locker. As the woman lit up and inhaled a deep drag, I wanted to snap a pic of Morgan's face, which looked like she just stepped in dog shit.

Morgan stepped a few inches away from the embers. "I thought this was a non-smoking venue?"

Jane flicked an ash. "Well, yeah, I'm the owner, so not all rules apply to me. And I've had a fucking terrible day, so..."

All Jane needed to do was whip out a flask and Morgan would roll over in her prudish grave. Maybe I was a sadist, but this awkward-as-hell moment was the most fun I'd had since arriving back home.

After walking down the path, Jane cut through the brush. My boots squished in the soggy grass, and I peeked at Morgan's pristine ankle wedges getting mud on the side. I withheld a smile picturing her scrubbing those with a toothbrush and a pile of baking soda when she got home.

Jane jutted her finger at a structure that could only be described as a run-down machine shed meets a Quonset hut. "There's the venue."

Yikes.

Morgan's throat rolled with a swallow as she stared at the rusted, metal-framed building. "Your website said it could hold three hundred people, correct?"

The woman inhaled a large puff, then flicked the cigarette into the grass. The airborne ashes flew and Morgan, most likely fearful a spark would land on her cashmere scarf and burn her at the stake, whipped her shoulder back.

The cigarette sizzled on the wet grass, but I still wanted to snuff out the smoke. With Peaches living on a hobby farm, and my aunt and uncle owning a tree farm, sparks were cancerous. I cracked my neck and exhaled, silently repeating Peaches's catchphrase: "Ain't your baby, Maury." AKA, mind your own damn business.

The doors screeched like a power drill slicing through sheet metal as Jane opened them, and I gritted my teeth.

Morgan stepped inside and froze. "Well, this has that... rustic vibe... people like."

Rustic was the understatement of the year. The place looked like an abandoned warehouse with a single string of white lights dangling from the ceiling—not even near the "finished and ready to serve" venue it touted on its website. A few folding tables and chairs were stacked against the wall in the corner next to a single wooden bench. The room carried a smell that I couldn't quite place—almost the sharp tang of garbage meets a dirty, wet mop.

I stepped further into the space and my boots stuck to the floor. Each sticky footstep echoed as I moved further into the space. *Gross.*

"Over here you have a bar area." Jane pointed to a standing table with a sink. "Bring your own. We don't have bartenders on staff. And I don't recommend drinking from the tap, so pre-make everything."

Seriously, how did this place pass inspections?

Morgan's lips remained pulled tight. "Do you have restrooms to accommodate that many people?"

Jane nodded. "Yep, I'll show you." She escorted Morgan and me past the "bar" area, and through the door to a small kitchen space with steel counters, a huge farmhouse sink, and one refrigerator. She pushed open another door and pointed outside to a wooden shed with a floppy sign that said RESTROOMS.

Oh no. This was surely the nail in the coffin. No way in hell would Olivia squat in her wedding gown over a toilet in the ground.

"Outhouses?" Morgan frowned.

"Yep," Jane said. "Good enough for the settlers, am I right?"

A few moments passed when Morgan crossed the grass. "Well, let's take a look."

She was not actually going for this, right? I tugged at her elbow and put my mouth up to her ear. Damn it if that vanilla rose scent didn't distract me for a split moment. "I don't think this is the right venue."

Morgan snapped her gaze at me. "Are you saying you can't shoot here?"

The blow to my ego was instant. "I can shoot *anywhere.*" Did Morgan even look at my work? I knew Olivia sent her my website last week, so had Morgan done even the smallest due diligence, she would know that I normally loved this style... making something that others don't find beautiful, into something beautiful. But for a wedding venue, this place wasn't right.

At the outhouse, Morgan opened the door for a peek. A putrid fog emerged and floated right over to me. I slammed a palm over my mouth and nose. *Don't puke.*

Morgan, who was clearly a poker-face champ, simply stepped back and clapped off her hands. "I think we've seen enough to decide. I'll check in with the bride, then keep you posted."

"Don't keep me waiting." Jane pulled out the pack of smokes and stuck a cigarette between her lips. "There's other people who want this."

I sincerely doubted that.

We walked back to the parking lot in silence. Morgan looked like a deflating balloon as she swapped crisp steps and straight shoulders with slow movements and a creased forehead. I wasn't actually feeling bad for her, right? Sure, this limited-option situation sucked. But Morgan looked like all hope was lost. Even though it had been fifteen years since I spent any significant time in our town, there must be other places. "So, what are the next steps?"

Morgan dug out keys from her purse. "Almost everything is dependent on the venue. I can't book caterers, liquor, decorators, DJ, literally jack shit without knowing the date, and I can't know the date until we book the venue."

I grabbed my helmet off the bike handle and tucked it under my arm. "It's gonna be fine. Something will work out."

"*Clearly*, you have no idea what it takes to pull off a wedding, not to mention in three months." Morgan's fingers gripped the top of her door frame. "Olivia and Tommy haven't even narrowed down the guest list or picked out colors so I can get even a semblance of a theme. I have to get invitation samples, flowers, guest gift ideas, the list is freaking endless."

Christ, that tone. I was just trying to make Morgan feel better after this disastrous meeting. I tugged on the helmet with a smirk, refusing to give Morgan even a morsel of satisfaction that her snarkiness was getting to me. "Cool."

"*Cool?*" Morgan glared. "You have no clue how complex planning a wedding is. You can't just wing it like usual."

Wing it. Well, it appeared Ms. Rose was, in fact, hanging on to some ancient bullshit. It had been a common theme in our previous relationship that I liked to "wing it." I was the dreamer. Morgan was the planner. Which was cute, for a while. A little salt to the pepper, a yin to the yang, a balance during those chaotic teenage years. And it worked, until "wing it" morphed into "irresponsible" and "not to be trusted."

And I wouldn't point this out now, but this wasn't my first rodeo. I had some idea of what it took to plan a wedding. "Fine, well, let me know when you find the next venue. You have my number." God, that stupid, sweet face looked simultaneously tough, sharp, and verging on tears. I needed to just drive away, forget this happened, let her figure this out solo. *Ughhhhh.* Sometimes, I seriously hated myself. I choked on the olive branch I was about to purge. "Let me know if you need help with anything."

"I absolutely do *not* need your help."

And I'm out. I kicked the side stand, pulled the clutch, and started the motorcycle. I revved it enough to be perfectly obnoxious, and sped out of the parking lot.

THREE
MORGAN

Why the hell did I say I didn't need Frankie's help? I blinked at the clock. It wasn't even 6:00 a.m. yet, and already the low but steady stress headache rumbled. By mid-day, it would most definitely rage against my skull—exactly what had been happening for the last three days since Frankie stomped her combat-boot-laden feet back into my world.

I eased myself up from the bed and checked my phone, hoping that a magical Google alert had popped up overnight, showing that a local-*ish* venue had space for a wedding in roughly ninety days.

Nope. Nothing but a text message from my brother from ten minutes prior.

SAM:

Call me when you wake up.

I bolted upright. Ever since his wife, Lisa, got a devastating breast cancer diagnosis ten years ago, messages like this made me assume the worst. I slapped at my phone to dial.

The call picked up after one ring. "Is everything okay?"

"Oh yep. Just need a huge favor." His annoyingly chipper voice rang through the phone.

"Don't do that to me. Messages like that freak me the hell out." I lowered myself down on my pillow. "God, it's early. Don't you sleep?"

"I have an infant, a toddler, and a first-grader. I never sleep." A slurping noise sounded through the phone. "Can you swing by the bakery and pick up two dozen cupcakes? Long story short but the dog chewed Henry's shin guards last night, we think the baby's got an ear infection so wifey has to take her to urgent care, it's Henry's teammate's birthday and our turn to bring treats, and I don't think they're going to get back from urgent care in time and—"

"How many cups of coffee have you had?" I dug a knuckle into the corner of my eye.

"It's a constant drip. I should IV it into my veins and save myself the trouble of brewing," Sam said before yelling something inaudible to either a dog or a kid. "You didn't forget the game today, did you?"

"I didn't forget." *Unfortunately*. I forgot nothing added to my beautifully organized, color-coded calendar, separated in categories of personal, professional, and family. But just because I had remembered it didn't mean the highlight of my life was watching a bunch of seven- and eight-year-olds run around trying to kick a ball into a net.

I loved those kids to the deepest parts of my soul. Sometimes, when I thought about what would have happened if Lisa hadn't survived her cancer and my nephews and niece would've never been born, an unbearable emptiness filled me. Every second not spent on my business, I spent with the kids, which was the only silver lining of my company's downslide these last few years. Absorbing the growth milestones of the little ones was a gift. Last month, I even increased my Google Photos storage because I couldn't bear to delete any of the gazillion photos Sam sent of the kids every week. Even through their messes, boogers, and germs, I couldn't get enough. However, I secretly looked forward to the time when they wanted to learn how to use a label maker, sort their clothes by color, or build a proper spreadsheet.

But watching them play sports was where if anyone questioned my love for them, I'd enter photos of me cheering from the sidelines as Exhibit A. I *hate* sports.

"Cupcakes, you said?" I rested my forearm against my eyes to block the rising sun. "I wasn't going into town today. You seriously owe me."

"You got the looks and the brains in the family." Sam chuckled. "The least you can do is pick up the cupcakes."

"That's true." I grinned despite myself. "The grocery store or Zoey's?"

"You think I want a mutiny on my hands? Zoey's obviously."

Good choice. Not that the grocery store didn't have some solid cupcakes in the bakery aisle, but Zoey's Bakery was the best in the area. Besides, I always liked to support queer businesses when I could, and being from a small town, the options were limited.

"I've got to run," Sam said. "You're the best."

"Yes, I know." I hung up the phone and dragged myself into the shower. As the steam filled the space, I tried to take the moment and relax, but my brain betrayed me as always and started whipping through a mental inventory. Planning weddings was often stop-and-go, with me simply waiting for the couple to make decisions. Thankfully, Olivia and Tommy were pretty quick. In the past few days, Olivia narrowed the wedding invitations to three choices. But last night, she'd texted me and said she wanted to add dried pressed flowers to the card. Good idea. Great, even. *If* we had more time or Olivia wanted to do it herself. Neither of which were going to happen.

My heartbeat kicked up higher, and I exhaled. *I got this, I got this.* I'd keep repeating that to myself until my internal organs heard the message and responded accordingly.

I squeezed out a dollop of my favorite vanilla rose shower gel and scrubbed the loofah across my elbows. *Dinner placements, DJs, wine glasses, appetizer, officiant...* I shook my head. Why again did I turn down Frankie's offer to help?

Oh yeah. Because Frankie sucks.

Was it immature to hold on to this resentment? Most definitely. But I couldn't shake it. The burn in my belly after seeing Frankie was so deep that it far surpassed grudge and was swiftly heading down the pike to full-on loathing. When Frankie left me, I cried almost every night for a full year. And after the tears stopped, I still thought of her. *For years.* And there were lots of reasons after that why I never had long-lasting, stable relationships—work, building up my business, helping my family—but if I dug deep, which was a very unpleasant thing to do, I knew it was because I didn't think I could open myself up again for that potential pain.

And seeing Frankie again, so aloof, so distant, so *uncaring*, solidified everything I had feared back then—I was not worth staying for, and Frankie was not sorry.

I think I hated her.

After the least peaceful shower time in existence, I shagged a towel through my hair, then typed off an email.

Hi Olivia,

Hoping by the end of the week we can have the following:

1. A solid count on the guest list
2. Your color scheme
3. Confirmation on who will be in your wedding party

Thanks!

Morgan Rose, Rose Events

But really, what we needed was a goddamn venue.

Ninety minutes later, desperate for coffee made with an espresso machine and not my pot, I headed out of my place. The car took two tries to start, *ugh*, but once it choked to life, I tapped on my favorite podcast, *Love 'Em or Leave 'Em*, and flew down the road to get cupcakes.

"Okay, everyone, our next question comes from Trisha," the podcast host, Ruby Reanne, said. "Let me read the email I received. 'Hi, Ruby. For the last few years into my eight-year marriage, my husband and I have gone from being nearly best friends to constant bickering. Although I'm not innocent in this matter, I feel like he picks fights, makes excuses to not be around me, never tells me I'm beautiful, the list goes on. For the last year, he has almost completely stopped contributing to the household chores, choosing instead to spend his downtime gaming or going out with his friends. About six months ago, a male co-worker and I started texting. It really started as work-related and soon morphed into something deeper. Although I have not, and will not, physically act on anything, I love these messages. They are an amazing distraction, make me feel better, and honestly make me less angry at my husband, which I think is good. Anyway, a friend told me I should tell my husband. I don't think I need to. I'm not doing anything wrong. So, my question is: Am I under obligation to tell this to my husband?'"

Ooh, this is a good one. I turned up the volume to hear Ruby's response.

"First, thank you to Trisha for this message. I always like to put myself in my wife's shoes—metaphorically speaking, of course, as she is tiny—or apply situations directly to me, to really understand how I might feel. But we need to call this what it is —an emotional affair. You are having an emotional affair on your husband. Yes, he sounds pretty whiny and pretty ridiculous and really needs to step it up in the husband department. For sure. But I will address the one question you asked: Are you under obligation to tell your husband. And my response is, if you think you're not doing anything wrong, why haven't you said anything yet?"

I pressed the pause button and parallel parked in front of the hardware store. I waved to Joe, the owner, who was setting out a display, and hurried into the coffee shop.

"Hey there, Morgan. Whatcha havin' today?" the owner, Connie, asked while wiping her hands on a towel.

"Morning, Connie." I dug out my credit card, smiling at Connie's accent. Minnesotans were known for their accents, but they were often exaggerated on TV and film. But Connie sounded like she was in the movie *Fargo*, and I swear I could listen to her speak all day. "Just a small Americano with cream please."

"Sure is warming up outside. I betcha this summer's gonna be a hot one." Connie poised her marker over the cup and scribbled on the side. "How are ya folks doing?"

"Ah, you know them." I waved the question away. Everyone knew everyone in Spring Harbors, so the answer was irrelevant. If something was going on with my parents, one of the locals would have said something on their morning coffee run, and the news would have traveled lightning speed to the rest of the town by noon. "I heard you're not doing the Summer Festival this year. You're going to have a lot of people missing your famous blackberry iced mocha."

"Oh, well, ya know. With my husband's back surgery and the kids off to college, there just isn't enough of me to go around." She tugged at her polka-dot apron strings. "That's all right, though. We'll give the business to some of these younger guys."

"That's pretty generous of you," I said as I shoved my wallet back in my purse.

Connie waved over the new barista. "Say now, did I introduce you to my niece here, Megan? Megan, meet Morgan. Morgan, Megan. And wouldn't ya know, your names are only one letter off."

Two letters, but I would never say that. I nodded at the young woman with the messy bun and tortoiseshell glasses. "Hey, Megan. You must be new. I'm here all the time and haven't seen you yet."

"Yep, just started two days ago." Megan shoved a mug under the filter as the water hissed through the beans. "School just got out, so I'm helping Auntie for the summer. Good to meet you."

The door chime rang, and a few heavy footsteps moved toward me. A moment later, I felt the energy of someone standing a few inches too close. I didn't even need to turn around to know which she-devil was at my back.

"Isn't this fun coincidence?"

Groan. I hadn't heard from Frankie since we parted ways at the Satan's Den Diner a few days ago, which admittedly surprised me. But also, why would I think I'd hear from Frankie? This was the woman who left for New York City all those years back without saying goodbye. I turned on my heels. "Two adults getting coffee at one of the three coffee shops open before nine a.m. is not that coincidental. This isn't New York when you probably don't see the same person twice in a lifetime."

Living in a town of under three thousand for my entire life, I constantly ran into people I knew. That was why I always had my face and hair done, and a smile plastered on top of the makeup, even when my insides were knotted. But I loved it here. This was home. The town was stable and supportive, always holding me in a protective security blanket.

But Spring Harbors was never enough for Frankie. She wanted out since childhood. The town... me... none of it was enough to keep her anchored.

"So feisty this early on a beautiful Saturday." Frankie reached in her back pocket and pulled out a wallet. "Looks like someone didn't get their neighborly May Basket."

Whoa. Years had passed since I thought about the May 1st tradition. As a kid it used to be one of my favorite events where I'd make neat little baskets of gold-wrapped chocolate, wildflowers, and a couple of my mom's homemade chocolate bars, and I'd ding-dong ditch baskets around the neighborhood. The last year I did it, Frankie and I were probably around thirteen or fourteen. I remember tripping while ditching, spraining my ankle, and Frankie giving me a piggyback ride back to my house.

"I'm not feisty." I gritted my teeth, then smiled at Megan, who called my name for the coffee.

Frankie ran her fingers through her dark cropped hair and stepped up to the register. She was always more masc than me— a tough, fast-as-hell, gym-shorts-and-sports-jersey-wearing girl— but the short hair with buzzed sides and the Harley driving would take getting used to. And I would admit this to absolutely no one, but the look suited her. Incredibly well.

I sipped the deliciously smooth drink and had every intention of bolting out the door when Frankie stepped in my path.

"I have some good news." Frankie shoved her wallet back in her pocket. "I'm taking Olivia and Tommy's engagement photos today."

I almost spit out my coffee over Frankie's brown leather jacket. "Wait, what? Why don't I know about this? They should have told me." I tapped my fingers against the cup. "Where?

How long does processing take? We can get these out with the invites if there's enough time." This was actually really good news. But did anyone even consider that I should have been told immediately? I checked my watch. "Dammit. I have to pick up cupcakes for Sam."

"Your brother?" Frankie tipped her head in thanks at the barista and grabbed her drink.

"Yes. His oldest is having a soccer game and he's on cupcake duty."

A grin tugged at Frankie's lips. "God, those were the days. Orange slices, tearing up the field, screaming with my buddies. Soccer was always my favorite."

Yeah, I remember. I must've sat through hundreds of Frankie's games over the years. Frankie was a phenomenal athlete—basketball, softball, hockey—but a star on the soccer field. Seemed like she could run for days without dropping. "Do you still play?"

"Nah." Frankie lifted the drink to her lips. "I had surgery about five years ago, and sadly, no more soccer for me."

I stopped in my tracks. *Surgery? What kind? For what?* No matter how many questions verged on the tip of my tongue, I kept my mouth zipped. It wasn't my place to ask any invasive questions, but it reiterated that a lifetime had passed and I no longer knew the person I used to know better than myself.

"Which place you grabbing the treats from?" Frankie held the door open for me.

"Zoey's Bakery, across the street." I stepped onto the sidewalk and jutted my head to the shop across the street with the pink-and-white awning and the obvious Zoey's Bakery written across the large front window.

Frankie glanced toward the store as if this was the first time seeing it. *God, she really doesn't notice things, does she? How has she not evolved as an adult?* I swear Frankie was perpetually in la-la land and completely unaware of her surroundings unless on a court or field, where she had magical laser focus.

"Zoey's Bakery, huh?" she said. "That's where the nail salon was, right?"

"That was like five years ago. Zoey's been here since then." Why did this annoy me? Not that Zoey took over the salon, but that Frankie didn't *know* Zoey took over the salon. When new stores opened in town, it was always a big deal. A write-up in the local weekly newspaper, a long line of locals cheering for them on their first day, homemade GRAND OPENING EVENT signs stapled into wooden light posts. No chance Frankie's ultra-hipster neighborhood in New York rallied like this.

"Cool." Frankie squinted into the sun. "I'll walk with you, and we can chat about the wedding."

Although this was the very last thing I wanted, I reluctantly agreed. Like it or not, I needed the details about the photo shoot so I could plan. The wedding time bomb ticked in my ear, and the more I could cross off my list, the better. Nightmares of being lost at a reception, dropping a cake, and sending out the wrong invites flooded me this past week, and I'd give my left pinkie to be able to sleep through the night.

I walked the sidewalk with Frankie and took grateful sips of the Americano. "Are you taking photos at the water?"

"Actually, no. At least not today." Frankie pushed the crosswalk signal at the lights. "We're going to go up to my aunt and uncle's place. Remember Pete and Patty? The ones with the Christmas tree farm."

"The one up by Maple Creek?" Talk about blast from the past. When I was a kid, my whole family would go there every year to chop down a tree and attach it to the top of my dad's car, Griswold-style.

"Yeah. I heard the place is kind of a wreck, but the land is still pretty. And I don't need a permit or have to worry about people getting in the way," Frankie said. "And, selfishly, I wanted to capture the place while I'm here. Sounds like they're going to be shutting down the farm and retiring."

"Really?" My heart sank. Sure, I didn't frequent the Christmas tree farm. For the last decade at least, I stuck a four-foot, pre-lit tree by my front window—which was more to not look like a bah-humbug to my neighbors, and less about my holiday spirit. But Pete and Patty's place was a local tradition, even if it wasn't what it used to be. "That's too bad. But also... good for them. Keeping up a tree farm has got to be a ton of work." I moved past the pride flag outside Zoey's Bakery and reached for the door handle.

Inside, I stepped into a mushroom cloud of dough and sugar scents. I inhaled, filling my lungs. *Yum.* God, I was a sucker for sweets. Chocolate, raspberry, vanilla, I'd even tried a pickle cupcake a few weeks ago that was surprisingly delicious. I breathed in one more time, then went to the counter.

Zoey glanced up from tucking edges into a pastry box. "Heya, Morgan!" She wiped her hands on her pink apron and moved to the counter. "You haven't been here for almost a month. Did we break up and I didn't get the memo?"

"Nah. I'll never leave your raspberry scones." I grinned. "Sam sent me to pick up cupcakes."

Although the queer community was small around here, it had been apparent from day one that Zoey and I would never be a match. Zoey was cute. Wavy dark hair, chunky glasses, bright blue eyes, a wide grin. I swear I'd befriend her properly if I had more time. But no spark ever existed. And even though I wouldn't call myself a romantic, I relied heavily on sparks and tingles to indicate if someone was a good match. The brain might lie, but the body does not.

"Sam's little guy has a soccer game, right? I got them ready for you right here." Zoey dug out a pink box from under the counter. "Lisa called earlier and said you'd be by to grab them."

Frankie leaned toward me. "Jesus, do you seriously know everyone in this town?"

Kind of, yes. I wanted to snark that Frankie would know everyone, too, if she didn't bust out of here like Spring Harbors was a jail, but I refrained.

Zoey tapped on the screen, her gaze flashing between Frankie and me. "Are you two together?"

"Definitely not." I stiffened, then softened when I looked at Frankie's deadpan stare. "I mean, yes, we're getting these cupcakes now... together." *But only out of sheer desperation to move the wedding-needle a fraction.*

Zoey swiped the credit card I handed her in the machine and smiled at Frankie. "Are you new to the area? Tourist? I don't think I've seen you around here."

"Um, something like that." Frankie's dimples deepened with her smile.

Are they flirting? In front of me? God, that smile, though. Honestly, it was unfair. People who had smiles like that made other people melt. That smile hid what a terrible, awful, horrible person Frankie was, and hopefully Zoey could see through those deep-set dimples' facade.

"Great place you've got here." Frankie took a step back and cast a gaze across the space. "Love the pride décor."

The tiniest swipe of blush crossed Zoey's pale cheeks, enough that I wanted to stomp out of the store. The very last thing I needed to see was another victim succumb to Frankie's famous charm. Christ, too many things hadn't changed with Frankie. She always had this way about her... someone who could talk their way out of a ticket or convince a teacher to swap a grade, which I distinctly remember happening at least twice our senior year, which infuriated me because I had done the due diligence of studying my ass off, and she'd done the bare minimum by charming the teachers. I called out my thanks to Zoey and headed out the door, with Frankie at my heels.

Outside, I balanced both boxes and my coffee as I scurried across the street.

Frankie held out her arms. "Let me hold one of those."

"I'm *perfectly* capable." I didn't need some motorcycle-driving, knight-in-shiny-leather-armor coming in and doing chivalrous things. Although it was pretty cumbersome trying to dig out the keys from my purse while propping the boxes on my hip.

I wanted Frankie to ask me again, so I could hand her a box. She didn't.

Frankie tossed her drink into the sidewalk wastebasket. "Hey, why don't you meet us up at Pete and Patty's for the shoot?"

I sighed. I had *so much* to do. However, it was nearly impossible to get Olivia nailed down for longer than a few short emails. At least if I were in person with Olivia, I could strong-arm her into making a few decisions. "Okay, maybe I'll try. Can you send me the details?" I opened the back door and slid the boxes on the backseat. "And, um, thanks." Ugh, if those words didn't feel like glass shards coming from my mouth.

In the car, I pinched the bridge of my nose and exhaled. The headache eased up, but the thought of spending the after-noon with Frankie kicked it back into high gear. I turned the ignition and... *Oh no. Oh, no, no, no.* A horrific sound like a metal fork scraping across something under my hood flooded the car. I pushed the back of my head into the seat. *Not now.*

A knuckle rapped on the window. "Need a ride?"

I stepped out of the car and pointed at the motorcycle. "On that death trap? Absolutely not."

Frankie shrugged. "Cool."

If she says that one more time, I swear to God... Frankie tugged on her helmet and flung a leg over the bike seat without so much as a second glance. *Dammit.* Sam would already be at the soccer game, and I sure as hell wasn't going to call my workaholic parents for a ride. I could Uber, but in this town, the rideshares weren't plentiful. I may hate anything sports-related, but the last thing I could bear to think about was Henry's disappointed cherub face when I didn't make his game or bring the cupcakes.

Crap. I really didn't want to do this. But... but I had no choice. "Frankie, wait!"

FOUR
MORGAN

The motorcycle boomed to life with a guttural roar, and I jogged over to it. Riding on the back of Frankie's murder-mobile was the very last thing I wanted to do, but my family needed me. I tugged on the arm of Frankie's leather jacket. "Um, I think I need a ride."

Frankie revved the bike. "What? I can't hear you."

Asshole.

I crossed my arms until Frankie killed the engine. "I'm sorry, *okay*," I said. This felt terrible. *God, I hate apologizing.* "I really need a ride, but I have to get the cupcakes to the game. Pretty sure I can't bring these on your motorcycle."

Frankie tapped the front of the bike seat. "I have to swap this guy out for Peaches's truck so I can bring my gear to the farm. I'll drop you off at the field, pick up the truck, bring the cupcakes to you, then we can ride together to the shoot."

That all seemed logical, but... this didn't even have doors! Much less seatbelts or a back-up camera or airbags. It was loud, and scary, and no doubt debris would get all over my clothes. I stared at the beast as my mouth turned dry.

Frankie lifted the helmet off her head and held it out. "Here. Wear this."

A warmth tingled in my belly with the offer. I had a small urge to say I'd be just fine, but the truth was, I didn't want to be splattered like roadkill across Highway 61.

Hair be dammed, I pushed the helmet on and threw a leg over the seat. *Hmmm.* The seat was surprisingly comfortable, but still, I was on a certified death machine. My throat cinched tight. I couldn't believe I was actually doing this. *Please don't pass out.* I left a few inches between us, and white-knuckled the side bars.

Frankie slid her ass up to me and held her back firm. "Hold tight on to my waist, okay? Try to stay in sync with me. If I lean, just causally lean with me. Don't wiggle or shift around or try to counteract the balance. And keep your feet on the stand the entire time, even if your body is urging you to set them on the ground."

Oh damn. That firm, demanding tone... Frankie was not messing around. And Frankie was *always* the person that messed around. Who was this all-authoritative and serious person? The unexpected sensation of Frankie being in control, and me most definitely *not* in control, deepened that belly tingle. I pushed forward until my chest was against Frankie's back and a heavenly scent of something dark and stormy wafted to my nose. I wrapped my arms around Frankie's waist and *my God...* Frankie may have given up on soccer, but she was clearly doing *something.*

Frankie heeled the kickstand and revved the motorcycle and *holy hell...* was this what motorcycles felt like? Why didn't every woman own one? Under my ass was a sturdy, constant vibration... *Oof...* It had been way too long since I had sex with something non-mechanical. I clenched my thighs as Frankie eased out into traffic. Thank God I was wearing jeans today, and not the maxi skirt I'd originally intended. The good people of Spring Harbors did not need to see my skirt hitching up my thighs as we flew down the road.

Once Frankie picked up speed, I fanned my fingers against her firm stomach, and I swore she flexed under the touch. *Show-off.* The wind whipped against my neck and lines of goosebumps skittered across my skin. But between my body pressed into Frankie's warm back, and the beaming spring sun, I was as cozy as if I was on my couch with a chunky knitted blanket.

The soccer field was less than ten minutes away, but by the time we arrived, my legs and arms were shaking like a nervous chihuahua's.

Frankie cut the engine and scooted forward. "Careful getting off."

For once, she wasn't trying to slip in a dirty joke. I tried to stabilize my gummy limbs as I slid off the seat. I tugged off the helmet and patted my head. "Thanks for the lift."

Frankie lifted her hand and gently swiped what must have been a rogue strand of my hair. "It was, uh, messed up," she said. When I lifted a brow, she grinned. "The hair. Not the ride."

Nope, I was not for a second doing this twinkling thing right now. Absolutely no chance. Frankie just did something nice, and I'd essentially had a three-hundred-pound vibrator underneath my hoo-hah for the last ten minutes. Whatever was happening inside me was simply a need for release from facing certain death.

Sparks be damned.

I smoothed back my hair. "Oh. Thanks." I glanced out at the field. "So, you'll be back before the game ends with the cupcakes? Please don't forget. I'm serious. The kids are really counting on them, and I can't let them down."

The smile dropped from Frankie's eyes. "I'm not going to *forget.* I'm gonna swap out the bike, then go back and get the cupcakes." She pulled on the helmet with one firm tug. "Toss me your keys."

I didn't mean to sound like an ass, but my job was to double, then triple, check everything. Throughout my entire adult life, I could never fully rely on anyone. I was responsible for one of the most important days of people's lives. And sure, things may have changed since I last knew Frankie, but back in the day she was queen of forgetting everything—her backpack, phone, water bottle for sports practice, extra shoes for the court. I swear half our relationship consisted of me running back to grab things for her, or making a bulleted list of items she needed so she could keep on track. *So, excuse me, Frankie Lee, for being a little paranoid that you'll mess this up.*

I handed the keys over and tried to muster up a half-assed apology, but Frankie took off without another word.

The screech of whistles blowing, soccer balls being kicked, and kids screaming snapped my attention away from Frankie's wordless departure. I hurried across the dewy grass to where the kids were stretching, and Sam was yelling something from a lawn chair. I poked my brother's shoulder, then plopped next to him on the empty chair.

"Didn't realize you rode with the Hells Angels these days." Sam nudged his head to the parking lot. "Where are the cupcakes?"

"Long story, but they'll be here." I dropped my purse on the ground and scanned the field. "Where's your wife?"

"She stayed home. The baby's still too cranky with her ear infection." He tugged down the lip of his baseball cap, creating shadows on his scruff. "Just like his auntie."

I ground my knuckle into his shoulder until he yelped. "Very funny. I don't have an infection."

"You don't need one to be cranky."

"Jerk." Not that I loved soccer, *at all*. But sitting in a comfy chair in the fresh spring air, and watching kids tear around the field was not the worst way to spend a Saturday. I waved at a beaming Henry, who was yelling "Auntie!" from the sidelines. "Where's the middle child? With Grandma?"

"Nah, he's at home with Lisa, too." Sam grabbed a water bottle from the chair cup holder. "The likelihood of Mom babysitting is right up with you mud-wrestling."

"Rude." I snatched the water bottle from him and gulped. "She's babysat before."

He snatched the bottle back. "Really? When?"

"Thanksgiving, right?" The whistle blew and the kids scrambled into a circle. I clapped for the kids, who high-fived each other, then ran up to the painted lines on the field.

"You mean when I ran to the store with Lisa for more wine and she had the kids, *with you*, for like twenty minutes?" he asked.

"I'll have you know I left the room to take a call, and I completely abandoned her." I grinned. "Seriously, how did she raise us? I really don't remember her being so skittish around kids. Didn't she even volunteer at the school sometimes?"

Sam's head swerved to look around a group of kids blocking his view of Henry. "I don't remember, but honestly, I think you ruined her. She's been scared of kids ever since she pushed you out."

I flashed him my most irritated glare. "First of all, I'm older than you. Second, I'm the easy one." I crossed my legs and dusted the side of my pants. *Crap.* Fresh dirt stains from the bike ride smeared across my calf, and my Tide stick was in my car. I moistened my thumb and tried to wipe them off before I gave up. Nothing screams professional like mud stains. "Ah, look at Henry out there. So cute. You know he's my favorite, right?"

Sam shook his head. "You know you're not supposed to have favorites, right? And for Christ's sake, when you do, you should never tell the parent."

"Can't help it. Henry's tough. Your other kids cry too much."

"They're *babies*." Sam took off his hat and lightly smacked me in the leg. He knew damn well that I adored my niece and nephews, but also that I had no desire to have my own. I might be a superhero-cape-wearing aunt, but I was convinced if I had my own children, I'd royally screw something up, and they'd need a lifetime of chocolate and therapy to erase the memory of my severe lack of motherly instincts.

God, I missed hanging out with my brother. Work always took more time than either of us had, but this little reprieve lifted my spirits. Sitting here, listening to him cheer for the kiddos, I wondered what my twelve-year-old self would think of Sam and me now. Growing up, we had as many screaming matches as we did hours of building forts in the living room. He was one year younger, annoying, and loud, but deep down even as an angsty teen, I still loved him. Sam was the only person who understood the pressure our parents put on us to succeed. Working to the bone was godly. Something to be proud of, to brag about to the neighbors. Our parents meant well, but growing up it seemed the vast majority of the family conversations surrounded praising someone who "never took a week off of work" to chastising the unfortunate souls who lost their business because "they must not have put in all the effort."

If Olivia's wedding didn't work, and I lost my business, I could just see my parents reacting to the news. They'd hug me, my mom would cry, and my dad would give me some awkward bro slap on the back and tell me to look on the bright side of things. But deep down, I knew they'd think I didn't put in enough effort, and that'd kill me.

Sam roared for Henry, then tapped his knee against me. "So, for real, who was the dude on the bike? You switchin' teams now?"

"So much homophobia wrapped up in one little sentence.

Truly remarkable." Oh, how my brother loved to push my buttons even with his pure heart. "It was... Katey. Who goes by Frankie now. I'm trying to honor the name change, even though I'm still getting used to it."

His jaw dropped. "Katey? You mean Katey Lee? Your ex-girlfriend from high school?" He leaned forward so quickly that his chair nearly tipped over. "Shut the fu—"

"Language." I shook my finger at him. "We're at a kids' game."

"No way." He leaned back, his eyes grazing the field. "What's she doing back in town? Didn't she move out east or something like a hundred years ago?"

She sure did. Discarded our plans to build a better life, to look for something more than me. Frankie was always obsessed with photography. When we were younger, she'd carry around a Polaroid and snap me doing random things. The amount of ink wasted on scowls or open mouths of protests would worry me, but Frankie always convinced me it was never a waste. Then she saved up for a Canon, and everything changed. When other kids got digital cameras or were lucky enough to buy the newly invented smartphones, Frankie refused anything but film. She had that thing strapped to her like an extra limb, filling it with yearbook photos, nature photos, sports photos. If she wasn't on the field herself, she was snapping photos of the field.

Back then, so many people told me it was young love, *kid* love, the kind of love that the moment I stepped into my freshman dorm room I'd forget. But I didn't forget—not for years. Not ever, actually. Every woman I was with was tainted with the ghost of mine and Frankie's relationship.

I avoided my brother's gaze and instead watched the kids chase a ball. "Yes. New York."

"Gross."

I laughed. "Right?"

Of course, the city itself wasn't gross. Not that I'd been

there, but I could understand the appeal. But being raised in Spring Harbors, with enormous yards and minimal traffic and quiet summer nights where the frogs sang symphonies and people caught fireflies in mason jars, New York was a different world. New Yorkers couldn't possibly understand the joy of the local restaurants that carried the best cream pie, or the ability on a bad day to drive to the old Blatnik Bridge to watch boats and fishers hauling in pounds of walleye, or stopping at a flea market to eat the best cheese curds of your life. Minneapolis was not nearly as busy as NYC, and after a weekend, I was exhausted and claustrophobic from the people, traffic, and tall buildings.

Sam cheered on the kids and settled back in the chair. "So why did you need a lift? Where's your car?"

I tried not to let the harness inside my chest tighten, but anything car related restricted my breathing. "Something's wrong with it. I have to take it in, but it's going to cost a gazillion dollars and take a week, and I don't have that kind of time." *Or money*. But I left that part out to avoid any chivalrous acts from my brother, who'd most definitely want to slip me some cash.

"I'd say you can bring it by, but I'm as useless as you are with cars," he said. "Ask Dad. He could probably help."

Nope. I loved my parents. But my golden rule was never to ask my parents for anything. Asking for help would lead into one of two things. One, they'd ask for help back with something that took twice as long, or two, it'd lead into some tired and thinly veiled "we're worried about you" or "you're not getting any younger... when are you going to settle down" type of conversations. Right now, I couldn't stomach either of those scenarios, even if it meant free car help.

I refocused on the game. "Come on, Henry!" I clapped as my nephew ran like a baby goat getting its walking legs, before he tripped and fell. My shoulders tensed until he hopped right back up and gave me the two-thumbs-up sign. I settled back into the chair and glanced at my brother. "Ah, look at him. He takes right after you."

"God, you're an asshole."

"Language." I lifted my finger to my mouth with a smirk. "Mom and Dad coming?"

"Nah." He clapped and hooted as some kid on the team kicked the ball farther than three feet. "Mom said they were gonna try, but you know them."

He didn't need to say more. Disappointment laced his voice, though he tried to sound nonchalant. Being raised by two German Midwesterners, the pecking order was work first, then church, then family. Watching a grandkid play soccer was considered a luxury, never to be indulged in until they completed all chores.

"They're going to run themselves into the damn ground," I said.

He nodded. "If you'd ever come project manage for them, they wouldn't do this."

"Oh, hell no. You're not laying this guilt trip on me." Fourth in the family pecking order—frugality. They could easily hire someone else to do the project management, but our parents lived by the motto of why pay someone for something when they could do it themselves. Every day while our father was out with the crew, Mom stayed at the store, answering emails and coordinating contractors.

Even though Sam had worked there since he was a teenager, he had a very Superman-like ability to draw clear boundary lines. When Lisa got her breast cancer diagnosis, and went through the radiation and double mastectomy surgery, everything changed. His life was no longer about work and supporting our family business. It was Lisa. Even after she went into remission, and by all accounts was fully recovered, he remained steadfast on his priorities. Then when they had

Henry, he told our parents his schedule was nine-to-five and no weekends, and they could take it or leave it.

They took it.

But I knew myself well enough to know I'd never draw that line. Once sucked into the family business, I'd never leave. Yes, my current schedule was punishing, but at least I was building and maintaining *my* business, *my* dream. Not theirs.

Sam cupped his mouth. "Yeah, Henry! Look tough out there!" He gripped the edge of his chair handles and swore under his breath at the referee. "So, what's Katey doing here?"

"*Frankie*," I said. "Her grandma passed, so she's settling her estate."

"That's too bad." The sun peeked through the clouds, and he tugged his hat lower. "Stuff like that's a beast. Her parents aren't doing it?"

I shook my head. When Frankie said her parents weren't helping, it wasn't a shock. Sure, I hadn't talked to them in fifteen years, but the town was small enough to hear through the grapevine if anything had changed—like consistent employment. They were nice-enough people, but flaky as hell. The type of parents with their lack of structure and rules that *seemed* cool growing up, but deep down I knew was a little icky. They skipped town a lot, threw back one too many at the local watering hole, and gave Frankie and Quinn Pop-Tarts for dinner.

Seeing the kids run around the field was pretty entertaining, more fun than I thought it would be, and the spring sun warmed my skin. During the winter, I dove full into hibernation mode, only poking my head out to hang out with Sam and the kids. Being holed up in my small townhouse for the last six months wasn't great for my soul.

I hated dating, but *really* hated it during the winter. The idea of getting all dolled up, then putting on scarves and hats and stepping into frozen tundra was terrible. And business was typically slow during that time, with only a handful of weddings around Christmas, New Year's, or Valentine's.

At halftime, as the kids sucked down orange slices, a blue pickup truck pulled into the parking lot and Frankie hopped out holding the cupcake boxes. *Whew.* I scurried over to her, meeting her halfway. "Thank you so much for doing this." As I reached for the cupcakes, the relief flooding me was probably not rational. Maybe unfair, and I didn't know the "adult" Frankie much, but I'd assumed Frankie would've totally flaked out and not shown up on time. Or ever, honestly.

Back in the day, Frankie was the worst for missing everything except her games. Date nights, study times, appointments, homework. Yes, I loved keeping a task list and schedule for myself, but when Frankie and I were together, I had this overwhelming anxiety to keep hers as well. My life revolved around reminders—reminding Frankie about her math homework, or that she had to babysit her sister, or that we promised to help Peaches clean her yard. Honestly, I wondered how adult Frankie made it on her own all these years without me being her personal assistant.

"It's all good, I've got them." Frankie waved away my hands. "Where we going?"

I pointed to the empty lawn chair. "Over by Sam."

As we crossed the grass to the field, Frankie's grin turned wide at my brother. "Sam Rose. Man, the last time I saw you, you were just getting your driver's license."

He grabbed the cupcakes from her with a thank-you nod. "Katey—sorry, Frankie. Last time I saw you, you were making out with my sister."

I landed a hard slap on his chest.

"What?" He shrugged. "Would it have been better to say you were snot-crying on the curb?"

I felt the blood rise in my chest. But if the comment affected Frankie at all, she didn't show it.

"See you still have that impeccable timing with humor, huh?" Frankie gripped the back of the empty lawn chair and watched the kids. "Which one of these little shits is yours?"

Sam pointed to the left field. "Number seven. Henry."

"Ah, he's cute." Frankie crossed her arms. "Must look like your wife."

Sam huffed. "Oldest joke in the world."

"I'm not joking, though." Frankie grinned.

It definitely felt like I was back in high school watching the two pick back up their love-but-mostly-fake-hate relationship. For a second, it felt like no time had passed. Sure, bitterness replaced sparkly feelings, but right now, it was a typical Saturday afternoon when my annoying brother and spunky girl-friend tried to out-jab each other.

With only one lawn chair, I stood next to Frankie. It took all of ten seconds for Frankie to get wrapped up in the game. "Come on, kids, you got this. Watch your instep! Dude, no. What are you doing? Don't use your hands!"

Frankie ripped off her jacket, tossed it in the chair, rolled up her sleeves and... *shit*. Frankie's white Henley was fitted, perfectly snug, and freaking hot. How did she get such defined forearms? Yoga? Weights? Carrying guilt for a decade?

Soon, Sam couldn't sit still and paced next to Frankie. Together they lamented about formation and push kicks and toe kicks and whatever-the-hell moves and agreed about not caring if the kids were in first grade, the ref should allow penalty kicks. When Henry made a goal, Frankie stuck two fingers in her mouth and whistled so loud it reached the clouds.

I checked my watch. "We should probably head out."

"Ah. We're good." Frankie waved me away without removing her gaze from the field. *Rude*. "We can leave in like five minutes."

My jaw flexed, and I sucked in my lips. People like Frankie disregarded time like they were brushing away a gnat. But time was *everything*. It maintained order. It kept things flowing. It showed *respect*.

Three minutes passed and my heartbeat kicked up an uncomfortable notch. "I really think we should go just in case we hit traffic."

Now Frankie flicked me a side-eye. "On the way to Maple Creek? Really?"

"Minnesota construction season, you know?" I tried hard to swallow back the annoyance in my voice. "You might have forgotten that while living in the big city." Minnesotans liked to joke that we had two seasons—Snow and Construction. But without knowing all the detours or road lane reductions, travel time could increase by ten or twenty minutes. And if that happened, we'd be late. And if we were late, whispers would spread of me being untrustworthy and irresponsible and incompetent and—

"Tommy and Olivia will be fine," Frankie finally muttered, breaking my train of thought. "Just a couple more minutes. Game's almost over."

The heartbeat now thudded in my throat. "I know I'm only tagging along, but these are *my* clients and if I'm present, I absolutely do not want to be even a minute late. Can we go? Now. Please." I was *not* letting anything ruin my chances at executing this wedding. Frankie's give-a-shit-less attitude would not poison my good name, no matter how hard she might try. I shifted toward Sam while tugging on my scarf. "Tell Henry I'm so proud of him."

Frankie grabbed her jacket from the chair and patted Sam on the back. "It was mediocre seeing you again."

"If by mediocre, you mean similar to the root canal I had last year, then agreed." Sam's eyes twinkled. "You two have fun. Mo—hit me up later if you want me to look at your car."

Frankie dug keys from her pocket. "It's just the spark plugs.

I ran to the hardware store before I grabbed the cupcakes and got a replacement. Should only take me like an hour to replace."

Wait... what? Frankie, a superb pain in my ass, had checked out my car, bought the parts, and was going to fix it? Everything stopped. But why? What did she have to gain by doing this? And yet, God, it'd be nice to have this fixed. "You... you don't have to do that."

"Yeah, I know." Frankie shrugged and unlocked the truck door. "But I figure forcing you to listen to Bon Jovi during the photo shoot will be a little payback."

My heart softened. More than I wanted. And way more than what I was comfortable with. I would not let my guard down, ever again. "You're *still* listening to them?"

Frankie climbed in the truck and fastened the seatbelt. "Greatest band of all time, and I'll never stop."

As we rolled out of the parking lot, the tiny flicker of hope I felt disappeared the moment I checked my watch. I gripped the handle and tried to breathe out a shaky breath. If we were even one minute late, no matter how kind Frankie had been this last hour, I would lose it.

FIVE

FRANKIE

Well, look at that. We're practically right on time. Not that Morgan's body language seemed to agree. On the way up to the farm, Morgan had remained almost totally silent, swiping manically on her phone and glancing at her watch no less than three billion times. If that didn't give me some serious relationship PTSD, I don't know what did. During our relationship, Morgan had never trusted me with anything—not buying our prom corsages, or making date-night plans, or filling up my truck with gas (*it only ran out once and she acted like it happened daily*). Nothing. Sure, was it nice sometimes? Yeah. My brain was like a ping-pong machine, and details and me were not friends. But did it also feel demeaning and frustrating? Yeah.

Morgan was almost as fidgety as me, which was not a good sign for someone normally borderline robotic. Thank God I'd run back to switch my motorcycle for the truck because when I got to Peaches's place, I realized I forgot to take my ADHD medication that morning. The beauty and curse of those meds—they kicked in right away. But then left my system just as quickly. Seemed like an invitation for disaster for someone like me—who was constantly forgetting tasks or procrastinating—to remember to take it when I was unmedicated.

I wasn't diagnosed with ADHD until I was twenty-one, when finally some of my doomscrolling on social media one day paid off, and I was inundated with "is this you?" type content. I saw myself in all of those ads and knew I had to make a change. As a kid I could never stay in my seat, often got in trouble for interrupting people or blurting out answers in class or constantly forgot lunch bags or backpacks at home. But as I entered into the professional world, the inability to complete tasks and forgetting things was no longer acceptable, and I was fired from my first few jobs after high school. I knew if I was serious about my photography career—which I was—I had to get some help.

The truck tires bumped over a gravel road, and I gripped the wheel. There was something so comforting about being behind the wheel in Peaches's truck—the same vehicle my grandma taught me to drive in at twelve. Yeah, country roads or not, there was nothing legal about me driving that young. But neither was my grandma refusing to wear her seatbelt and taking small sips of strawberry schnapps from a flask. "It's not even real alcohol," Peaches used to say while smacking her bright-pink-lipsticked lips and checking her reflection in the vanity mirror.

Thinking back on it now, everything about that sounded unethical and dangerous. But that was just who Peaches was.

I'd started sifting through all the things in Peaches's house, but I'd barely made a dent. I had been prepared for Peaches's death. Ready, even. And yet, two days ago I bawled in the kitchen over a stack of old *Good Housekeeping* magazines. Every item replayed a memory. The bags of scraps used for quilts, the clunky wooden sewing machine and drawers of threads, plastic Cool Whip containers used for Tupperware. Tucked away in a mothball-smelling closet were a million knitted blankets, sheets, and pillows, like an army of children might arrive and need to take a nap on her green shag carpet.

But selling this truck was going to break my heart. I ran my hands across the steering wheel, the familiar ridges massaging my palm. Every time I was in town, I slipped into the truck like a bath. The torn seat, the smell of the years imbedded into the fake leather, the clunky shifting gear, was like home. The truck itself carried memories, and I glanced at Morgan more than once to see if a flicker of those flashed through her during the drive. For all I knew, Morgan didn't remember the truck at all.

But surely, she remembered *a* truck, right? Sophomore year, during the fall, crisp orange and brown leaves passing by as we drove up the hill in Duluth for the million-dollar view of Lake Superior. Unhinging the tailgate, gathering blankets and candy. Staring at the water until the sky turned dark, then lying back on the truck bed and gazing at the stars. We held hands and talked about our dreams, and whatever cliché existed about the first time in the back of the vehicle didn't apply. It was magical. Trembling hands, nervous fingers, the chill in the air matching the goosebumps on skin. The stars and moonlight providing just enough light for two self-conscious girls exploring bodies for the first time.

So yes, I would sell this truck last and only to the right person.

Branches tapped on the window as I navigated down a road. A hand-painted wooden sign and an arrow said: Greenburg Farms—This Way.

"Almost there," I said as I swerved around potholes.

"I saw the sign."

God, that tight tone was ear-scratch-inducing. My jaw clenched. After ten minutes of one- or two-word answers, to a full-on dead stop, I was over the attitude. "What's your problem? Are you pissed that I asked you to come along?"

Morgan pulled her lips into her mouth. "I'm not *pissed*."

I tossed a "bullshit" side-eye.

Morgan exhaled through her nostrils. "Look, I hate being late. *Hate* it. If we're... if *I'm*... late, it's rude, shows the other person that their time is not as valuable as mine, and throws us off schedule. When that happens, it's hard for me to get back into a rhythm."

Ah. That old bitter anxiety bug was clearly gnawing on Morgan's nerves, and although I didn't fully understand, I wasn't a totally un-empathetic human being. Sure, I might fret a bit at situational things... like if the magazine would offer me a job. But as long as I had food in my belly and a roof over my head, I wasn't anxious.

But I definitely remembered this from our childhood—Morgan completely freaking out waiting for test scores, asking me if she sounded stupid when she did the dreaded class presentation, biting her nails as she waited for the college admissions response even though she was a straight-A student. The closest I ever came to that was junior year when my team was one game away from going to state in basketball, and we were down by twelve with four minutes left.

A few wild turkeys waddled across the road, and I skidded to a stop. Freaking wild turkeys? How did I forget they just roamed free like this? "We're like two minutes late."

"Five," Morgan snapped. "They may be your friends, but they're not mine and it's totally unprofessional. I'm going to be mortified when they're standing there waiting for us."

Jesus Christ, this one. Morgan may as well take a bullhorn and announce to the townsfolk that she thought I was an irresponsible failure. "They're not standing there waiting for us. What do you take me for? I wouldn't actually be late to a meeting with a client, friends or not." I gripped the shifter and jammed it into first gear. "I wanted to get here at one thirty, to scope out the place and bring in my equipment. Olivia and Tommy won't be here until two."

A silent *Oh* left Morgan's mouth in what I could only assume was an apology.

At the end of the path, I navigated the truck through an open rusted metal gate that looked like it was two seconds from falling over. Down the drive in front of a gray barn, I pulled over and killed the engine.

"Wow." Morgan slammed the truck door closed and stood, hands on her hips.

Uff-fucking-da. "Wow" was right. This place had gone downhill in a hurry. Granted, nearly twenty years had passed since I'd last stepped foot onto Pete and Patty's property, but I remembered it being filled with life. Back in the day, it was the land of strung holiday lights, music, and kids climbing on bales of hay.

The once sturdy barn which doubled as a small gift shop was faded and cracked with years of rain, snow, and hail. Broken chairs and tools scattering the lawn made the space look like a junkyard. Weeds twisted up the five-foot tall wheels of a tractor to the left, the formerly pristine trimmed bushes were overgrown, and dozens of dead hanging plants littered the fractured patio area. *Yikes.*

The maple trees sagged, low and sad, like they carried the memories of the joy-filled days of being tapped for syrup but crumpled under the weight of abandonment. I squinted against the sun and surveyed the rest of the property. Thankfully, the pines were still beautiful. But everything else was a disaster.

"I remember coming here." Pebbles crunched under Morgan's feet as she moved toward the barn. "It's, uh, changed. A lot."

Must've been during sophomore or junior year when I brought Morgan out here during the holiday season. Layered up like the abominable snowman with scarves and hats, we strolled hand in hand, drank hot chocolate with marshmallows, and waited for our turn to hop on a hayride driven by my uncle.

Morgan tapped the railing on the side of the barn. "It's still beautiful, though."

Um, what? "Beautiful?" No way did I just hear Morgan, who was literally wearing a white peacoat and some sort of sparkly pendant, call this place beautiful. Sure, my job was capturing the beauty in traditionally unbeautiful spaces, but this was on an entirely different level. "Are you being sarcastic?"

Morgan stuffed her hands into her jacket. "Not at all."

"This place looks like it's verging on being condemned by the authorities."

Morgan arched a brow. "And people think I'm the dramatic one. Have you never heard of rustic chic?"

"Sure. Pretty sure they're not talking about... this, though." I waved my hand toward the barn. As if on cue, a gust of wind kicked up and blew a chunk of something—God knows what— off the roof and onto the mushy ground.

Morgan stepped closer to the opening. "Come on, let's look inside."

The splintered wood barn doors with deep gouges missing were cracked open. To avoid my palms getting stabbed by a million slivers, I tucked my hands into my jacket sleeve and pulled.

"Oof." Morgan scrunched her nose. "It could use a little airing out."

What in the tetanus shot was happening in here? The place smelled like a combination of cat pee, mold, and ripe pungent compost. If I thought the outside was a hot mess, the inside was worse. Busted-up garden tools and machinery, a tossed-aside rusted sink, and dozens of broken mice traps were scattered across the barn, as if my aunt and uncle finally just gave up trying to trap any rodents.

Buckets, overflowing totes, and piles of God-knows-what covered with tarps filled the "gift shop" space, which I remembered as shelves flowing with wreaths, crocheted items, and blinged-out ornaments. No chance in hell would I lift the fabric and check what was underneath.

Morgan took a tentative step. "Guess you won't be taking any pictures in here, huh?"

Captain Obvious to the rescue. "Probably not." I stepped back into the fresh air and tried to remove the stench singeing my nose hairs. When Pete and Patty said they spent the summers on their lake home in Brainerd, but welcomed me to use the property for pictures, I was bummed. Would've been nice to see them in person after all these years. But now, I was grateful I didn't have to come up with some words on the fly about their rotting farm.

Morgan and I walked the property, finding some hidden gems. Sunbeams funneled through the lush greenery like a golden kaleidoscope, and I started envisioning the outside shots. The property itself really was beautiful, *thank God*, with rows of Christmas pine trees, sitting rocks, majestic oak trees, and a small shed that actually had the "good" rustic vibe.

Ugh. When did I become the photographer that liked to shoot farmhouse chic decor, but only if the "farmhouse" was in an Upper East Side penthouse? Minnesota had a lot of beauty, of course, but maybe seeing the New York city skyline for the last fifteen years had made me forget the quiet beauty in rural America. "Let's head back to the truck. I need to grab the stuff before Olivia and Tommy get here."

Morgan nodded but remained uncharacteristically quiet as her eyes darted across the property—probably scared that a rabid raccoon was going to get muddy paw prints on her white jacket. *Whatever*. Who the hell wore white anyway? It was the least practical of all the colors.

Back at the truck, the tailgate screeched as I dropped the latch. I tugged off the tarp and pulled out the totes carrying lenses, tripods, a reflector, and champagne for a celebration picture. I strapped a bag to my back and tucked items under my arm.

Morgan stepped in front of me and held out a hand. "I can help, you know."

I tried to swallow back the smirk. "You're wearing white."

"In all fairness, when I left the house this morning, I didn't know I'd be going to a farm." Morgan brushed her palms against the front of her jacket. "But we're good. Give me some."

In a stroke of photography luck, the bright sun hid behind a cloud. I snapped a couple of pictures and viewed the finder to check the exposure. As Morgan cupped her hand around her face to peer through a barn window, I used her as a test subject and snapped a few more.

The barn, as beat up as it was, translated a little better in the photo. I clicked at different angles, the trees, the outlines, and finally hung the camera from my neck. "Hey, can you step back and face me for a few test shots?"

Morgan clapped the dust from her hands. "Sure."

Beautiful or not, Morgan had zero clue how to pose. She kept her arms militant on her side, then shifted to pop them on her hips. I almost wanted to tell her the pose didn't matter since these were test shots, but it was too amusing seeing her try. "Forward a little, good, back," I instructed. God, this was fun. I actually didn't need her to move at all, and any moment now she was going to catch on. "No, two inches forward, two inches back."

"Christ, really?"

Now Morgan was rocking a super-*Vogue*, grumpy-model look. *This* was more authentic. I snapped a few more pics, then put her out of her misery. "Just be natural. I don't need you to pose."

The camera shutters were always a rush, like playing photography slots, never knowing which picture would be the treasure. I kept snapping when, finally, Morgan released whatever monstrosity was happening in her face and studied the barn door. And if I didn't have the camera, I wasn't sure I would've caught the slight parting of the plump lips, or the twinkle in her eyes as she stared at the wood.

I stopped snapping photos and slowly lowered my camera, taking in the sight. *God, she really is beautiful.*

A car door slammed in the near distance, and I twisted my neck. "They're here."

"Good." Morgan started walking toward the path. "Because I have an idea."

SIX

MORGAN

Throughout the years, I'd been present for close to a hundred wedding photo sessions. But normally I was running around the venue telling cake vendors where to set up, making sure the wedding party wasn't dipping too early into the champagne, and decorating like my life depended on it. I'd sneak quick peeks out the venue window but never found the picture-taking session to be all that interesting.

But today, I very reluctantly admitted that watching Frankie work was a thrill. As the camera clicked, even with the cloud cover, Frankie's eyes lit up with specks of amber and gold, becoming nearly honey-colored. After Olivia and Tommy arrived, and some pleasantries exchanged, Frankie flipped a switch. She was professional, engaged, her deep-set dimples fully on display—and someone I realized I didn't know. Teen Frankie wouldn't have had a quiet command over people like this or listened without interrupting. She would've charmed, sure, bulldozed, definitely, been loud, of course. But now she was gentle, empathetic, completely in control. My brain couldn't fully process what I was witnessing.

"Tommy, amazing. Head up, tilted like this. Okay, look into

Olivia's eyes. Think about the things that you love about her... think of your first date. Great, great." *Click, click.* Frankie rested her camera for a moment and shifted the couple. *Click, click.* "Let's head to the back."

I followed a few steps behind. The attention to detail Frankie took to capture photos was intense, and yet another thing I would have never put in the same sentence—Frankie and attention to detail. She tugged on sleeves, adjusted finger placement, swiped tiny hair strands that I hadn't even noticed. An hour in, and I was impressed. Not that I'd ever tell her that. Because no matter how impressive Frankie might be, she was still awful. Still the one who cared so little about anyone but herself, proven time and again.

The property behind the barn was stunning. *So much green.* Cedar and pine, underbrush lining the area, long swooping branches. Twigs crunched beneath my feet as I walked the path to the hundred-year-old oak tree with the two-seater wooden swing.

Tommy tugged at the rope, and the crackle of wood echoed in response. "Not sure we should sit on this."

"Dang." Olivia flipped her long, dark hair over her shoulder and frowned. "I really wanted to get this picture."

Frankie approached them, and even though I couldn't hear everything being said, it was obvious Frankie was in charge. Even Frankie's normal fidgets were muted and her body calm. The photo session wasn't part of my job description, but I always felt a deep sense of obligation that every aspect of the weddings I planned had to be perfect. The weight of this pushed on my shoulders, often waking me up at night in a sweat, but evened out as I checked items off the task list. But now, watching Frankie be in control, was... liberating. I inhaled a deep, pine-scented breath.

Whoa. Olivia and Tommy must both be professional squatters because the position Frankie had them in looked awkward as hell as their butts hovered over the seat and fingers gripped the rope. How Frankie would translate that into a good photo, I had no idea. But after spending time here today, no doubt Frankie could pull it off.

"Damn. Feel the burn." Tommy laughed as he stood. He grabbed Olivia, gave her a quick peck on the cheek, and whispered something in her ear that had Olivia beaming.

After spending an hour with Tommy, I came to a few conclusions. One, he was a nice-enough guy. Two, he really loved Olivia. Three, he could give an absolute shit less about any wedding details.

"Little break time. I need to set up a few things." Frankie crouched and dug through a tote.

Perfect. My turn. I stepped towards the couple, fingers crossed. *Please give me something.* "Are we any closer on the headcount? We really need a ballpark figure to help narrow down the already limited options for venues."

Olivia grimaced and glanced at Tommy. "Less than three hundred. I hope?" She tucked a long dark lock behind her ear. "If it were up to me, I'd say thirty."

"It *is* up to you." But sadly, I knew what Olivia meant. A decade in this business and one thing was consistent—the day was *rarely* about the individuals getting married. Everyone lobbed their opinions, from attendees to food. "You're the ones getting married."

Tommy chuckled and wrapped an arm around Olivia's waist. "You don't know our parents. We've both gotten the 'it would mean a lot to us if you'd invite...' and they rattle off some random names that we've never heard of. Just today my mom asked me to invite her former co-worker. I've never even met the person."

"I don't care, honestly." Olivia leaned her head on Tommy's broad shoulder. "One, two, a thousand. I just want to marry my love."

I swallowed back a surprising blip of emotion. *Love.* What a concept. All these years, after Frankie, the only things I loved were my family and my job. I'd dated enough, but never had that spark, that zing, that fire, I had with Frankie. Maybe I didn't give the other women enough of a try. Maybe I didn't give myself enough of a try. But now, watching these two... the looks, the natural support, the clear respect and adoration... would that ever be me?

Before I got emotional—and even worse, unprofessional—I cleared my throat. "Have you thought any more about colors?"

"I like green." Tommy dug the toe of his boot into the gravel.

Olivia groaned and gave me an overexaggerated eye roll. "I showed him sage, kelly, forest, seafoam... nothing."

"Green is green. We can do hot pink for all I care." His smile dropped and he raised his hands. "Wait, that sounds awful. I care. I promise I do. Just... not about the shade of green."

If I had more time, this would be kind of funny. The color indifference from one member of the couples I helped was almost a tradition. But I had zero time, and every decision held up another. *Ninety freaking days.*

Frankie crossed back towards us. "You guys ready for the next round?"

For the next hour, she guided the couple everywhere from the shed, to sitting on top of the gate, to leaning against trees. After another half hour passed, Frankie looked energized, and the couple fatigued. Frankie seemed happy to snap photos for hours, but if she didn't pick up on the obvious social cues, I might need to butt in and set the couple free.

Finally, Frankie pulled out the champagne—the last shot of the day. Tommy and Olivia shook the bottle and popped the top to squeals and laughter. Bubbly liquid blasted in the air like a fire hydrant, and even though I caught unexpected liquid shrapnel, I laughed.

"You guys did amazing." Frankie scrolled through a few photos on the camera. "These are gonna be beautiful. Give me at least a week or two to edit, and I'll send them your way."

As Tommy helped Frankie carry things back to the car, I strolled next to Olivia, kicking small rocks out of the way.

"It's so quiet out here." Olivia pulled in a deep breath as they approached Frankie and Tommy loading at the truck. "I love Duluth, but I can hear the traffic from our apartment. But out here... it's just so peaceful."

"It really is." The pinecone scent was rejuvenating. And past all the junk littering the ground, the budding trees and swaying tall grass *were* beautiful. Acres and acres of beauty...

The idea had crossed my mind when we arrived but firmed when Frankie was shooting pictures. *We can do this*. At the truck, I tugged Frankie out of earshot of the couple. "What if we had the wedding here?"

Frankie looked at me like I had just sprouted fresh alien ears. "*Here?* As in funky smelling, broken windows, probably wild animals burrowed in places I don't want to think about, *here?*"

Absolutely. The overflowing piles of broken junk shifted from daunting to manageable. The trees looked alive, green, welcoming. This could work. "Do you think your aunt and uncle would be open to it?"

"Christ, I don't know." Frankie blew out a slow breath. "Maybe? But... how would that even work? I mean... look at this place."

I *had* looked at this place. For the last two hours, I scoured the property. With each glance, the place transformed from "broken" to "opportunity." Would it be a hell of a lift? Yes. Did I have a million things to do besides help fix up the venue? Double yes. But could it be done? I was pretty sure. "Leave the details to me. I want to see what Olivia thinks."

"And Tommy," Frankie said.

I withheld a chuckle. "Yes, and him." I raced back to the couple. *Please, please, please go for this.* I tried to calm my breath before reaching them to not seem too overexcited, but I almost couldn't help it. This place was *the place.* "I have an idea. If we can make it work, what do you think about having the wedding here?" I tried to gauge their thoughts with the glances they shared. "Obviously, we'd need a crew. It'd take a ton of work, and probably a chunk of money, but you have a pretty hefty budget. We could swap the cost of fixing up this place and a small stipend in place of a larger rental. And, you know, the golf course you originally wanted to rent would probably cost about the same."

Several moments passed, and with each one my heart thumped stronger. Tommy's head tilted from side to side as Olivia paced with her lips pulled tight. I could almost see Olivia's wheels turn as she looked across the property, at the barn—that seemed no longer so *broken* as it was *weathered*—and back at her fiancé. My belly fluttered while my mind shifted into fifth-gear overdrive. This would solve 90 percent of our problems. The only issue would be time and crew. But my parents owned a remodeling business... Pete and Patty's place had a shed... We could rent high-quality portable toilets that flushed and had sinks... Since their tree farm was already a licensed business, they probably had the right insurance and things.

Maybe. *Hopefully.*

I eyed Frankie's neutrally frozen face. Probably scared to skew Tommy and Olivia's response. But dang it, right now, Frankie better skew.

Tommy grabbed Olivia's hand. "What do you think?"

Olivia ran her tongue along the inside of her cheek, then glanced at Frankie. "You think your aunt and uncle would go for this?"

A long moment passed. "Maybe?" Frankie said. "My

parents said they've been talking about retiring, so they might either be super open to it because it will up the value if they sell or totally opposed because of the hassle."

Please. I pulled Frankie to the side in case I had to get on my knees and beg. "Would you talk to them?" I gripped Frankie's forearm like my nephew Henry pleading for a holiday gift. "I'd take care of all the details... the cleanup, the hiring, the prep. We could use that big machine shed to store the... leftovers. The only thing we might need from them is signatures. But they could sit back and do nothing."

My voice was rushed, but I couldn't help it. Right now, everything hinged on this space working. Absolutely no other options, existed. If Frankie didn't think this could work, we were done. The wedding could not happen the way the couple wanted, I would lose my wages, and my business would officially close.

For the love of God, this had to work.

"I don't know about this..." Frankie said, her arms crossed. "That's a ton of work."

I gritted my teeth. "*Please*, Frankie. I'll handle everything. You know me. If I put my mind to something, I'll do literally everything to make it work."

A scoff left Frankie's mouth. A real, genuine scoff, enough where I flinched and took a step back like she'd flicked me on the forehead.

She dipped her head at me, her whiskey-brown eyes narrowing. "You *must* be joking."

Heat filled my face. That tone was like a punch to the gut, a cross between condescending and incredulous, and I felt it directly in my core. I tossed a quick glance at Olivia and Tommy, who were thankfully in a quiet discussion out of earshot.

This right here was not about our past, what may have happened, who let who slip away all those years ago. This was about my business and livelihood, not that Frankie knew that, and her family friend getting married. I opened my mouth to snap something snarky back but instead pulled in a deep breath through my nose.

"Listen. Whatever history we have, right now, can we please bury it? I think this place is our last option. All I'm asking you to do is have a conversation with your aunt and uncle." I twisted the rings on my fingers. "Please. Just ask them. Not for me, but for Tommy."

Frankie tipped her head at Tommy and Olivia. A moment passed, then two. Frankie nibbled on the inside of her cheek and finally her shoulders softened. "Fine, I'll talk to them," she said. "But that's it. I want nothing to do with this after that. I'll let you know what they say, then after that I'll see you in August."

I walked past the crisp American flag next to the even crisper pride flag waving in front of Peaches's house. God bless my grandma, the first in the neighborhood to raise a pride flag outside her home the moment I came out at twelve. I'll never forget biking here after school one day and watching Peaches hoist that thing tall and proud, the rainbow waving majestically in the wind. Throughout the years, as Peaches's garden overgrew, her lime-green couch sunk, and the crank on her windows stopped working, she still replaced both those flags with new ones every two years.

I tossed my keys on the side table and looked around the space. No matter how many times I entered the house, the smell covered me like a warm weighted blanket in the middle of a snowstorm. The scent of my grandmother's Elizabeth Taylor Passion signature perfume, cinnamon from decades of baking, old carpet, and dusty furniture imbedded into every fiber. I wanted to capture it in one of the thousand mason jars Peaches had in the basement and bring it with me when I returned to New York.

After being back for over two weeks now, I thought I'd be

further along with packing up Peaches's house, but I swore it looked the same as when I started. But every item held a memory, and every memory deserved to be honored. For years, I smirked about Peaches being a hoarder and holding on to things like random container lids with no containers. And here I was, looking at the same box of multi-colored crocheted granny squares that I'd been staring at all week, refusing to add them to the donation pile.

I flopped on the guest bed I'd been staying in since returning to Spring Harbors, and the bed springs croaked in response. My parents had reluctantly offered me a room in their house, but I figured I'd be dragged into some MLM presentation with my mom or forced to join my dad at the pawn shop. Renting my dad's Harley for a hefty fee for the summer—even though he could no longer ride—was a favor enough. Although Peaches's ghost lingered the halls, sleeping at this house was a safer bet.

Last night, I got ahold of Pete and Patty and chatted with them about using their property for a wedding. At first, it was a quick and resounding no. To which I nearly said, "Oh, thank God," and hung up. But guilt gnawed at me. I could see the desperation in Morgan's eyes, and only marginally cared to help her if I was being honest. Was there a little lingering bitterness between Morgan and I? Obviously. And her lack of options wasn't my problem. I was hired to shoot the wedding and engagement photos, not make sure they had a venue.

But I'm also not an idiot. I'd seen Woodlands and could recognize that the likelihood of other options existing were minimal if nonexistent. And Tommy's mom had been solid to me growing up. A neighborhood woman with a kind smile and a lush strawberry field who liked to bring buckets of the fruit to our house. She was someone who'd often "pop by" when Quinn and I were little, probably noticing our parents were gone and we were too damn young to be alone. And it didn't sit right with me that she might not have a place to properly watch her son get married.

So, I pressed Pete and Patty some more, asked what Morgan could do to sweeten the pot. Was it money? Making sure certain things weren't touched? Preserving the land? Finally, it boiled down to this: The amount of shit they accumulated over the years overwhelmed them, but they didn't have the energy to sift through it all. Some of the items were valuable, some had family history, and most was junk.

So, they'd agree to Morgan's rental fee offer and remodeling idea on one condition: I had to be there every step of the way to oversee, to make sure that Morgan—a family outsider—didn't throw anything meaningful and respected the property.

I shifted my focus back to everything I needed to do today, and grabbed my phone and called my sister.

"Hi, you've reached Quinn," she said after two rings. "Sorry to have missed your call, but I am currently tits deep in a heaping pile of unread emails and Slack messages. I'll call you back when I'm dead. Beep."

Oh, Quinn. I missed the dramatics. "You know voicemails don't actually beep anymore, right? Mom may still have her answering machine from the nineties, but we do not."

"Whatever. You've abandoned me just like our childhood cat and the last delivery guy who promised to come back with the egg rolls he left at the restaurant. It's been a week and I'm still waiting by the fire escape window to see if he'll pull up."

I stuffed a second pillow behind my head and tried to wiggle into a comfortable position. "First off, our cat was Mom's cat and lived till he was nineteen. Second, when was the last time you had a homemade meal?"

"Hmmm," Quinn said. "When did you leave? Then."

"Yes, but I froze like ten fresh meals for you. Lasagna, soups, enchiladas—"

"I know, and I love you for that. But for real, I've stayed in the office late every night this week and have already eaten by the time I get home. Don't worry. I'll gorge myself this weekend."

The sound of slurping came through the phone and even though it was seven p.m. East Coast time, I'd bet good money it was an iced triple espresso.

"All right, scale of one to ten," Quinn said. "How are things going with... *ahem*."

That was a loaded question. Better than expected. Worse than expected. Every moment was this weird mash-up clouded with a lifetime of memories while starting fresh ones with someone I didn't know anymore. Morgan was cranky, angry, stubborn, then had these flickers of sweetness, and none of this was doing anything positive for my insides. "You can say her name, you know." I put the phone on speaker and interlocked my fingers behind my head. "Is it a real one to ten or can I include negative numbers?"

Quinn released a low whistle. "Shit. That bad, huh?"

Yes and no. Definitely and not at all. Seeing Morgan again was certainly stirring something, and I didn't like it. Memories suck. I wasn't happy being smacked in the face daily with reminders of why I left this place. Growing up, the only place I had felt confident was on the field or with Morgan. It took years to shake that self-doubt and evolve into who I was today.

Back then, I hid my insecurities by being the loudest, holding my head high, and fighting with anyone who dared to talk shit. More than once, I got a technical foul by ramming into a bully on the basketball court. I specifically joined co-ed hockey because of the rush of hurling full speed ahead and body-checking a dickhead into the wall. But with Morgan, this beautiful blonde, rigid angel, I was authentically myself. And I always thought I was enough.

But when Morgan wouldn't come to New York, that fragile ego shattered with the realization that I *wasn't* actually enough.

Finding my new identity in New York, moving from being Katey with the long hair and gym shorts and little direction, to Frankie Lee, an admired, respected, even successful photographer, helped assemble those shattered pieces. I finally became the person I knew I was—someone who loved as hard as I hated, who cried as hard as I laughed.

"It's not bad so much as it's… a lot," I finally said, tugging at the carnation comforter on the bed. "We had the photo shoot with Tommy and Olivia at Pete and Patty's on Saturday."

"Oh, you went there?" Quinn's voice rose. "God, that place was magical. I loved it so much as a kid."

"It was definitely something, but I wouldn't call it magical." I rolled to my side on the thin mattress. *Ouch.* The stupid spring dug into my hip. I flipped over, gave up, and paced. "They're clearly overwhelmed and haven't kept up the place. The barn is filled with so much crap I'm worried a dead body might be buried in there, and the yard is practically destroyed."

"Shut up. Do they still do the Christmas stuff?"

"Only the trees." Maybe my memories were muted, but I swore as a kid they had endless rows of giant pines. But on Saturday, I only saw them if I stood at the top of the hill. "No gift shop, nothing. They have a little bit of new growth planted, but that's it."

Quinn paused. "Damn, that's depressing. It's like my one happy childhood memory."

I dug my thumbnail at a tear in the wallpaper. "Pretty sure your happiest childhood memory is when you were the first one in your grade to wear a bra."

"Really? That was the *worst.* And thanks for bringing up that lovely little morsel. I can practically feel the underwire dig into me." Quinn groaned. "What sort of nefarious shit did we do in our past life to be all boobs and no ass?"

"Speak for yourself." I laughed, but Quinn was spot-on. I'd grown comfortable with my body over the years, appreciating the natural ability to maintain muscle. But seeing people like Morgan, whose curves spanned from hell to heaven, sometimes that little insecurity bug nipped at me. "Anyway, long story short, since Tommy and Olivia can't wait to get married, but also have zero time, they've hired Morgan. She's scoped every place within two hours' drive for a venue and there's literally nothing available."

Another slurp sounded over the phone. "So, what are you guys going to do?"

In the kitchen, I slid out a stool from under the kitchen island. "Well... Morgan wants to fix up Pete and Patty's barn and have the wedding there."

"That's a freaking *huge* undertaking," Quinn said in between sips. "Why's your voice all cranky?"

I placed the phone face up on the counter and rested my head on the cool countertop. "Because Pete and Patty would only agree to it if I oversaw the entire thing."

"Shit."

My sentiments exactly. A tiny part of me was almost excited about the idea. Being stuck in Peaches's house all day wasn't doing a lot for my mental health. I needed to be outside, moving, and in the sun, not inside packing boxes. But being stuck with Morgan for the summer sounded nearly as suffocating.

"Doesn't something like that take years?"

"You'd think, but Morgan is like Ms. Speederton and is already knee-deep in moving this along. Ever since I offered to talk to Pete and Patty, I'm dodging calls, texts, and emails like a boxer in the ring." I wasn't even exaggerating. In the last two days, I'd received dozens of messages. Everything from her ideas on hiring a few folks from Morgan's parents' crew, bringing up an electrician from Brainerd, and, after making ten phone calls, finding a guy in Minneapolis who had an in-stock window to replace the broken one in the barn. "Why not use a single mode of communication and send one update a day? I feel like I'm playing whack-a-mole on messages."

"Well, as a *premier* and *highly sought-after* executive assistant—who's also seriously cute—I can tell you there are very specific reasons why you'd use different modes of communication." I could almost hear Quinn smiling over the phone. "For someone who shuns nearly everything digital, like you, that sounds seriously overwhelming, though. For real. I feel for you."

I stood, moved toward the coat closet and fiddled with the squeaky door handle. Of course, part of this was simply seeing Morgan's name pop up over and over on my screen. Even though the shock dulled, I always tensed before pulling up the messages.

"So, what are you going to do?" she asked.

"Honestly, I don't know. If I'm the reason that Tommy doesn't get the wedding he and Olivia want, I'll feel like shit," I said. "But spending a summer with my ex is not how I envisioned this trip back home. I'm trying to put things to rest, not stir up any drama."

Maybe I was the asshole here, though. Besides packing up Peaches's house, I did have the time. And it was pretty obvious that Pete and Patty's place was the couple's last option. Working outside for the summer sounded pretty damn good, too. But inside, I knew I was holding back because of this deep-seated anger towards Morgan. When she broke up with me all those years ago, I held on to that grudge like a bulldog. She crushed me, to the deepest part of my soul, and still had not apologized. Doing her a massive favor like this felt like I was tipping the scales in her favor again. Doing what she wanted to do, because she said. Just like when we were together.

"I think you'll make the right decision," Quinn said.

She didn't need to say any more. I knew exactly what she meant. *Dammit.*

"All right, blue-whale-in-the-room question."

I grinned. "You do know the phrase is *elephant* in the room, right? I'd hate for you to be in a boardroom and drop that little zinger."

"Um, yes, but a blue whale is bigger than an elephant, so I'm starting a trend," Quinn huffed. "Besides, the people at work are humorless, so I test things on you to see if they'll land in the real world."

"It didn't land."

"Good to know." Quinn sipped again. "*Sooo*, have you heard from the big dogs yet?"

The big dogs. AKA *Birch & Willow*. My dream. My *love*. Even though it had only been a few weeks—and they said it would take at least a month or two—I had a delusion that my portfolio and interview chops blew everyone else out of the water, and the hiring manager had slammed her hands on the desk and loudly declared, "I don't need to see any more. We found the one!"

I lowered myself to the ground and ran my hands through the shaggy carpet. "Not yet."

Quinn paused. "It's going to happen. Lunar year, moons aligned, stars everywhere, *going to happen*."

"Oh no. You've been watching too many reels while I'm gone."

"Well, what the hell else can I do at night when you're not here to read me a bedtime story?"

I chuckled. "By bedtime story, you mean our true crime docuseries on Netflix."

"*Obvi*," Quinn said. "For real, though, you're super gifted. It'll happen, manifesting or not. You got this."

God, I missed my little sister. When she moved in with me after everything that went down in New York, it had been a mutually beneficial financial decision. But now I couldn't imagine a better roommate. "I really don't hate you."

"I really don't hate you, either," Quinn said. "I gotta go."

I treated myself to a few more moments of quiet before diving in to organizing. *Okay, okay... where do I start?* Closets, bathroom, kitchen, or garage. *Oh!* Linen closet.

The closet held ratty towels tumbling over themselves, bins of products and medicines, rags, a half dozen empty spray bottles. I popped my hands on my hips for a moment, then started dropping towels into a bin.

Wait. Towels would make a good insulator for glass. I slid the box against the wall and moved to the kitchen instead but pivoted. The kitchen had too many items with too many memories, and the linen closet had no emotional attachment. I could do everything else besides the towels.

Good plan. I snapped open a garbage bag and moved to dump the container of meds into it. *Wait. Can you just throw expired meds in the garbage, or would that seep into the landfills? Is this something I should turn in to the local fire or police station? The last thing I need is to mess with the pristine air around here and have karma pay me a visit.*

I googled expired medication disposal. Christ, there was a ton of information. Articles on state rules and guidelines, prescription meds vs syrups vs pills, landfills, and poisoning the earth and...

Maybe I should just finish the kitchen. Or maybe I should take down all the paintings. Yes! Good idea. But would I want to keep any of them? Hmmm. I might want to, but we don't have a ton of space in our two-bedroom apartment. Maybe I'll ask—

Stop it. God damn my brain sometimes. I grabbed a notepad from the nightstand and scribbled.

- Bedroom
    - Closet
    - Dresser
    - Wall

- Kitchen
  - Cabinet
  - Right side drawers
  - Left side drawers
- Linen closet
  - Towels
  - Linens
  - Medication

There. My brain finally decided to settle and I traipsed into Peaches's closet. The smell of mothballs, cedar blocks, and unwashed sweaters from the '80s filled my nose. *Oof.* I grabbed a large box for donations, tugged off the clothes from the hangers, and started piling up the garments. I stretched all the way to the back and froze. A plastic bag. Who knew what the hell might be in here. All of this felt a little bit like going through someone's underwear drawer. Chances were if it was stuck in the back of a closet in the bag, I probably shouldn't look inside. I took a breath and opened.

"Huh."

Inside was a sombrero, black wig, mustache, wide tie, white shirt, and embroidered belt. *Oh Lord,* I remembered this cringeworthy outfit. Peaches had worn it to hand out candy at Halloween the year I turned fifteen. I'd gently told her it was bad to appropriate a culture like that and kind of racist.

Peaches had waved those words away. "Nonsense. You know how much I love Mexico." She proceeded to talk about her favorite Mexican restaurant, her best friend, Maria Lopez, who she had coffee with every morning (*who was the one who gave her the outfit in the first place, she'd tsked*), and how she celebrated Cinco de Mayo every year. In my heart of hearts, I knew Peaches was not trying to be hateful but was too old and stubborn to be taught anything else.

My lips trembled. I distinctly remembered being at a party

that night, Morgan somewhere else, when someone offered me a fruit juice with rum. If I closed my eyes, I could still remember the burn, then the elation, then the severe nausea and shame. At midnight, I'd called Peaches begging her to pick me up and not tell my parents. I'd been bawling while puking outside in the bushes, totally convinced I'd get a minor consumption arrest and Coach would kick me off the team for drinking.

Peaches had come tearing around the corner, threw me into the truck, and let me sleep it off. She gave me a one-time-only get-out-of-jail-free card. "I'd pick you up anytime, no questions. But I can't be hiding shit from your parents."

Thankfully, Peaches never had to repeat that moment. The sight of fruit-juice-and-Halloween-candy-laden vomit was enough for me to not drink again until I was legal.

A tightness gripped my chest. I missed Peaches. *So much*. I slumped back on the faded yellow daisy comforter and put my head in my hands. What I would give to talk Peaches one last time and get some no-bullshit advice on what I should do about this summer. I came here to officially bury my past, settle Peaches's affairs, and only return every few years for an obligatory weekend visit with my parents. Not spend the summer dusting up terrible memories with an ex who changed the trajectory of my heart.

Staring at the yellowish stain on the popcorn ceiling that had been there since I was a kid, I imagined Peaches standing in the doorway with her faded blue nightgown, bonnet in her hair, some nightly cordial in her hand, waiting for me open up on whatever was bothering me.

"I don't like to pry," she'd always say, knowing damn well that was her way to pry.

I didn't need to imagine too long what I'd say to her if she were here. And I knew what her exact response would be.

EIGHT
MORGAN

Satin button-down pajamas do not get the love they deserve. Sure, on movies or TV shows they might show people wearing them, but I've never known anyone besides me who actually owns a pair. Most stick with cotton, a more practical and breathable material. But with the temperature rising just a touch every day, my satin-pajama-wearing nights would be coming to an end any day now.

Two days had passed since the engagement photo session with Frankie, and I needed to do everything possible to take my mind off the fact that my fate rested in the hands of a woman I didn't trust. So, I slipped on my pajamas and grabbed an over-stuffed bowl of cereal for dinner (*don't judge*), sunk into the couch, and clicked on my favorite guilty pleasure, *The Real Housewives of Salt Lake City*. No matter how entertaining, though, I couldn't stop thinking about Frankie.

After the engagement photo shoot, she'd brought me back to my car and fixed my spark plug on the side of Main Street. It went way above the call of duty, and I almost hugged her right there in front of the coffee shop but refrained. I did, however, offer to buy her dinner, which she declined, lightning-fast.

It wasn't *dinner* dinner. It was more an "I'll pay your labor with food" type of offer. But the snap rejection... *Whatever.* Frankie could think what she wanted and let her ego get in the way of what was clearly, obviously, meant as a friendly gesture.

I really needed to stop dwelling on that interaction.

Another thing I should stop? Practically salivating while watching Frankie take charge not once, but twice, that day. I was the least submissive person I knew. I was the one in charge, *always.* But during the photo shoot, then while fixing the car, having Frankie be totally in control made places tingle that definitely should not tingle for a terrible, awful ex-girlfriend.

I crunched into the Honey Nut Cheerios with extra honey swirled on top—Henry's and my favorite—and tried to pay attention to the TV but couldn't. Had Frankie talked to Pete and Patty yet? What did they say? And more importantly, why wasn't Frankie answering any of my calls or texts?

As much as I wanted to hate Frankie, I didn't. She wasn't a bad person, so I didn't want to believe this ghosting was a way to somehow retain control or get back at me for what she perceived as past relationship mistakes. She knew how important this was, right? Not only for me, but for Olivia and Tommy. Yesterday, I made a final, last-ditch effort call to a similar farm two and a half hours outside of town—way further than Olivia wanted—and they were not interested in having people on their property.

So, I was done. My business livelihood hung on my ex-girlfriend, who I barely knew. I grabbed the honey bottle and squeezed more on top of the milk and cereal, and took another bite.

Who was Frankie, now? What made her go from Katey to Frankie? When she left, she was a hyperactive, inattentive, totally unpredictable wound-up ball of energy. Which, I hated to admit it, could be very fun. She'd kept things interesting during our relationship for sure, convincing me to do things I'd never normally do. Skinny-dipping in a lake at night (I still cringe about the amount of lake beasts that could've eaten me alive), getting my ear cartilage pierced, which hurt like hell, making out in a truck a block away from my parents' house.

But now, she was a bit more serious, more laid-back, perhaps even more responsible? She'd showed up with Henry's cupcakes, she snapped photos like a pro, and when I finally took the time yesterday to dive into her website, it was extremely well-thought-out, with a portfolio of hundreds of gorgeous pics. A very, very small part of me wanted to get to know the new Frankie.

And then I'm zapped back to her hardly responding to my messages. Perhaps I sent ten too many. *Perhaps*. But I wanted her to know how buttoned-up I was in case she forgot, so she could ease Pete and Patty's minds that I'd make this work no matter what. She needed to see I had contacts, and knew how to run my business, and could succeed. All I needed was a chance.

I scooped a heaping spoonful and bit into the cereal when my phone buzzed.

FRANKIE:

Confirmed. They're in.

My fingers tapped the call button before I could stop them. "They said yes?!" I asked with a mouthful of food. I muted and crunched as quickly as I could, then swallowed.

"First, it's customary to text someone that you'll be calling first, otherwise you give off some seriously boomer vibes," Frankie said on the line. "Second, it is *really* customary to say hi first."

I wanted to say something snarky but couldn't. In the past forty-eight hours, Frankie had saved my ass not once but twice. I hated how much I loved it. "Hello. Top of the morning to you, my fellow lady."

"Whoa."

Something that could only be described as a chortle sounded through the phone.

"Wait a second," Frankie said. "I'm not a comedy connoisseur or anything, but I *think* you just tried to be funny. I need a moment alone with my thoughts to consider the enormity of this situation."

"You're a dick. Please, I'm dying to know everything." I clicked pause on the TV. Frankie didn't need to know my preoccupation was indulging in what surely was going to be a screaming match between some self-absorbed rich ladies. "What did they say?"

A *goosh* sound of a pop can opening sounded over the phone. "Honestly, they were a little reluctant at first. Not because they don't want to help us out, but because the whole concept was overwhelming." A gulping noise sounded. "But we chatted money, about their right to veto anything, and confirmed they won't be asked to lift a finger."

My chest lifted. "Perfect. And they were cool with it? Should I contact a lawyer to draw up some paperwork?"

"Nah. I think that's the piece that freaked them out the most. Contracts and legal stuff. They're 'handshake deal' type of people."

I bit my lip. Of course, not hiring a lawyer would save money. But handshake deals were nerve-racking, even though that was common practice around town. "Okay. What else?"

A long pause followed. "There is one caveat on all of this, though, and they won't budge." I swore I could hear her swallowing through the phone and the hair on the back of my neck stood up. "They refused to do any of this unless I'm there, every day, overseeing everything with you."

My stomach dropped. *Every* day? Together? Frankie and me? I fanned the bottom of my pajamas, which were quickly turning into a thermal body wrap. "Every day?" was all I managed to squeak out. I hadn't spent any significant amount of time with Frankie in fifteen years. What if she actually had evolved into a terrible human being? Was she still late all the time? What happened if she didn't show up, or completely flaked out, or left—as she was obviously known to do—would the word-of-mouth-only contract then be null and void?

God, it was hot in here. I unbuttoned the top two buttons and rolled up my sleeves. Throughout my life, I'd faced enough adversity. The love of my life leaving without any warning. Opening my own business. Watching my brother and his wife fight a cancer battle. Tiptoeing on the edge of losing my business. If I had to work with my ex-girlfriend to save my company, I would.

"*Every* day," Frankie repeated.

I flicked the side of my thigh, my brain verging on a full-on breakdown. "And, ah, what do you think?"

"What do I think about working together every day on the first summer I've had off in my entire life? Peachy."

It sounded like she had a teasing tone to her voice, but I didn't know adult Frankie that well, and this could be her being passive-aggressive. "So, you'll do it?"

"I didn't actually say that. I'm just repeating what they told me," she said. "Do you even want to work with me this summer?"

Knots filled my stomach. *Want* was a very strong word. And the answer was, no, I did not want to work with Frankie this summer. I'd never worked with a partner before, and if I was going to, my untrustworthy, impulsive ex-girlfriend would be the very last person I'd choose. *This is to save my business... This is to save my business...* I exhaled the taste of eating crow— which was a seriously disgusting term—and swallowed. "I, ah... yes, of course, I'd love to work with you. It'll be... fun... to take this time and catch up."

Puke. This felt more terrible than not having a venue. So many seconds ticked on my analogue clock that I wondered if

Frankie heard me at all. I was just about to see if the phone disconnected when a soft exhale sounded.

"I didn't hear a please."

God, she sucked. *Inhale for counts of four before spouting off.* "Please."

A moment passed. Then another. "I like pleases to be accompanied with a 'pretty' and 'with a cherry on top.'"

Well, if this didn't just flash me back to the past. We used to do this to each other—when Frankie really wanted me to go to a game, she'd say this to me, or when I really wanted to do a joint book report, I'd say this to her. I'm not sure if she remembered that or was just teasing. Either way, I gritted my teeth. "You are the biggest asshole in the world." A smile escaped. "You're going to make me beg, aren't you?"

"Sure am."

Now this time, the smile in Frankie's voice was undeniable. She was officially, 100 percent the worst human alive. "Pretty, pretty, pretty please with a freaking bowling ball-sized cherry on top, will you help me out?" The words tasted icky. After this, from now until eternity, I'd fly solo.

"Wow, that was a lot of emotion, and I felt it right here. Oh, I'm tapping my heart for reference," Frankie said, clearly loving every painful moment of this. "For real, though, my aunt and uncle love their place, but I get the sense they are over it." She took a loud, sharp breath. A few moments passed before she spoke. "Look. I know you're ambitious. But we're talking about not only cleaning out that massive disaster station but also remodeling a broken-down barn in less than three months. Can you even find a crew that quick?"

"Don't worry. I've totally got this." But those words prickled the back of my throat. Supplies, permits, workers, equipment, design, on top of planning a wedding, in *ninety days*. If given more time, no problem. I do this stuff in my sleep. I've planned hundreds of weddings. But ninety days to remodel *and* plan?

Yes, I'd sent Frankie at least a dozen texts these last two days talking about my contacts and how I would make this work if Pete and Patty agreed to it, but that was me in fighting mode. This was now reality. I scratched at my neck. We were out of choices. Marlboro-gate was the last real venue available, and no way would I have the wedding there.

"Are you sure?" Frankie said. "This is a ton of work, not to mention a gazillion moving parts."

It's like she can read my mind. "I can handle it." *I absolutely cannot handle it.* Why did I say that? My belly churned with the undigested cereal, and I pushed the bowl to the side. Floor measurements, plumbing, new windows, cleaning, junk removal... *My God*, where would we put all the stuff? All moisture depleted from my mouth and skyrocketed to my forehead. "I've got this," I choked out.

"Cool."

Ugh, I wanted to pluck out Frankie's annoyingly beautiful brown eyes with that word. I hated this so much... this need, this dependency, on someone else. These things always ended in a disaster. It's why I never took on an employee, it's why I owned my own business, it's why I stayed single all these years. Dependency was an unsteady, splintered crutch that could break at any time.

"I mean, *we've* got this," I said, fanning my notebook across my face.

Here we go. Like it or not, for the next three months, Frankie and I needed to be locked at the hip.

I tossed the bag on the counter and dug out ten rolls of packing tape, and a twelve pack of Sharpies. From here on out, I had zero excuse to not have tape or markers. In less than two weeks, I'd lost them all. Yes, there was a huge amount of crap scattered across Peaches's place, but it's like some packing-supply goblin crept in during the day and ate up the materials. I popped open a drawer next to the dishwasher to add the pens.

"Seriously?" I groaned. In the drawer sat one of the missing tapes. Who knows when I did that? I really needed to be more organized, but the piles surrounding me made me want to choke.

In the field shooting or while editing, I know exactly what I want to do. My beautiful gift of hyperfocus takes over and I can manage massive amounts of work in a short period of time. But clutter and making a ton of decisions, and being surrounded by so much stuff, pushes me heavy into decision paralysis. Some-times, I love being in control. But times like this, I'd give anything just to have someone tell me what to do.

Which... will be my next three months. I really should be careful about what I wish for. Morgan clearly had no problem telling me, or anyone else, what to do. I'd already fielded about ten text messages from her today, one email, and dodged a call from her at the store... which reminded me... *Oops. I forgot to call her back. I'm sure she'll call any minute now.*

This, I remember well from back in the day. Morgan always on my ass for something or another. Remembering my gym bag, or to study for some assignment, or to return a library book. Sometimes I hated it, and sometimes I loved it. A cross between feeling insulted and cared for, and depending on my mood it could swing one way or the other. But I understood it came from a place of love.

Growing up, it probably looked to outsiders like I was the tough one. Just because I loved sports and could tackle the shit out of anyone. But I always cried just as easily. Still do. Morgan was always more emotionally strong and stoic. But I can't help but think of the way she was at her nephew's soccer game. Back in the day, I was the one who'd babysit for pocket money and Morgan didn't like kids. She always said they were too loud and messy, which wasn't a lie, but I sort of thrived on that. But at the game, I saw this softness, almost motherly side to Morgan, and I couldn't help but wonder what else changed about her over the years.

My phone buzzed. I glanced down. *I knew it.*

MORGAN:

I'm setting up a goat delivery for the second week of July.

The sheer randomness of her messages, like I'd been floating around in her head all day, jolted me from my thoughts. We hadn't even reached day one, and she wasn't running anything by me that I was supposed to oversee. Honestly, I was kind of relieved.

I hovered my thumbs over the screen.

My phone rang. Before I even said hello, Morgan cut through. "I'll have you know goats are an extremely effective way of clearing weeds and brush from land. It's so overgrown that we can have them do the work before the landscapers come in. Cost effective and environmentally friendly."

Huh. "What do they do with the goat poop?" I was not even kidding. That seemed... not ideal when talking white bridal gowns and fancy shoes.

"Really?" Morgan said in a deliciously irritated tone.

Too easy. Morgan was like poking a bear but knowing that bear was as tough as a kitten. It had quickly reverted into my favorite pastime. "I'm dead serious. What happens to the poop? Hell if I'm going to be on duty to pick that up, and for some reason, I don't imagine you doing it, either."

A loud, grumpy sigh sounded over the phone. "I believe the goat owners usually collect it and dispose of it or make fertilizer."

I could almost see Morgan squirm when talking about shit while most likely amid ironing. The visual was glorious. Somehow, I needed to figure out how to bottle this up and bring it with me back home for fuel on gloomy days.

"Anyway, I'm just letting you know to keep you informed. You can tell Pete and Patty if they ask," Morgan continued.

"Permission granted." *Poke the bear.* "The goat herders should be fine."

"They don't herd... Whatever." Morgan tapped something. "Quick recap on things."

No problem, I'm free. Thanks for asking. Morgan probably expected people at her beck and call, but I didn't work that way. A hefty protest hovered on my lips, but I stopped myself. I agreed to help, after all. But if Morgan wasn't paying me a stipend, and Tommy didn't need this, I might have bolted by now.

"So, the yard crew is mostly locked in place. My dad thinks between him, us, and a couple of landscapers, they can get the yard in shape in about a week. Today's May 10th, Olivia and Tommy finally confirmed the date August 5th. So, we have exactly... eighty-seven days."

So far, Morgan seemed more calm than stressed, but that was not a lot of time. *At all.* As a freelancer, most of my deadlines were self-imposed, and very intentionally with a tight turn-around. With my type of brain, time was not my friend. Time bred procrastination and scattered thoughts. *Lack of time* drove me. Short deadlines kicked me into overdrive, a hyper-focus where I could carry out damn near anything. But a wedding and remodel in less than ninety days? That was too extreme, even for me.

"The lawn will wait until the week before the wedding. We talked about seeding and paving a path, but that's too ambitious. Also, we need to be respectful to Pete and Patty and run certain things by them that you might not know what to do, without overwhelming them." Morgan took what seemed her first breath. "We'll be mostly cleaning up the yard, trimming bushes, seeing if we can revive that old fountain in the back of the property and bring it up front, clearing their defunct pond, all that jazz. Also, the remodeling crew is confirmed, but they're finishing up a few other gigs. My dad did some fancy footwork just to get them here, but they won't be able to start for a week. The best thing we can do is to start clearing stuff ourselves to save time."

I almost snorted out a laugh picturing Morgan in her white peacoat and crisp blouse moving mouse traps and broken appliances out of the barn. "*You're* going into that dirty old barn to clear stuff out?"

"*Yes*." Morgan huffed. "God, you really don't think highly of me, do you?"

It wasn't that I didn't think highly of Morgan. The woman could do things with a spreadsheet that left me slack jawed. But a spreadsheet was no use when you opened a kitchen cabinet to a heaping pile of mouse droppings. I could just picture Morgan running and screaming from the house, arms flailing. Morgan, at least the Morgan I knew, was never a "pull your sleeves up and get dirty" kind of girl.

"*Whatever*," Morgan finally said after I refused to respond. "At minimum, we need to decide what exactly we're doing, what objects your aunt and uncle want to save, etc."

With the phone pressed against my ear, I paced the avocado-green carpet. Morgan was always the worrier. Not me. And yet, my heartbeat pounded with the amount of work in front of us. "Do you really think we can pull this off in time?"

"Yes, I really do," Morgan said firmly. Whatever keyboard tapping was happening on the other end of the phone stopped. "How are the photo edits coming along?"

My jaw tensed. "Why are you asking?" I already knew why she was asking. She absolutely thought I was slacking and wouldn't get them done in time. "Just so you know, I've been working as a freelancer longer than you've been running your business and know how to deliver on time."

A short catch of breath came over the line. "I was asking because I was curious. That's all. *Jesus*."

Okay, so perhaps I'd overreacted. But only a little. "The edits are going amazing, actually," I said after a recalibration moment. "I think I'll finish tonight." I settled my shoulder against the wall. Anything photography related, besides waiting to hear from the magazine, of course, was an instant stress diffuser.

"Oh! Really? I'd love to see."

My heart lifted at the genuine tone. Morgan was actually

interested in what I did? Shocking turn of events. Back in the day, Morgan never cared much about my "hobby." She'd look over my shoulder, murmur things like "looks great" or "good job" before diving back into her studies. "Okay, cool. I can try and send you some later today or tomorrow."

"Great," Morgan said. "I need to check how these will look on the invitations I have in mind. A few sample pieces would be awesome."

And my heart sunk. Morgan wasn't interested in my work per se, other than that I provided a means to an end.

"Hey, are you at Peaches's?" Morgan asked. "I'm headed to the craft store, but could stop by after if you're free?"

My neck grew warm. Morgan, here? In Peaches's house? I wasn't sure why, but the idea was suffocating. This house was big enough for sure, but this was my special place. The place that held the tears and the memories. I wasn't sure I wanted to share this space with Morgan.

"Besides, I have a little something for you."

The sheepishness in Morgan's tone sparked some curiosity, and soon that overtook the icky feeling. "Sure. Yeah, I'm here all night."

Morgan has a little something for me. Hmmm. Maybe she stumbled across an old photo of us? Or, highly unlikely, but perhaps she broke down and wrote an apology letter from all those years ago.

The curiosity turned into a spark, which I tried, but miserably failed, to squelch.

I held my breath as Frankie stared at the three-ring binder. A couple of moments passed with Frankie's eyes doing calisthenics with all their squinting. Another moment and instead of shifting to excited, or heaven forbid, grateful, Frankie frowned.

"*This* is your gift for me?" Frankie asked.

The words stabbed me in the chest. I lifted my chin, high. "I never said I was giving you a gift." Although that was exactly what I had intended. After Frankie denied my offer for dinner the other night—to pay her back for working on my car—I wanted to do something nice. "I said I had a little something for you. And here... is *a little something*."

It was actually more than a little something, but hell if I'd divulge that information. I knew Frankie was not a big fan of electronics unless it came to photo software. So, I spent almost two hours putting together a binder for Frankie, *with color-coded tabs, dammit,* so Frankie could keep on track with renovations and wedding items via paper.

"Um." Frankie chewed on the side of her lip. "Thanks?"

The sting was fierce and sharp. "Well, I just thought it would be easier for you because you hate emails. But just throw it away if you don't think you'll use it." *Ungrateful.* Not only had I color-coded, but I also did it in a rainbow theme—reds and oranges for house stuff, yellow and green for wedding stuff, and the blue and purple for contracts and vendors. I spent so much time filling it out and printing off pages to help keep Frankie organized, and I naively thought Frankie would be happy. The back of my eyes stung, but I moved my head and scanned the house, needing a distraction from Frankie's horrible, rotten, terrible face.

Peaches's house. Wow. The memories here were nearly as thick as they'd be at Frankie's parents' home. The place looked the same, as much as I remembered. Nothing was updated, yet it was all preserved, like I stepped into an early '80s museum. The green carpet, the honey oak kitchen cabinets, the daisy wallpaper... untouched. "I can't believe nothing has changed."

Frankie tucked the binder under her arm. "I know. It's like a shrine to the eighties. If you click your heels three times and sing the lyrics to 'Take On Me,' pretty sure Molly Ringwald or Bruce Willis will appear."

My body betrayed me, and I smiled. I hated smiling at Frankie's humor and loathed that throwing on the charm came so easy for her. I dropped my grin and crossed the room to the patio door. The backyard also looked the same, with tall pine trees, saggy crabapple tree branches, and budding lilacs. "No way. She still had the tire swing?"

Back then, when I needed to get away from my work-obsessed parents, or take a break from studies, I'd meet Frankie at Peaches's. We'd tear around the yard, fill our bellies with stale candy and fresh cookies, and climb in the tire hanging from a rope on the tree. The tire looked smaller than I remembered, and I tried to picture myself squishing in it now to swing. Most likely I'd end up with a hefty rope burn and a trip to the chiropractor.

Frankie slid the binder on the counter. "Remember when your foot got caught?"

"And I fell flat on my face? Um, sure do. I had to wear a Band-Aid on my face for like a week, which is one hundred percent the most embarrassing place for a Band-Aid." I stepped back and crossed my arms. "I totally blame Peaches, though. She let us sip Kahlúa in our coffee. Thinking of that now, it was kind of problematic that she let two underage girls drink in her home, huh?"

"Oh, Peaches." Frankie lifted a box off the stool at the kitchen counter and offered me a seat. "I wonder where the lifetime of bad decisions my dad made ever came from."

Being around Frankie lately, there'd been a couple of those "remember that time" type conversations, and I wasn't sure I liked it. I spent years burying the pain I felt after our split. Reminiscing was doing something funky to my insides, and I liked it as much as I didn't like it. "Anyway, I just wanted to drop by and give you that binder. I thought it might be easier for you to have everything in one place, but you can disregard it if it's not useful."

"No, no, it'll be great." Frankie's eyes softened as she patted the top of the binder. "Sorry, my reaction was... off... earlier. It was just unexpected, that's all. I'm sure it was a lot of work to put together."

Putting together the binder *was* a lot of work, but I didn't want to dive any deeper into why Frankie's reaction upset me so much. Because really, was Frankie's ingratitude the real issue here? Or was this about the need to be seen and validated, for Frankie to think that I had my shit together and she could wallow in everything that she gave up when she left?

Nope. I wasn't doing this. I refused to overanalyze this situation any more than I already had.

Frankie reached for the shipping tape and pulled a box close to her chest. "What are you up to for the rest of the day?"

Contemplating every argument I've ever made since the seventh grade and wondering why I left out valid points. "Olivia wanted to see a sampling of different table settings and name cards. I'm gonna press some flowers, do some fancy fonts, make a few mock-ups." I gripped the side of the box as Frankie taped. "I have a trunk full of crafts items waiting for me to have a stroke of wedding-inspiration."

Frankie scribbled a note on top of the box. "Do you need some help?"

Right now, at least two dozen boxes littered the kitchen, open cabinet doors showed dishes stuffed on every shelf, and a heaping pile of clothes was scattered on top of the kitchen table. I almost suspected ultra-tough, ultra-cool, ultra-don't-give-a-shit Frankie didn't want to be left alone. Fascinating. "You seriously want to do crafts with me?"

The corner of Frankie's lip lifted. "If you can go into that rust-infused barn with your golden Gucci shoes on, I can help iron flowers or whatever crafty crap you need me to do."

Damn her being the *tiniest* bit charming. "First, I don't own Gucci shoes." Only because I couldn't afford them, not because I didn't want them. Obviously. "Okay, then. Looks like we're doing some crafts."

After dragging in two boxes and clearing off the long coffee table, I sank into the worn green couch next to Frankie and started giving directions. An hour or so passed of reviewing different design websites, organizing plate settings, and rolling a few scrolls, when we moved to name cards. I glanced at Frankie, who was writing—in near perfect calligraphy—"Olivia & Tommy." Who knew someone with such a rough exterior could have such delicate penmanship? And was this a newly developed talent? I certainly didn't remember this skill from high school. Frankie was always rushed, running late, flying by the seat of her pants. I assumed her handwriting would be scattered and messy.

Time passed with me rearranging place settings while Frankie snapped photos from various angles. I frowned, adjusted, frowned again. Where was that damn "it factor"? Everything was just "fine." But with my business teetering on closing for good, I didn't have the luxury of "fine." I needed perfection.

How would the community react if I failed? I could almost hear the whispers at Connie's Coffee, or Zoey's Bakery, or Sunday after mass. "Can you believe that poor Rose girl had to shut down her business? Couldn't keep up with the fancy Dreams Events place." Of course, most would be sympathetic, some even slightly militant, droning on about how they don't appreciate big money coming into our town and running out the little guy.

Sure, God knows I'd engaged in concerned community discussions, aka gossip, myself over the years. But being on this side felt terrible, no matter how good the intention. I had no choice—I had to nail this wedding.

A cramp buried itself into my shoulder blade, and for a flicker of a second, the thought of Frankie's strong hands working out my shoulder kink sounded heavenly. I mean, the strong-hands part sounded heavily. The fact that those appendages were attached to Frankie sounded terrible. I pushed a finger into the pressure point and rotated my arm. Soon enough, I'd have to take a break before my bones crumbled.

Frankie was gluing a small baby's breath stem into cardstock, her eyebrows knitted in concentration. I really, *really* didn't want to admit it, but having someone helping with this work was kind of nice. "You said the photo edits were coming along?"

"Yeah." Frankie blew on the glue and tossed me a quick side glance. "Want a sneak peek? Just, ah, to see how we'll fit it into the invitation?"

Did Frankie just swallow? "Sure."

She jumped up from the floor. "I'll grab the iPad. Be right back."

Okay, that tiny crack in Frankie's voice, plus the way she scurried from the room was... unexpected. Frankie had zero reason to be nervous, if that was even the correct emotion I sensed. She was a gifted photographer, obviously, since she made it in the big city on talent alone. Why would it make her nervous to show me the photos?

A moment later, something cool touched my arm. "Cream soda, huh?"

Frankie nodded and slid back onto the couch. "Peaches has cases of these downstairs. She stocked so much of this stuff, I wonder if she was preparing for an apocalypse."

I wiped a thin layer of dust from the top of the can with my sleeve. "Just soda and canned veggies, huh?"

"Yep." Frankie stuffed a marigold couch pillow behind her back. "I feel like I can't throw them out. But who knows how old they are, so I don't feel right in donating. I'm making it a personal mission to drink as much as I can while I'm here before I dump and recycle." She tipped her can in cheers. "Fair warning, though. You're about to experience the saddest fizz of your life. I had one yesterday, and it sounded like it just gave up."

Frankie wasn't wrong. The normally gratifying *cacoosh* sound when I cracked open the pop was a forlorn hiss at best.

The iPad fired to life and Frankie tapped on the screen. A moment later, stunning, *truly stunning*, photos filled the screen. The colors were bright, enhanced, but still looked genuine. Olivia and Tommy's candid photos by the barn transformed something broken down and rotting into something more historic, something with life.

"Oh, go back, I love that one." I leaned forward and pointed at the screen. And when I did, the side of my knee grazed Frankie's knee and my breath hitched. For a damn knee. God, I was seriously over my adrenal system not listening to a single thought of reason. Frankie seemed to not notice, or if she cared at all, she didn't show it. She didn't break stride, nor move, as she continued swiping through the photos.

The kicked-up heartbeat cooled. I propped my elbows on my knees and returned to my focused, non-ridiculous, professional self. For ten years, I'd worked with wedding photographers, and none of them came close to what Frankie captured here. Even the posed ones didn't look cheesy or awkward.

And then an image of myself popped up, one that Frankie must've taken when testing the shutter speed. I had my arms crossed, peering into the distance like I was contemplating the fate of the world. Streams of the sun highlighted my blonde strands, and even with the serious expression, this might be one of the best pictures I'd ever seen of myself.

Frankie tapped off the screen. "I'll delete those test shots."

"No... no... it's okay. You could even send this one to me if you wanted." I had no idea if the forced nonchalant tone landed. The flat cream soda on the coffee table was a perfect escape. I gulped back the sugary substance and dabbed the side of my mouth. "Frankie... these photos are beautiful. Olivia and Tommy are going to love them."

A small grin appeared, enough to show Frankie's dimples. "Thanks."

Damn those dimples. When we met as kids, I remembered asking my mom how I could get dimples myself. They were the most beautiful thing in the world, like a secret compartment unlocked by the power of a smile. As we grew older, the dimples still held a power over me, a sort of lesbian kryptonite that could make me melt.

I scooted toward the edge of the couch, needing distance. "I thought you didn't shoot people."

"I don't shoot people. I may look like I can hand someone's ass to them in a bar fight, but I'm a pacifist right here." Frankie tapped her heart with two fingers.

God, she was really going to make me drag this out, wasn't she? "You know what I mean. You're really... gifted. I mean, I knew, but I guess I didn't know."

Did I know? No, I couldn't have. *Right?* The memories were hazy. If I knew Frankie was that good, I would've treated her dream of becoming a famous photographer differently. Things would've been different. Maybe.

No. I have to stop. Nothing would have been different. Frankie could've developed this talent here... she didn't have to move to New York to do it. And honestly, it was so long ago. Why do I even care? I don't care.

"Well, thanks," Frankie said. "I really love what I do."

I flicked the top of the pop can. "Do you work? Like regularly?" Fine, I marginally cared. But that was it.

"Yes... and no." Frankie slid the iPad to the center of the table. "I'm freelance, but I usually stay pretty booked up. The schedule works for me, and is perfect for times like this, knowing I was coming home for the summer. I just didn't book myself with any appointments except this wedding." She glanced out the window for several long moments before her knee stopping bouncing next to me. "I'm actually interviewing for a different thing."

"Oh yeah?" I said between sips. "What's that?"

"Permanent staff at *Birch & Willow*. Not sure if you've heard of them."

Not sure if I've heard of them? My mouth dropped at the rate of my eyes skyrocketing. The magazine, the brand, even the freaking website, was everything. "Shut up!"

Birch & Willow was incredible. The photography was stunning, of course, but I loved their products. Chunky knitted blankets, live-edged cedar coffee tables with their minimalist stamp, hand-carved stone vases. I even splurged a few years back and purchased several hand-dipped, soy-based candles that smelled like mandarin, figs, and greens. Although they were so expensive that I hadn't lit them yet and just occasionally walked by and sniffed.

And Frankie landed an interview with that company? I didn't know the ins and out of the photography world, but *Birch & Willow* probably only chose the best of the best. Having spent years developing my own brand, I knew having a strong, recognizable brand that straddled the line of bougie (but not too bougie) while flawlessly conveying beauty, minimalism, and class was tricky as hell. But *Birch & Willow* had succeeded and became a household name—even if not all households could afford their products. "Okay, I've got to ask. Was the process grueling?"

Frankie sunk deeper into the couch. "You have no idea. First, I'm not used to interviewing at all. Normally, I just send a portfolio, or people check my references, and call it good. But I swear given the opportunity they would've asked me for my blood type and what type of porn I watched."

I gobbled down everything Frankie said about all the prep she completed just to land the interview, pulling every string she had and dropping *all* the names. When Frankie talked about going to the headquarters (which was not too far from Times Square, apparently) and spending a full eight hours getting to know the creative team, I inched closer.

"Anyway, yeah, it's definitely a chance of a lifetime." Frankie stood and adjusted her jean legs. "So, we'll see. Who knows, I may have scared them off the moment I strutted in like a badass with all of this." She swiped her hands down her torso and grinned.

No matter how cavalier the voice, or the actions, I could see through the bullshit. This carefree attitude was the exact same one I flexed around others when talking about not caring about my five-star reviews, knowing damn well the power it held over me. I gathered the craft items into the totes and followed Frankie outside to my car. "Okay, tomorrow, bright and early at

Pete and Patty's. I know I said around eight, but in full transparency, I'll probably get there at seven."

Frankie swiped her hands down her face. "God, that's early."

"You have until eight, though."

"Gee, thanks. How overly generous of you." Once the items were securely in the trunk, Frankie slammed it shut. "And, uh, thanks for the nice things you said tonight. I forget under that Rambo-Barbie exterior, there's still a hint of sweetness."

"Jerk." I didn't know what possessed me, maybe the ghost of a past relationship, or the fact I had very few close friends, but I threw my arms around Frankie and hugged. Only a split second passed before Frankie squeezed back. Her dark and stormy cologne drifted from her neck and *dammit*. Maybe it was because Frankie was so strong, or because it had been a long time since I'd been held, but my body melted.

Stop. I stiffened and did an odd one-arm bro tap on Frankie's shoulders. "See ya tomorrow." Pretty sure I could not have made this encounter any more awkward if I tried. I peeled out the driveway, my face so hot it felt like it'd bubble. I pushed a palm into my forehead and exhaled.

What in the hell am I doing?

ELEVEN
FRANKIE

A small container of food, some tools from Peaches's shed, and cleaning supplies filled the truck's passenger seat as I made my way up to the tree farm. Who knows what I'd do when I arrived, but I wanted to be prepared.

Not wanting to think about the hug from yesterday, because absolutely nothing good would come from diving into that pond, I turned on Ruby Reanne's podcast, *Love 'Em or Leave 'Em*.

"Okay, all, a listener emailed this to me last week, and I had to jump on it," Ruby said in her signature smiling voice. "'Hi, Ruby, I'll keep this short but looking for your advice here. I've been married to a wonderful man for ten years and have never lied to him. But I'm lying now.'"

Oh, juicy. I turned up the volume.

"'My husband thinks he has a good singing voice,'" Ruby continued. "'And he doesn't. It's truly terrible. I think he struggles with tone deafness or voice dysmorphia or something. And if he only sang around the house, that would be fine. But he told me he wants to develop this singing hobby into a career. He even recorded demos, sent audition tapes to every show you can imagine, and next week he's trying out as the lead singer in a band. But, as the rejections trickle in, he asked if I thought he had a good voice and if he could make it in the business. I dodged the question, but what should I do when he asks me again? I know your motto is honesty is the foundation of relationships, but I'm torn. I don't want to lie, but also I don't want him to feel humiliated if he auditions and gets laughed out of the club. Sincerely, a New Jersey Wife.'"

I turned left onto the county road and leaned in to hear Ruby's response.

"So, honesty *is* the foundation of everything. You cannot have a healthy relationship built on lies," Ruby said through the speakers. "Being married to Amelia has taught me this a million times over. *Now*, that being said, I'm reminded of a few things. One, several years back, Amelia forced me to listen to this new singer, Billie Eilish, and her song 'Bad Guy.' I did *not* understand the appeal at all."

Say what? Ruby was just knocked down ten points. She better redeem herself, stat.

"I thought Billie was too breathy, spoke more than sang, and her style was not at all my cup of tea. I told my wife this. Mind you, I consume grunge and metal the same way I consume coffee, and it was just... different. But, before you grab the pitchforks, hear me out. *I thought Billie didn't have a good voice.* Can you believe that? Considering I am now one of her biggest fans, I'm shocked that ever entered my mind."

Thank God Ruby restored my faith in her. I'd really hate to stop listening to the show.

"Next point. Bob Dylan. I mean, notoriously not good voice, right? But he's one of the most respected artists ever. So, who are we to judge? Maybe even if your husband doesn't have a traditionally good voice, he can still make it in the business. There's an audience for everything, you just have to find it. Final point. I'm reminded of a time when Amelia wore one of these poofy shirts that were apparently all the rage. I thought she looked like a pirate. But when she asked, 'How do I look,' I said she looked beautiful, because I didn't want to hurt her feelings or sleep on the couch. So, to recap, voices are subjective. Maybe his voice is good and you just can't hear it. Second, *every once in a while*, it's okay to lie. In this case, lie like a damn doormat. Tell him he's wonderful. Let someone else tell him he sucks. It's going to hurt either way, but he can be hurt by them and not you."

Huh. Solid advice. I cracked the window as I weaved up the winding road into Pete and Patty's. The phone rested in my palm. *I shouldn't... don't do it...* but I couldn't help it. I slowed to a stop and held my breath as I swiped through emails. No new messages from *Birch & Willow*. I exhaled. I was not the praying kind, but another week or two of silence and I may dig out one of Peaches's rosaries.

Less than five seconds after getting out of the vehicle, Morgan marched towards me with a frown visible from across the valley.

"You're late."

If this was the attitude on the first day of this massive project, I would seriously consider telling Morgan to screw herself. After all these years, Morgan still hadn't dropped her holier-than-thou attitude when it came to things *she* thought were important. Time, rigid schedules, college... it didn't matter. If it was important to her, then it was clearly important to everyone else. How had she not evolved over the years and realized that other people had different priorities? The self-centeredness was truly remarkable.

I was about two seconds away from saying something snarky but goddamn... Morgan was in denim overalls, tennis shoes, with her blonde locks tucked in a red bandanna. She looked like an even sexier version of Rosie the Riveter, and I was totally disarmed. Unfair playing field, unfair advantage.

I glanced at my watch. "I'm exactly on time. It's eight a.m. You said be here at eight."

Morgan crossed her arms. "Which is late."

Whatever. No matter how hard I tried, I'd never get her logic. But for now, I'd play nice. Besides wanting to do Tommy's family solid, the distraction from waiting on *Birch & Willow*'s response, plus taking a break from packing up Peaches's house, was exactly what I needed. I lifted the mug in my hand. "I brought you coffee."

Morgan's frown flipped, and she reached out her hand. "You're forgiven."

I scanned the property. *Jesus.* Did the place look this bad when we took pictures, or had Pete and Patty somehow accumulated even more shit? Every imaginable busted, rusted, and broken thing was piled high on the lawn. Was that a freaking toilet in the middle of the yard? I squinted. Yep, sure was. I followed Morgan across the marsh and tried to keep up with her mile-a-minute talking about the plans for the crew that was already clearing brush, the process we'd follow for organizing and cleaning the barn, and how she was going to attempt to fire up the abandoned bulldozer, so we didn't have to rent one.

Two guys dragged what looked like a broken-down table saw from the junkyard pile, while another guy banged on the window frame. Sam rounded the corner, his hat tugged low, and his shirt already smeared with dirt.

"Kat—sorry—Frankie." He removed his hat and swiped his forehead with his shirt. "Not very good seeing you."

"Same." I sipped from the mug, the warm coffee sliding down my throat. "Similar to the feeling I had when the Wolves bit it during March Madness."

Sam shook his head. "I still have nightmares. I mean eight minutes is like—"

"Eight years, right? And then he gets it and—"

"Totally chokes." Sam flung his hand. "How the hell could he get a charging call—"

"*That* one was on the ref. He was plowed into—"

"He didn't even have a chance. But the D they were playing was—"

"Guys. Really." Morgan stepped in between us with a scowl. *God, she's cute when she's angry.* "Can we please focus on the barn?"

I saluted the drill sergeant and tilted my head at Sam with a grin.

Morgan put me on moving duty with a couple of the guys, which was fine enough. I loved hitting the gym and lifting weights, but I'd much rather work out by doing this stuff, or a fierce game of one-on-one. Less boring, same effect. And *way* less time being in Morgan's presence, thank God.

Hours soon passed as the spring sun beat down, becoming a shade too hot. For every minute spent piling usable items for Pete and Patty to go through, I grew even more nostalgic. This place used to be everything. Sleigh rides, a laughing Santa taking gift wishes, a bonfire crackling in the background, the smell of mint and chocolate and snow.

I hauled pieces of metal, mouse traps, dirty rugs, and too many unidentifiable things to the dumpster. The loud noise of chainsaws and men yelling at each other poured over the area. The dumpster filled quickly, taken up by several old mattresses and a box spring, and I started a new pile next to a haystack.

The work was hard, but rewarding, and I couldn't help but getting a kick out of Morgan heaving and dragging a wheelbarrow full of broken jars to the dumpster. "Need some help?"

"No, I absolutely don't," Morgan huffed, then stood with her hands on her hips, probably trying to figure out how in the hell she was going to dump the contents into the dumpster. I almost stepped toward her and offered to lift it, but *nah.*

Morgan said she didn't want help and who was I to overrule the queen?

But too many minutes passed, and what was once amusing was now inefficient and no longer funny. I tugged my work gloves tight. "For Christ's sake, just let me help." I crossed the lawn to Morgan. "Sam! Can you give me a hand?"

In no time flat, Sam and I lifted the wheelbarrow and dumped it out, and Morgan returned to the barn. I sipped water and watched as one of the crew members hooked a broken snowplow up to an ATV and drove it down the valley.

I walked back up the incline toward Morgan as a crew member pushed past me with a hand-held snowplow. "Where are they putting those snowplows?"

Morgan wiped her hands on a towel. "For right now, anything that can't be put in the dumpster, we're putting down the hill where wedding guests can't see it." She shoved the towel in her back pocket and cocked her head. "I've instructed the guys to make a 'possibly salvageable' pile and a 'definite salvage-able pile' for you to look at and review. I know you are supposed to be *in charge*, but I made some executive decisions on things like broken glass, plastic pots, rotting wood, and mice traps. I'm assuming that's okay with you?"

First of all, Morgan did *not* just put air quotes around "in charge," did she? I exhaled a little bit of fire from my nose and swallowed back the deep desire to remind her that I was the one doing her the favor, not the other way around. How did all these little incidents take me right back to being sixteen? Like the time when my teammates and I decided to do a carwash fundraiser to pay for us to go see the Timberwolves at the Target Center. Morgan wanted to "help out" and ended up being so militant about signs and advertising and getting customers, she even pissed off the coach. We did, however, make enough money to pay for the band to come with us, too, but Christ, her delivery still sucked.

"It's fine. I'll deal with it," I finally choked out, and nope, I also wasn't going to admit that a part of me was deeply grateful she started the piles, because I would've taken a look at the overwhelming amount of items and probably panicked. But she still should've asked.

I spent the next twenty minutes hosing out some kids' wagons, which would make a great photo op prop for the wedding, when Morgan stepped out of the barn, picking off debris from her overalls.

"I'm starving," she said. "Want to take a break? I brought sandwiches."

Okay, so maybe she's not that terrible. "Yeah, I could eat." I thought about bringing lunch but got distracted last night with packing Peaches's Precious Moments collection and didn't get to the grocery store. Before I left this morning, I ended up stuffing a few protein bars and a bottle of water in a bag.

After washing our hands old-school-style with a garden hose and some lilac soap Morgan brought from home, I popped down the tailgate and hopped up on the only surface I was confident sitting where I wouldn't get glass shards stuck in my ass. I bit into the sandwich, which was way more delicious than the protein bars.

God, this sandwich was delicious. Turkey, sprouts, mayo, and mustard made the perfect combo. There was a small deli outside of my apartment in Manhattan that had the best pastrami on rye, but it didn't nail the turkey sandwich like Morgan did. "So, I sent the main pics to Olivia last night."

"Great. She needs to buckle down and choose the photo she wants for the invitations ASAP." Morgan cracked open a bottle of water. "If we don't get those out by next week, we'll miss the eight-week mark."

"Then what?" I asked, swallowing back the sandwich with a swig of water.

Morgan stopped the bottle mid-air before taking a drink. "What do you mean, *then what?*"

Whoa. Did her tone really change like that? The question still stood. This fascination/obsession with time and following certain archaic rules was so over the top. No wonder Morgan always looked stressed out. If she could lighten up just the tiniest, she'd probably be happier. "I mean... then what? Seriously. What happens if the invitations are sent at seven, or even four, weeks before the wedding?" I took another bite and shifted the food to the side of my cheek. "No one will die, you know? This isn't life or death. It's not like we're pediatric surgeons or something."

Morgan's face flamed. She tossed her sandwich aside and jumped off the tailgate. "You literally have no respect for what I do."

Was she actually serious? I had God knows what sort of rat-infused rust, glass shards, and splinters all over my clothes, my muscles were on fire, and not that I'd ever say anything, but I'd way overexerted myself these last six hours and tonight I'd have to ice my knee for an hour. And Morgan was saying I had no respect? Screw her. Seriously.

"What the hell do you mean, no respect?" I snapped. "I've busted my ass all day to help *you* make this day great. It's not like anyone from the wedding will say 'great job, Frankie, you really cleaned the hell out of that place.'"

"That is not the goddamn point! You're always late for everything, and you have this... attitude... this, ugh, all-encompassing ... *vibe*... that you just don't give a shit." Morgan's hands jutted with every sputtered word. "I can't rely on you, and yet I need your help, and I'm totally trapped."

Maybe "rely" was a bit of a trigger word after hearing that a million times over in my life, but I hopped off the truck, hard, and landed *just right* on my bad knee. An electric white heat shot through my leg and I clamped my teeth together.

I never asked to be born with the brain I had, and no chance in hell would I admit to Morgan the shame I carried for years when I'd forget things, or not finish tasks, or get so focused on something that I lost track of time. It took years in therapy, reading every article I could on ADHD management, and a solid medication regimen, to let some of this go. And in a snap, Morgan threw it in my face. "You're fucking ridiculous, you know that? People bend over backwards to do everything you want them to do. You just think because you're beautiful, smart, organized, and have never made a mistake since you were ten that everyone needs to fall in line. News flash—this is not the military. I do *not* have to listen to your orders. I could walk away this second and not give you or this place another thought."

Shit. That was too far, and definitely not true. But the fire was ignited, the words just exploded, and I was at the end of the goal line refusing to lose to my opponent.

Morgan stepped forward, her eyes blazing. "Well, at least I know some things never change."

The words landed with the intended sucker punch, and my gut dropped. As Morgan stomped away, I flashed my gaze between Morgan, the barn, and the truck. It would be *so easy* to tear out of the driveway and go back to Peaches's. But if I did that, I'd be no better than what Morgan said. Yet, the idea of continuing to work with Morgan for the rest of the summer constricted my chest so tight I needed to cough.

I kicked at a rock embedded in the tire. Right here, right now, was a fork-in-the-road decision. Stay or go.

And I had no idea what I was going to do.

TWELVE
MORGAN

My ears perked at the sound of Frankie's truck firing up, its shoddy, rattling muffler echoing across the valley. But when the distinct crunch of gravel sounded, I peeked out of the barn door at the dust kicking up from the back tires as Frankie tore out of the property, and my heart sank.

She left. *Again.* Just like that. Yet again, I wasn't worth helping, worth staying for. My lower lip trembled, but I sucked it into my mouth and bit it to make it stop. But... why did I say those things to Frankie? What was wrong with me? Frankie was a goddamn workhorse, lifting and moving as much as the crew. And instead of saying thank you and essentially paying her back with a turkey club, I railed into her about being late.

And Frankie wasn't even late. Not technically, anyway. Ugh. I made Frankie feel like shit, and for what? Because the tension of executing on an impossible timeline was building, brimming, bubbling over, and I had to lash out at someone, something, and Frankie was an easy target? When did I become this person?

I tugged on my work gloves and returned to the barn. *Am I*

even allowed in here without Frankie? I seriously hoped that Pete and Patty didn't mean that Frankie had to literally watch over me—which was a joke anyway. Frankie was the least responsible person I knew. It's like asking a toddler to babysit a college kid. She couldn't even make it a full day without storming off like a child.

She's coming back, though, right? Dammit. What would I do if she didn't? Beg Pete and Patty to let me have the wedding here anyway, even though they explicitly said only if Frankie were involved? Work through some magical third party like Sam or Frankie's sister, Quinn, who could negotiate a truce between Frankie and me, and she could come here after hours and sift through the items I wasn't sure I should throw?

No, no. She'd come back. She had to. There was no way she'd do this to Tommy and Olivia. *I think. I hope.* But then again, she did it to me. All those years ago...

I kicked at a small piece of broken pallet and surveyed the area. Nothing good was going to come from me sitting here wallowing and wondering if Frankie was coming back. I needed to just plow through this and keep my fingers crossed we'd make this work.

Okay, okay. I can do this. The corner of the barn held dozens of boxes of old Christmas decorations. Some good, some broken, everything filled with years' worth of grime. Inside one tote, I nearly gagged on the smell and made an executive decision to toss the entire thing. After lugging it to the dumpster, I prayed it didn't contain some special family heirloom.

How did Sam do this type of work every day? I twisted my back until it popped like gunfire, then returned to the barn.

So many things to do. Tools, dirt, broken windows, junk pile, junk yard, trim trees, trim bushes... My chest squeezed. I scooped up broken glass and dumped it in the trash. Place settings, flowers, wedding cake, invitations, call the florist, find a

DJ, arrange table and chair renting... My heartbeat quickened, throbbing in my throat. It was too much. I couldn't handle this. I put a fist on top of the broom handle and leaned my forehead against the top.

"Dude, you workin' or what?" Sam's voice sounded behind me.

I breathed in a sharp breath and jabbed at a dirt pile with so much ferocity, I almost broke the handle in half. "That's all I ever do. Work, work, work. There's nothing else in my life *except* for work. Sorry I had the audacity to take a two-minute effing break!"

"*Whoa.*" Sam gripped the handle, and when I yanked it away, he tugged tighter. "You're not mad at the broom, so let's go easy on it, okay? We already know you could totally take it on in a street fight."

Even Sam couldn't get me to crack a smile. Even though six of us worked for hours today, we didn't even make a dent in the overflowing piles of shit. *Why did I think this was a good idea? Why did I ever say yes to Olivia? God, maybe I should just quit and work for my parents.* Sam seemed happy enough. I could give up my business and stop having the stress of doing everything alone, stop crumbling under the burden that every damn decision might make or break my business, stop shouldering the responsibility of people's dreams.

The tears broke through and I covered my face.

"Oh shit. Oh, okay. You're crying. Um, yep. I got this. I'm a dad now." Sam tapped me on the back like he was burping a baby. "You're good. You're fine. It doesn't hurt that bad, right?"

I swiped the tears with the back of my grimy hand. "First, I didn't scrape my knee." I sniffled. "Second, have you read even a single article on parenting? You should validate kids, not tell them it isn't that bad."

Sam leaned the broom against the wall. "Come on. Why don't we take a breather on the bench and crack a brewski?"

"Beer's gross." My nose dripped. I wiped it against my forearm, something I never thought I'd do, but I was filthy and disgusting, and didn't have any Kleenex.

"Good, 'cause I don't actually have any with me. How 'bout instead, we take a break, and we split the bars Lisa made."

Bars? I lifted my chin. "The ones with the cornflakes, peanut butter, and chocolate?"

Sam grinned. "Is there any other kind?"

Even if my brother wasn't the most emotionally intelligent human I'd ever met, ten minutes later, with my cells buzzing from the pound of sugar I just ingested, I felt better. Sam didn't ask any questions, most likely knowing I'd talk when I was ready. Instead, we sat in silence, the sun warming the back of my neck, listening to the crew chain up yet another piece of machinery to haul away.

Sam dragged a napkin down his face, then balled it in his palm. "So, you think Frankie's comin' back, or should I see if Mom can find another crew member?"

I shrugged. Frankie didn't have a great track record for staying. And if I dug deep, which was a miserable thing to do, I myself had a pretty solid track record for pushing people away. With that combo, chances weren't good Frankie would be returning anytime soon. Frankie would most likely fulfill her commitment to her family friend to be the photographer and probably figure out a way to sift through the junk piles, but that might be all.

"We can't ask Mom. This is already a huge favor to get these guys half-time." I drank half a bottle of water, then used the rest to rinse the stickiness from my fingers. "I'll figure it out."

Those were the words. But the reality was I had no idea if I could figure it out.

Sam pushed his fist into his jaw and cracked his neck. "All I know, is once you set your mind to something, no snowblower, bulldozer, or pack of rabid wolves could stop you." He nudged his shoulder into mine. "I *know* you'll figure it out. Let me know if you need me."

He walked away without another word, surely exhausting the last of his brotherly love for the day.

I spent the better part of the next hour moving scraps of pallet wood to the side of the dumpster, and with each passing minute my heart sank deeper. I really didn't mean to lash out at Frankie. It wasn't Frankie's fault that she shined a mammoth-sized spotlight on my insecurity. But still, I wanted Frankie to care. I *needed* Frankie to care. I just didn't know why.

But now was probably the time for me to be the responsible adult and apologize. Like it or not, if we were down a body, I had to figure out a plan. I pulled out my phone and hovered a finger, so close to dialing. *Ugh. I can't do it.* Why did this hurt so much? Anger I could deal with. A solid emotion that I knew how to handle. But this ache, low in my chest, hadn't happened in a lot of years, and I *hated* it. I stuffed the cell back in my over-alls. *Who has time for this crap?* I stormed back into the barn and continued gathering old cleaning products for the hazard dump run.

Another hour passed. Sam left to work at our parents' shop and fatigue kicked in. I moved to the small tool area and popped my hands on my hips. Screws, nails, and every bolt imaginable overstuffed the space. If Pete and Patty were anything like my parents, discarded gadgets were sacred ground. Although Pete and Patty clearly subscribed to the "never throw anything away because you may need it" rule, with tools, that particular rule was gospel.

"See you tomorrow," a crew member yelled into the barn, and I waved. The sounds of trucks starting and gravel crunching and truck doors banging swirled outside. I wasn't going to lie— being alone on this farm was going to be creepy as hell.

The evening sun was still bright enough, thank God, so the

demons lurking the woods couldn't get me quite yet. But the second the sun started setting, I was out of here.

Something sounding like a twig cracking jolted me, and goosebumps rose on my flesh. *No, no... just my imagination.*

A moment later, a shadow appeared, and that definitely wasn't my imagination. I reached for the item closest to me—a three-foot-tall, dusty, plastic candy cane—and held it above my head.

"Better watch out with that thing. You could take an eye out," Frankie said, her hands up in surrender. "Okay, maybe not an eye, but you could definitely hurt an elf."

Frankie. Came. Back. Relief flushed through me, superseding the anger I felt when she stormed off. *Dear God, please let this mean she'll stay, and I can pull off this wedding.* I dropped the plastic candy cane onto the bench and tried to maintain at least a partially neutral face. She didn't need to see that I was damn near soaring that I wasn't alone with coyotes or bears or that the demons wouldn't snatch me on the way to the car.

"I'm really sorry about what happened earlier," Frankie said as she stepped into the barn. She shoved her hands in her pockets and kicked at a loose pallet piece. "I let my emotions get the best of me and I shouldn't have left the way I did. Super uncool of me, and totally unfair."

And now, Frankie *apologized?* Holy hell, it was a Christmas tree farm miracle. Sure, Frankie used to apologize all the time—sorry for being late, sorry for forgetting something, sorry for bolting off to practice. But I don't ever remember her apologizing like this, with maturity and genuine remorse. Maybe it was time to shake the picture of the teen Frankie from my mind, and start to understand this new, adult Frankie.

The golden evening sun broke through the door, highlighting Frankie like a halo. I'm not sure if it was from the way she looked in that light, or maybe the physical and emotional exhaustion of the day, but I wanted to leap into those chiseled arms.

"I'm sorry, too." I inched a few steps closer, twisting my hands. All the pressure of these last few years weighed on me. If I wanted to have a healthy working relationship with Frankie, now might be the time to come clean. I could tell Frankie about the dreams I had for my business and the nightmares that plagued me about my business plummeting. The pressure to always have a smile, that my business was my *everything*, and knowing this was my very last chance of making it work made me want to shrivel up in the fetal position.

Or... maybe I could just say "welcome back."

Yes, that was a better plan.

"I have something in the truck, but if you don't come now, it'll be destroyed." Frankie stepped back and waved toward the vehicle.

Intriguing. I like it. I arched a brow and followed her to the truck. When Frankie bent over to grab it, I definitely didn't peek at her perfectly firm ass in the jeans and instead stood back like a proper lady.

"Mint chocolate chip?" I asked after she handed me a cup of dripping ice cream. "My favorite." I had reached my sugar limit for the day, but sugar was like sex. Once I had a little, all I wanted was more.

The sweetened coolness slid down my throat. On the lawn, I scooted up until my back rested against a hundred-year-old oak tree with the width of an entire soccer team. An abnormally quiet and reserved Frankie sat next to me, taking small bites of the dessert.

"How did you remember what kind of ice cream I liked?" I asked, taking another scoop. I had absolutely no idea what Frankie's favorite was, but that wasn't something people normally remember about an ex, right?

Frankie shrugged and swirled her spoon. A long moment passed before she glanced up at me through the shadow of the tree. "I remember a lot of things."

Well, shit. So did I. Heaviness filled the space between us, and I focused on the melting dessert in my hand, and not all the things that needed to be said. Where would I even begin? A lifetime had passed since Frankie and I knew each other. And for everything I thought I knew about her, there were probably a million things I didn't. She'd lived in New York City her entire adult life, had interviewed at one of the most highly respected lifestyle companies in the country, and drove a damn motorcycle. Who knew what other things had changed besides her name?

"Look, how I left wasn't cool," Frankie said. "I told you I'm here to help, and I am. I'm all in." Several pauses passed as she twisted the band on her watch. "But for real, I'm not sure what set you off. Maybe I said something more insensitive than what I realized? If we're going to work together, we *have* to communicate. Just say something if I upset you. I promise I'll listen, but you cannot let things fester and then blow up. And I'll do the same, and try to be more conscious of my words, and not stomp off like a baby, okay? It's not healthy for either of us."

Wow. Frankie talking about feelings and communication was, frankly, kind of hot. Where was this woman fifteen years ago? Tree bark scratched into my back—not an entirely unpleasant sensation—and I sighed. "You're right." Ugh, how I hated those words. "So, where do we even start?"

Frankie dangled the spoon for a moment and grinned. "How about a friendly game of truth or dare?"

I chuckled through my nose. "I'm too tired for dare. How about just truth, but using the old-school twenty-questions game, rapid-fire-style?" Did Frankie remember? One night, probably in the seventh or eighth grade, we had a sleepover at my house and watched *Mean Girls*—which I only remember because Frankie decided she wanted to be Lindsay Lohan for a hot minute and dyed her hair to red—and we stayed up late playing twenty questions. Over a bowl of buttery popcorn and stuffed in our sleeping bags, I learned more about my best friend during that night than I learned about her since we met in kindergarten. It was also the moment I realized I loved her more than a friend, although it took me more than a year to confess my feelings.

"Twenty questions? Jesus, that's a lot. How about we start with one?" Frankie swirled the spoon in her mouth, then added another scoop.

Probably a good point. Twenty questions seemed a little ambitious. "Okay... how about you tell me about how you went from Katey to Frankie."

"*Damn*, nothing like diving into the deep end with that one, huh?" Frankie said, leaning back into the tree. She licked the corner of her lip and took a deep breath. "There's a lot to that, way more than what we have time for today. And, if you really want to know, I'll tell you some day."

"I really do want to know," I said, pausing on scooping up more ice cream. But more than the name, I wanted to know where this new calmness came from. Was the maturity age related or something bigger?

"Let's just for now say that I needed to shed my past, my parents, everything about who I was in Spring Harbors, and find out who I was on my own in New York. What I loved, what I wanted to do, the type of person I wanted to be." Frankie peeked at me through her long lashes. "And I started with changing my name."

Ouch. She didn't need to say much more. Shedding her past absolutely included me. We were each other's everything, for years. No doubt I was an anchor holding her back in the life she didn't want anymore. I exhaled through my nose and tried as hard as possible to not take the words personally.

"Your turn." Frankie set the bowl on the side of her leg and crossed her arms. "When I knew you, you were always a perfectionist. But, with this wedding, it seems... extra. Like this level of intensity that, if I can be totally honest, is probably not healthy."

I wanted to glare or say something snappy about the perfectionist comment, but I couldn't. Frankie was right, and she told me to call her out if she said anything insensitive. But this wasn't insensitive, it was the truth. I've been this way since I could remember, but also who wouldn't want to be a perfectionist? Why would anyone live a life where they were not putting their best foot forward? That concept never made sense to me. Frankie was like that growing up. Unless she was on the field, she just didn't care. Half-assed homework assignments, missing classes, wanting to make out in her bedroom instead of study. That part I obviously didn't mind, but the point still stood.

"Opening a wedding planning business was my dream for years." I licked the spoon, then scooped it back into the ice cream. "I wanted people to think of their wedding first, then me second. I thought there'd be nothing more amazing than creating a fantasy and making their day the most special one of their lives."

Frankie pulled her legs up to her chest and rested her forearms across her knees. "I can understand that. Being part of someone's dream day sounds rewarding."

"It is. But also... the pressure that comes with this job is intense. Sometimes I feel like I can't breathe. I don't want the couple to know that, though, so on top I'm like cool and calm, a duck flowing above the water. But beneath I'm frantically paddling, you know?" *All right, too much honesty. Reel it in.* "If anything's off, anything I do that messes with this day, it can affect the couple for life. I mean, they'll get over it, I assume, but knowing that I might be the one that taints their dream day... it's just a lot." *So much for reeling it in.*

Several moments passed where I wasn't sure if Frankie would say anything at all. Honestly, I probably deserved it. The universe officially revoked my cool-as-a-cucumber badge for how I lashed out at her earlier. Frankie was out here, busting her ass, for an incredibly meager salary and I highly doubted it was because she'd receive the same job satisfaction as me executing this thing.

"I don't really know anything about you now. Not really anyway," Frankie said as she shifted against the tree. "It's like you're stunted in my mind as a seventeen-year-old, but there's a lot about you that seems different."

I lifted a brow. *Do I really want to know what this is?* "If you say anything about my crow's feet, I'm whipping this spoon at you." This earned me a soft chuckle and a peek at those glorious dimples.

"I think you've earned every single one of your smile lines and should wear them proudly. As did I," Frankie said.

She's not wrong. Ever since Lisa got sick, my mentality on aging shifted. Age was a gift, and one that I'd never take for granted. Not everyone was lucky enough to watch their face evolve. "Okay, so then what has changed?"

"I mean, your fancy-as-hell wardrobe for sure. Pretty sure you used to live in leggings and couldn't walk in heels for shit." Frankie grinned, and I was definitely going to wipe that off her face later. "But there's more. The old Morgan would not have hopped on the back of a Harley in a two-second decision because she didn't want to miss her nephew's soccer game. Or wouldn't've looked at this insane pile of stuff and thought 'opportunity' instead of disaster or wouldn't've kept a straight face when opening up that outhouse at that diner."

"Oh God, that was so gross. I have no idea how I kept it together."

"So gross," Frankie said. "But also... don't hurt me for saying this... there's a level of despair to you that I don't remember, either. Like a heaviness. The spark, the fire, doesn't seem to be there anymore."

I hate that Frankie was right. That these last few years, the toll of losing everything I worked so hard for had worn me down to a fraction of who I used to be. After Frankie left, I did recover. Sure, I never met another love of my life, but I did become a fully functioning human again. Watching Sam and Lisa struggle through her breast cancer and coming out the other side gave me a new lease of my own life. I took nothing for granted, I filled myself in the love of my niece and nephews, I buried myself in my other love—work. But seeing that love being ripped away from me chipped away at who I am.

I set my empty bowl to the side and crossed my ankles. "This discount wedding and event center, Dreams, opened up a few years ago. They have cheaper prices than me, and their showroom's beautiful, but there's nothing personal about the coordinating experience. You'll maybe talk to five different people. You might start with one coordinator and get switched to another. The turnover is pretty high, but still, I can't compete. And... my business is tanking."

Well, shit. There it was, out in the open. Not even my family knew of my struggles, even though it didn't take a genius to figure out why I was free during the spring weekends to babysit, when that used to be a rarity.

Frankie's eyes crinkled sympathetically, while kindly sparing me the full-on pity look.

"That sucks. I can't even imagine how hard it is when you put your heart into something and watch it fizzle," Frankie said. "But you're really talented. Maybe this is just a rough patch."

"Maybe." I shrugged, but it wasn't a rough patch. The fee from this wedding was the only thing keeping me afloat right now, until I figured out a new business model or decided to completely close up the shop. God, I was just so freaking tired. Not from today, although that, too. But from the fight in me, the drive that had pushed me to succeed. The fire that had always been there was flickering out and I couldn't stop it. All I wanted was to slip into a twelve-hour coma where I slept without waking up with a palpitating heart. "Honestly, it doesn't even matter."

"*Of course* it matters." Frankie crisscrossed her legs and leaned towards me. "I'm really sorry if I ever gave you the impression that I don't value what you do. That's the furthest thing from the truth."

The words filled me in a way that I needed more than I knew. I took off my handkerchief, smoothed back my hair, and reattached it. "Frankie, can I say something?"

"Yeah, of course," she said. "What's up?"

I rested my head against the bark for just a moment. "I know you and I have some differing thoughts about being on time and things..." Frankie's jaw flexed, and I almost stopped myself. But if we were going to work together this summer, I needed to call it out. "But if you are not a few minutes early, my anxiety flies through the roof. And I know it's not your problem, it's mine, and I totally get that. And out here on the farm, it's not the biggest deal in the world. But if we have a meeting somewhere, or there are clients involved, if you could be there like five minutes early, it would mean a lot. Just so I'm not worried, or thinking maybe you forgot or something happened..."

Frankie's jaw relaxed and she nodded. "That's totally fair, and I'll definitely make a point to be early when meeting with clients."

And I've officially exhausted all my emotions for today. I stood and dusted off the seat of my pants. "Ready to get back at it?"

Frankie nodded, lifted herself from the ground, and followed me back into the barn.

"Where did you go this afternoon?" I asked, picking back up the broom.

Something clouded Frankie's face, a look that I couldn't put my finger on. But the light in her eyes dimmed, and Frankie gazed at the floor. She didn't say anything for so long that I almost apologized for being nosy, when she sighed.

"There was something I had to take care of." Frankie grabbed a box and carried it outside without another word.

THIRTEEN
FRANKIE

The Blatnik Bridge never seemed to disappoint. Seeing sunrays bounce off the glassy water while anxiously waiting for a cargo boat to open the bridge was a chef's kiss. I took a deep breath, the freshwater-infused air prickling my nose, and dangled my legs off the tailgate.

I couldn't believe I'd been back in town for almost four weeks now, and after the blowup with Morgan last week at the farm was the first time I'd gone to the bridge since I was a teen. This place was damn near heavenly. The white noise of traffic above, the lack of horn honking (unlike New York), the tall grass waving in the breeze, provided a perfect serene background. Which meant this place also provided the perfect opportunity to clear my mind and think.

And that was exactly what I did for hours that day. Sitting under the bridge, it felt like I contemplated every life decision I'd ever made. I revisited what made me leave this town, why I loved New York so much, why I didn't just hire someone to take care of Peaches's house, and why the hell I was spending the summer with my ex-girlfriend who tugged at my heart while simultaneously driving me up a wall.

That afternoon, after being seriously—and *fairly*, I might add—annoyed as hell at how Morgan snapped at me, I'd called Quinn. She cut me off from my rambles about not understanding the big freaking deal about getting invitations out by an arbitrary deadline and point-blank asked me, "How would *you* feel if someone who wasn't a photographer said, 'Who cares if the lighting isn't great? It's just a picture.'" I both loved and hated my sister for calling me on my bullshit. I didn't like not being right, and I definitely didn't appreciate Quinn's refusal to coddle me.

But it was the phone call I made *after* my conversation with Quinn that really sealed the deal in my decision to return to the barn and help Morgan finish what we started. I pinched the bridge of my nose. I really didn't want to think about that conversation, nor about how different my life in New York would feel when I returned. I was here with Morgan, and right now, that's what mattered. Not the drama back home.

The low horn of a cargo ship passing through the waters sounded, and a little jolt went through me. Who knew watching a boat trudge under a bridge would be so interesting? In New York, I loved the action, the hustle, the energy. The city was invigorating, had its own personality, and had a strong pull that made you believe if you moved fast enough, you could achieve your dreams. In the city, I could eat anything I wanted, from dim sum to sushi to the best steak in the world. I could go to Broadway, sit in a whiskey and cigar bar, or dance and scream under the flashing strobe lights and with the best EDM DJs in the world. Not that I'd done that since my mid-twenties, but I could if I wanted to. Spring Harbors had none of this for me, at least not at the scale I'd become accustomed to.

But, in New York, I never took the time to do anything like this—sit and watch bridges. Or stare at squirrels running up trees in Peaches's backyard, or learn the name of the barista at a local coffee shop. The pace here was different. Not better, not worse, just fundamentally different.

And I kind of loved it.

I rolled my head, trying to remove the tension from my shoulders. Morgan and I had busted our asses these last nine days and *finally* made a dent in the space. But I was making next to zero progress on Peaches's house, which was the whole point of me taking this time off and coming here. After lifting heavy tools and junk all day long, when I returned to Peaches's house at the end of the night to tackle the mound of shit waiting for me, I was too exhausted. I usually ended up spending the evenings icing my knee and watching as time slipped by at a furious rate.

When I tore my ACL during a "friendly" co-ed soccer game by plowing into some assholes on the opposing team who needed to be taught a lesson, I knew my days on the field were done. But rarely did my knee act up how it had this week. At this point, I might need to hire someone to help me clear the house, which would be totally financially counterintuitive to helping Morgan clean out the barn.

So maybe I should just stop helping Morgan? She could hire someone else with what she was paying me, I could swing by a few nights a week and look through the potential salvageable items, and I could finish what I came to Minnesota to do. Although that was by far the most logical plan, I didn't like it. But I didn't want to contemplate *why* I didn't like it.

My phone rang and I dug it from my pocket. "Hey."

"Hey," Morgan said on the other line. "I just got off the phone with Olivia. A little change of plans for tomorrow."

Knowing Morgan, *little change of plans* could mean just about anything. I lay back in the truck bed and closed my eyes. "For the love of everything holy, please tell me we're not going back to the barn. You said a day off. No, wait, you *promised* a day off. You told me you had to get liquor-permit appeals and court stuff and other paperwork things that I one hundred percent didn't pay attention to. I need a break from moving rat-poop-infested junk. Please. You are *killing* me." I added an extra-heavy whine to my words for good measure. "In fact, I think I'm already dead. I'm the ghost of Frankie and not a real person. Does it feel breezy? That's my spirit haunting you."

"You are the most dramatic human alive, and that's saying a lot since I grew up with Sam," Morgan said with a smile in her tone. "Take a breath. We don't have to go back to the barn until Monday."

Thank God. "Oh, okay, cool. Then what's the plan? You up for a quick skydive?" A playful smile tugged at my lips.

"Not this week. Maybe next," Morgan said without dropping a beat. "Long story short, Tommy and Olivia had hired a choreographer to teach them a wedding waltz. They were supposed to meet him tomorrow, but that person backed out. Flu something or other. Doesn't really matter. Bottom line, we're going to meet them on campus at noon."

I propped my elbow up on the truck bed and switched the phone to my other hand. "I fail to see why we would need to meet them at all since the person backed out."

"*Because* I'm going to show them how to do the dance. We thought it might be nice for you to capture some of the practice photos," Morgan said. "I gotta run. But be there tomorrow, noon, on campus near the Old Main Park."

I was about to respond when Morgan cleared her throat.

"Sorry," Morgan sighed. "What I meant to say was, it would be great if you could meet us tomorrow on campus to capture the memories. But also, you're under no obligation. But if you *wanted* to, we'll be there at noon. Will that work for you?"

Well, if there wasn't something damn near endearing listening to Morgan trying to act like an empathetic human. Having someone else in her space, working alongside her when she'd been working solo, would take a bit of getting used to.

Except for the initial rough patch, Morgan had handled the change better than most.

I took one last look at the bridge and hopped off the truck bed to head home. "No place I'd rather be."

And I actually meant that. Ever since the call I made last week, being alone with my thoughts, questioning if I made the right decision, thinking of my past in New York, was the very last thing I needed.

The only question I had now was if I was obliged to tell Morgan the truth.

Every part of my body ached with fatigue. I rolled out of bed burrito-style because my ab muscles hurt too bad to sit upright and sniffed the lingering peppermint in the air from the muscle-relaxing lotion I applied last night. T-minus seventy-six days until the wedding and I *needed* this day off from manual labor.

But Frankie and I had kicked butt and taken names. Frankie was an absolute workhorse and had shown up five minutes early every day since our blowup the other week. It was clear she was pushing herself to the limit, also. When she started limping yesterday and finally told me that she'd torn her ACL a few years back and it sometimes flared up, I ordered her to sit in a chair with her leg propped up, applied ice, then cut the evening short so we could go home.

These last ten days, with the help of Sam and the crew, we'd almost completely emptied the barn. A few piles lingered that needed to be moved into the large machine shed as well as the two full extra-large dumpsters. But I could see past that. Somewhere between the cracked windows and janky doors and special smells, I knew we'd transform it into something beautiful.

Beautiful... but potentially very, very hot. The barn had electricity but no air-conditioning, and in Minnesota, that was a risk. Olivia's parents were generous, but no way would they spring for air-conditioning installation. So, we'd open windows, fill the space with fans, and have one portable air conditioner at the bride and groom's table while praying it didn't top a hundred degrees with massive humidity.

In the shower, I leaned my head against the wall. I hurt, I was tired, but I was still making it. And one amazing thing had happened yesterday—I booked a New Year's Eve party, which was normally not my thing as I typically did weddings only. But the caller seemed frantic and paid a deposit, and at this point I couldn't be choosy.

The hot water beat against my shoulders. I tried so hard to let my mind go blank, and yet it reverted to Frankie. It felt like a barrier had broken between us, which was great for a working partnership. But these feelings were not going away. They were dangerous, stupid, damn near self-flagellating at this point since I knew Frankie was going to return to New York. Last time, she'd blindsided me. This time, I recognized the inevitable heartache if I gave in, even for a moment. Thankfully, Frankie didn't seem interested in anything but rebuilding a friendship.

God, those muscles, though. What did she have to do to get arms like that? The ones with the dip at the bicep where you could see the actual shoulder curve and a shadow? Yesterday in the sun, when Frankie whipped off her shirt to just a tank to haul piles of wood, I almost choked.

I dug a thumb into my neck and rubbed, but dipped my hand lower to my center. Right after I started circling myself, I stopped. I was *not* going to start the day by jacking off to a vision of my ex, no matter how much I craved relief.

After the shower, I slipped on a sundress and put on my face. Damn, it felt good, for the first time in a while, to not look scrappy. I bolted out of the house, grabbed coffee at

Connie's place, popped into Zoey's to double-check about the cake tasting next Tuesday, and made it to the courthouse for the daily liquor license appeal by ten. By eleven, an hour early, I pulled up to my alma mater, University of Minnesota Duluth.

Over the years, I'd visited campus to see a speaker, attend a concert, or watch a play. But a good five years had passed since I'd stepped foot here, and it all felt the same and yet totally different.

Back then, my freshman year looked nothing as I imagined. Frankie had crushed me to the deepest part of my soul when she left me and broke the promise of attending UMD with me. Fueled by the heartache, I focused all my energy on studies. When classmates were doing keg stands and beer pong, I was in the library reading about the Civil War. When they went to football games, I was at home debating which extra course credits I should take to graduate early.

The campus still held the magic I felt back then, the promise of financial independence, a future in business, an independent life. Stepping onto the grounds, surrounded by the gold-and-maroon emblem flying on the flags, I still felt that touch of school spirit, the drive to succeed. My chin lifted as the sun beat against my bare shoulders, and I strolled around until it was time to meet Olivia and Tommy.

At the Old Main Park, I flipped through emails. *Boring, boring, boring... Oh, thank God!* The electrician confirmed he could come to the barn on Friday to do a preliminary check on what might need to be upgraded to get a day event permit. I exhaled. This just bought us a little bit of time. I scrolled through a few more, when footsteps approached.

"Damn. You clean up nice." Frankie set her helmet and backpack on the bench and flopped down on the bench next to me. "You've been wearing a bandanna for so many days I forgot you were blonde underneath there."

I rolled my eyes. "I didn't even hear your death trap pull up. Where did you park?"

"Over on the east side. I've actually been here for an hour, walking around, taking pictures of the campus." Frankie's gaze traveled the grounds. "God, I forgot how beautiful this place was. I haven't been to this campus since..."

I knew what Frankie was going to say before she finished. Frankie hadn't been here since we toured the campus together, back when we were seniors. This would've normally lit a fury in me, but today I wasn't going to let anything ruin my good mood. Although it wasn't a real day off, sitting on a bench basking in the warm sun with the quiet sounds of a summer campus was close enough.

"Super-cute dress, though. You look good." Frankie shifted her focus to an approaching Olivia and Tommy.

Thank God. Because the blush that was working its way across my cheeks was mortifying. *I really need to get out more often. One compliment from my ex should not push me to near giggles.*

"Hey, guys." I lifted myself from the bench and gave the couple each a quick hug. "Any updates since yesterday, or are we still on that one-hour deadline to nail this thing?"

"Sadly, exactly fifty-five minutes." Olivia frowned and set her water bottle on the bench. "But we think if you can teach us the fundamentals, we'll be able to practice on our own."

"Got it." I switched into focused mode and positioned the couple to learn the dance.

Frankie, the pro that she was, snapped pictures from a respectable distance, and soon I didn't even realize she was there. These pics may or may not make it into any memorabilia package, but they'd be good to have to capture the pre-wedding days.

"Okay, Tommy, arms up." I lifted my arms so he could mimic. "You're the lead, so you will step forward into the box as

I step back. Olivia, arms here. Let him take the lead, because if you push, it could knock you all off balance."

I called out the instructions, which seemed simple enough. Step forward, right foot to the side, together. "On a count of one, two, three, okay? Right foot, step back for four, side five, and close six."

Tommy stepped on Olivia's toes at least twice, and Olivia nearly tripped over herself. "Wait, what? I'm not following."

Oh boy. Fifty-five minutes would never be long enough. "This is a basic box step." I air-sketched a box at the ground. "Literally, like you're drawing a box."

"But the box is drawn upside down for one of us," Tommy said as he moved to step but froze before clanking into his fiancée. He tried again and started chuckling. "I feel the need to call out that I am top of my class. I'm not getting this, but if we need to talk about the cardiovascular system, I'm game."

Olivia planted a fat kiss on his lips with a grin. "For the record, we could just rock side to side, and you'd still be the sexiest man alive."

"God, I love you." Tommy kissed her hand and took a step back.

Their love really was sweet to watch. Even though the couple was clearly under a tremendous amount of pressure, they made the time to laugh with each other. I'd bet good money that both of them would make excellent doctors, always cool under pressure.

I, on the other hand, was not nearly as calm on the inside. Yes, this worked out today to meet them and give a lesson, but we had zero time to spare. The urge to clap my hands and get them to focus burned through my arms, but I smiled instead. "Now, bend your legs, down, up, up, down, up, up. Slide, stay smooth. Oh... Ouch... Try again."

Frankie released the camera and inched closer to us. "Tommy, lower your elbow. You're blocking Olivia's face, which is fine for today, but you don't want that on wedding day."

Oh, good call. They kept trying, but dear God, Tommy had two left feet and two left hands. "Huh?" he kept asking, over and over until finally I called a time out.

They were never going to learn this in time. I could pull up a video and show them a demo, but my screen was small, and that might not be efficient. "You know, you guys don't have to do the formal dance if you don't want to."

"Sure do." Olivia grabbed the water from Tommy and gulped. "My mother had a long list of requirements, and this was one of them. I swear each minute that passes, the more this day becomes for other people and less about us."

Frankie put down the camera and joined them at the bench. "Well, I say you should add some touches to make it your day. Spice up the old waltz. Add a dip, like a good one."

Tommy hopped up and held his hand out for Olivia. "Come on, let's try."

Jesus, how can he seriously be that terrible of a dancer? Olivia was petite, and it looked like he was about to drop her. I shot a glance at Frankie, who mouthed, *Yikes.*

"Okay, how about this," Frankie said, setting the camera on the bench. "Morgan and I can demonstrate."

Wait, what? I lifted a brow. "You know how to dance the waltz?"

Frankie grinned. "And the foxtrot, and the tango, and a little bit of the merengue, although I kind of suck at that one."

Wow. Why? How? There really was so much that I didn't know about Frankie. Sure, we went to prom and homecoming, but we danced like any other awkward seventeen-year-olds who had no clue what they were doing.

Frankie held out her hand, and I gripped it. I hated how easily my palm slid right into Frankie's, and the warmth that slinked through my arm. Taking the leader position, Frankie held me firmly around the small of my waist, and my breath stopped. In a snap, we were not in the middle of a college campus with a few uninterested bystanders tossing glances our way. Olivia and Tommy were nonexistent, and the only thing I heard was the soft thumping of my heart.

It was a silly dance, meaningless really, yet my body responded differently. I hated reading into everything, but I was closer than needed, snugger than needed, and Frankie's thumb was gently gliding on the top of my dress. Maybe Frankie didn't know she was doing it, maybe she did. No matter what it was, enveloped in strong arms, being supported, felt really freaking nice. For years, I was responsible for everything. But right now, for just for a moment, someone was taking the lead, and I could breathe.

"See this?" Frankie asked the couple, pointing at her arms. "There's a flow, a glide, to the movement."

My God, Frankie had moves. Fluid, swaying moves, and I wanted more. When Frankie fanned her fingertips across my hips, I fell into a daze. A tender, incredible daze and I didn't want it to stop. What was happening here? Everything was warming and tingling, the sun making my skin dance, but the fingertips making my body flush. I needed to stop these thoughts, and yet... maybe... no. We couldn't, right?

"And then, what if you added something like this?" Frankie spun and dipped me. Deep, quick, and for a second, I felt like I was falling. But I wasn't. I was safe in those arms, and when my eyes fluttered up to meet Frankie's, her breath hitched. Frankie's gaze dropped just a second to my mouth, and I felt that look in my toes. Frankie's eyelashes dipped and grazed her upper cheek, before she scooped me up and stepped a solid two feet away. It was a fleeting moment, but a definite, *definite* moment.

"So, there you go." Frankie cleared her throat as she moved to grab her camera off the bench. Her phone rang and when she peeked at it, she tensed and declined the call. "Does that make sense?"

"Yes, I think so." Tommy stood and wrapped Olivia in his arms.

For the next thirty minutes, Frankie continued snapping photos as I called out instructions. Frankie's phone rang a few more times, and every time it did, the couple broke their stride. Finally, she put it on silent and tossed it next to her helmet.

The couple started understanding, and the harder I tried to concentrate on them, the more I kept stealing glances at Frankie. This was completely bananas, right? Yes, we had a fleeting moment on this random Tuesday afternoon, but was this flicker, this *rumbling* in my belly really warranted? I should let it go.

Or... maybe I could offer to buy Frankie a drink and have a talk? Despite spending almost a month together, we still hadn't hashed out our past issues. Was it silly to focus on that, or smarter to seek some closure that I clearly still needed? But... then what? Entertain a friendship, maybe more? No. No definitely not. I didn't want more. I was pretty sure. But that mouth, though. That look that Frankie passed me meant something, and maybe a conversation wouldn't be the worst thing.

The obnoxious sound of an alarm cut through my thoughts, and both Tommy and Olivia switched from smiling wedding prep mode to medical school mode.

"Thank you so much for this, both of you. We have some work ahead of us, but this feels like a really good foundation." Tommy grabbed his backpack and water bottle. "We'll practice at home and make you proud."

"Or at least make you not cringe with embarrassment." Olivia chuckled and tossed her bag on her back. "We have to run to get to a lecture in ten minutes, but I'll email you later."

"Sounds great," I said, gathering my bag. "I have faith in you two." A white lie never hurt anyone.

Frankie, who clearly didn't actually silence her phone but put it on vibrate, flinched when the phone started buzzing against her helmet. She tapped it off again and packed up her camera into the case.

This was the time. I should ask her out for a drink. A talk, a *real* talk. I didn't know how to say it without making it sound like a date, when my insides were screaming at me to actually ask Frankie for a date.

I couldn't believe I was going to ask Frankie Lee on a damn date. I'd lost my mind.

I wiggled my toes inside my shoes and waited until Frankie finished packing. As I strolled quietly next to her through the courtyard, I froze. Frankie had turned down my offer for dinner after she fixed my car. God, that was so embarrassing. *Do I really want that humiliation again?* Definitely not.

But this... this was different. There was a *look*. An absolutely, without a doubt, clear and definite look. No one tosses that unless they are interested in the other person. "I have some good news. I'm going to make an appointment with Delilah at the florist shop for Thursday afternoon, so we can take that morning to recover from working at the barn." I grinned, but my smile dropped when Frankie said nothing and stared straight ahead. "Also, we have confirmation from Zoey about the cake tasting—" Frankie's phone rang again, and I swore to God if Frankie didn't just answer the call, I was going to answer it myself. Clearly, whoever it was had some sort of emergency, so why didn't Frankie just pick it up? "Jesus Christ, who keeps calling you?"

I wasn't sure how to define the look that passed over Frankie's face. Sadness maybe? Sheepishness? A touch of nausea? But whatever it was, the energy coming from Frankie wasn't good, and my insides heated.

Frankie stopped walking and focused on the ground. She looked up, faced me, and inhaled a sharp breath. "My wife."

And the world stopped. No way did I just hear Frankie right. Her *wife*? Frankie was *married*? My stomach turned inside itself, and I thought I was going to puke. Oh God, I was the cheater-*est* of the cheaters. Every childhood Sunday school class my parents forced me to attend smacked me square in the face. The good Lord was looking down on me, shaking his head and wagging a finger. Even though it'd been twenty years since I stepped foot inside of a church, the second I got home, I would scour the parish directories to find a priest on call for confession. "Your... *wife*?"

Even saying those words out loud cut in a way I didn't expect. Not an overwhelming jealousy, although some was there. More of a recognition that Frankie truly lived an entirely different life away from me. That, for better or worse, Frankie got over me in a way that I never got over her.

The silence grew between us, with unreadable expressions and a chin dangerously close to trembling. "You... you're married?" I choked out. "I can't believe you didn't tell me you were married."

Frankie shrugged and resumed walking. "You never asked."

And now my face flamed. "Really? We're going to play this game now?" I probably didn't have the right to feel as upset, or as lied to, as I did right now. But I couldn't help it. No matter how talented, or how good at dancing, or how many ice creams she may bring me, Frankie hadn't changed. Not one damn bit. Lies and secrets, just like back then. When Frankie refused to respond, I whipped my keys from my purse and kicked up the pace. "Whatever. I guess you don't owe me an explanation."

Frankie maintained the stride and straightened her shoulders. "You're right. I don't."

With that, she spun on her heels and walked away.

FIFTEEN
FRANKIE

Five miles outside of the campus was as far as I could go before I knew I needed to pull over and get off the bike. I pulled into the parking lot of a small diner and killed the engine. Distracted motorcycle driving was dangerous as hell, and no matter how shitty I felt, I didn't want to die on the road.

The blinking, cheery FRESHLY MADE PIE! sign was in direct contrast to my insides. I bit my trembling lip, fighting back tears. A while back when I made the fork-in-the-road decision with Morgan, I knew that I first had to take care of something back home. And now I needed to finish this, for good. I exhaled a shaky breath and called back. The phone call lasted less than two minutes, and none of it was a shock.

I knew the divorce was coming. I was the one who asked for it and finally called the lawyer during the "fork-in-the-road decision night," letting him know that I'd sign the papers that evening. But hearing my wife... my *ex-wife*... now, on the phone letting me know she signed as well and the divorce was final, was a nail in the coffin.

It had been a long time coming. Savannah and I had been separated for over a year when my ex, ripping the silent but weighty Band-Aid off, moved out of our apartment. But our relationship had quietly died a couple of years prior. There was no dramatic breakup, no scandal, no cheating. Just people evolving and lives changing, where we didn't fit together anymore. The only reason our divorce dragged on was because the breakup mirrored our relationship—neither one of us wanted to hurt the other and both avoided confrontation like the plague. Finally, before coming to Minnesota, I'd filed the inevitable.

I needed to get out of here. In a convenience store next door, I stopped for a few bottles of water and snacks, strapped the backpack to the seat, and flew up Highway 61. The warm wind hit my arms and chest, giving me space to calm down. Keeping my eyes fixed on the road, I weaved between the lines. I needed to feel the pull of the machine below me, needed to be able to control it.

Oh, the scenery, though. *Beautiful.* The winding roads, the forested hillsides, Lake Superior as large as an ocean. There was a stillness to the area, so much different than the hustle of New York. Yes, I loved that within walking distance of my apartment I could get groceries, a bowl of pho, and pick up a prescription. Everything was available in the micro-community nested inside the massive metropolis. But here, the land was expansive, lush. *Quiet.* Minnesota allowed my brain the freedom and space to just let go.

An hour later, I pulled into Black Beach. Definitely not the quietest place in the world as locals and tourists alike loved the dark, volcanic rock- and mineral-crusted sand, nested along massive rock formations and rustic driftwood. I maneuvered the bike into a spot and grabbed my bag. I hiked up a small, rocky path, and ducked under low-hanging branches until I settled myself on a large rock. The serene water below was so calm, so clean, it looked like a photo.

"*Fuck*," I whispered into the wind. I pushed my thumbs

into my temples until the pounding released, then picked up my phone.

"Oh no." Quinn answered on the second ring, with the sound of a clicking keyboard in the background. "Calling without sending a text first. You okay?"

"The divorce is final."

"Ah." The clicking stopped. "How do you feel?"

I picked up a stick and drew a circle in the ground. "Mostly relief." I could officially move on with nothing hanging over my head. Besides these last couple weeks when I spoke to my ex-wife about legalities, I hadn't even talked to her since last Christmas, when we exchanged an obligatory *Merry Christmas* text. Sure, having everything finalized felt good, but there was nothing joyous or celebratory about the occasion.

A few years ago, Quinn and I went to a divorce party in Queens. The entire evening was reminiscent of a bachelorette party. The ex-bride sported a sash with DIVORCEE splashed across it, we downed tequila shots, and at the end of the night the group gathered by a fireplace on top of a swanky rooftop bar and burned a copy of the marriage certificate. At the time, I'd thought, *Now that's how I'd do it if something happened with me and Savannah.* Ring in my new life.

Now, though, the idea of celebrating this felt awful.

"Besides relief, what's the other emotion?" Quinn asked.

I flicked a rock into a branch and sighed. "Failure. None of this feels good."

And that was the truth. Ultimately, I was glad the marriage was over, as sad as it was. I'd fallen out of love long before we'd even separated, which was unfair to us both. At the end, it wasn't even like we were friends. No fighting, just avoidance. Long days of making excuses for not being together. I stayed at hotels near where I was shooting, even though I could have easily made it home on the train. Savannah crashed at friends' houses or slid quietly out of bed before I woke up in the morning. So many nights of us going to bed back-to-back with paja-mas, when we used to be pressed together naked. But should I have tried harder? The love was gone, but maybe I could've been a companion, worked on making Savannah happier?

As soon as those thoughts drifted in, I stopped them. Savannah deserved to be loved, *really* loved, by someone. And honestly, so did I.

"Listen to me." Quinn paused. "*You* didn't fail. The marriage didn't work out. It wasn't a failure. It was a good rela-tionship for you, at the time, and now... you're both in different stages of life. Right?"

I shrugged, even though Quinn couldn't see me.

"Besides, to be totally honest, I never really saw you and Savannah growing old together. I just didn't think of her as the one for you, you know? She was wonderful, of course, but I'm not convinced she was ever really your person."

The reality in those words hit hard. I met Savannah after I'd been living in New York for five years. The short, hot-pink pixie cut had caught my attention. Savannah smiled with her eyes, was filled with a joy that intoxicated me. And, Christ, we laughed a lot, at least in the beginning, and usually at the dumbest shit, like movie one-liners we'd work into conversa-tions. When I met her, for the first time since leaving Minnesota, the hurt and heartache I'd been lugging around from my breakup with Morgan dissipated in her presence.

But then, as quickly as it ignited, the magic changed. The friendship stalled, and we both spent too much time pretending everything was okay.

"Did you tell Morgan?" Quinn asked. "Maybe you could take the day off from wedding stuff and just wallow?"

"Yeah, I told her today." *Sort of. Kind of. Not really.* God, sometimes I really hated myself. Why did I act that way? What a shit thing to say: *You never asked if I was married.* Did Morgan deserve to know? Maybe, maybe not, but either way my shitty response wasn't kind. I really needed to process what possessed me to lash out like that.

Look at me, processing my feelings. My therapist would be so proud.

"Hey, I think I need quiet time," I said. "I'm going to find some skippers and go to town on Lake Superior."

"Skippers! God, the north shore has the best rocks. Okay, make it a good one. Love you."

I hung up and tossed a rock into the lake, watching the ripples interrupt the smooth water. Dammit, I really didn't want to think about my snap reaction to Morgan. If I buried my head under the black lava sand and just listened to the water, I could also not think about the way Morgan felt in my arms.

Morgan. Why didn't I tell her about Savannah before today? Sure, she'd never asked, but usually people offered up that information. She probably had a right to know. Maybe. Right? *God!* Why was I overthinking this? If I bumped into a high school friend today, would I tell them that I'd separated from my wife and had filed divorce papers? Probably not.

But Morgan was more than a high school friend, and I damn well knew that. And we'd spent all this time together this summer. And... no matter how much I was running from it, the dormant spark had re-lit, and all the denying in the world wasn't going to change that.

Not doing this. I gripped the stepping rocks with my feet as I slowly made my way to the beach. At the bottom, I slipped off my boots, rolled up my jeans, and dipped my toes in the water. *"Shit, that's freezing."*

Once the shock of the ice-cold water prickling my skin wore off, I dug around for skippers. As I flung them, skimming them on the glass-like water, I tried reasoning the feelings. It was familiar, that's all. Like going back home and overeating your mom's legendary tater-tot hot dish, knowing it's terrible for you, but the nostalgia felt too good in the moment. Maybe Morgan was simply the human equivalent of comfort food.

Dammit, though, she didn't deserve how I reacted today. But having her close, smelling that vanilla rose on her neck, feeling that curvy waist as I dipped her, zinged through me. That plump bottom lip and her pouty mouth was just so there, so prominent, begging for a kiss. I wanted to know if they still tasted the way I remembered. So, when Savannah called, it was like being thrown into an ice bath after having warm feelings, and Morgan got the brunt of the shock. But at minimum, Morgan deserved an apology.

When my feet nearly turned numb and my rotator cuff ached from skipping rocks, I knew exactly what I had to do. I grabbed my phone and dialed Morgan.

The most hyper-responsive, efficient person I knew didn't pick up.

SIXTEEN
MORGAN

Frankie has a goddamn wife.

I blinked at my bedroom clock, refusing to move my body until the time hit a respectable 6:00 a.m. Damn my brain, nudging me awake an hour ago and refusing to let me rest, swirling with the same thoughts since Frankie dropped the whole "I have a wife" bomb three days ago.

Each day, I thought I'd cool down. I mean, honestly, did I have a right to be this mad? But every day I got more upset. The guilt was thick, and I tried to review our every single interaction to see if I inappropriately flirted.

Where was the wife, anyway? She obviously didn't come with Frankie to Minnesota. But now I wanted to know why... why the wife wasn't here, why Frankie never mentioned her, why Frankie grinned at me with those stupid dimples making me all gooey, why Frankie looked at me the way she did when we danced. I didn't imagine that. It was like I was being lust gaslit or something, and even though I sometimes read into things, I wasn't reading into that look.

I deserved to know. Didn't I? Wasn't that something that

should've come up while hauling wood piles or sifting through table settings? Sure, I hadn't asked, and Frankie hadn't asked if I was in a relationship. So really, maybe I misread this micro-lust bullshit happening in my body, and *Christ*, that was embarrassing.

But also, thank God Frankie was married because the last thing I needed was a summer fling with an old high school girlfriend. Sure, I was in a different space from when I was eighteen. But I could only imagine tripping over myself, falling back in love, and getting my heart broken, yet again, by the same woman.

So, no. I should be grateful Frankie was married. Damn near ecstatic, honestly. So why did it hurt so bad?

6:00 a.m. hit and I dragged myself into the shower. Just because I couldn't sleep didn't mean I didn't have the urge to wiggle under the covers and eat Cheetos and watch terrible TV all day. This wedding was the only thing stopping me from sinking into a deep dark wallowing tub.

The water beat on me and I breathed through the vanilla steam. At some point, I really did need to talk to Frankie. But since the day at the campus, I ignored Frankie's two phone calls and one *I think we should talk* text message. Instead, I sent a text later that evening, telling her I didn't need help for a few days, to take some time off and ice her knee, and I had it all under control.

Which was both a truth and a lie. *Of course* I had things under control. Controlling every detail of the wedding was the only thing giving me a reprieve. But I was buried under an avalanche of renovation and wedding stuff. Fortunately, the crew was ahead of schedule, and Olivia had picked out the invitations. I spent four hours yesterday hand-addressing each one and bringing them to the post office while absolutely not imagining what Frankie's wife looked like.

I stepped out of the shower and threw on the *Love 'Em or*

Leave 'Em podcast as I dried my hair. The voicemail segment began, where Ruby replayed a message from a caller to her listeners. This was always gutsy—what if the other person involved in the relationship was listening?

"Hey, Ruby, here's my question," the caller started. "I've kept something from my partner, which I don't think is that big of a deal. But the situation is snowballing and I don't know how to fix it."

I grabbed a round brush from the drawer and popped up the volume two notches.

"A few weeks ago, this cute guy at work flirted with me. At first, I thought he was just being nice. But it was a definite flirt, and I thought it was a one-time thing. However, he's still doing it, and I'm feeling pretty guilty. Anyway, I'll never act on it, of course. So, my question, do I need to tell my husband? Is there truly an obligation to tell my spouse *everything*? It's harmless and I'm not sure what good would come out of telling him."

Hmm, telling people the truth. What a novel effing idea. I shut the drier off and moved to the flat iron.

"Thanks to the listener for this question. I think I need to open up live calls one day because I have *sooooo* many questions," Ruby said. "So, the answer is tricky. Do I tell my wife, Amelia, everything? Of course not. It would take forever to give a play-by-play of our days. Not to mention I'd bore her to tears. And sometimes I've withheld things. For instance, last year she tried what she called 'strawberry blonde highlights.' She came home from the hairdresser and asked... *Is this orange? Does it look terrible?* And the truth was, yes, it was orange and yes, it looked terrible. But did I withhold that? You bet your bottom dollar I did. I haven't stayed married for the last thirteen years by sharing *everything*."

I smoothed the iron through my hair waiting for Ruby's response.

"But you're asking if you have an obligation to tell your

husband that this man flirted with you? My question back to you is, why, on the first day that it happened, did you not run home and say, 'You'll never believe what so and so said,' or 'How do I handle this.' Because quite often bodies don't lie. And you said you were feeling guilty, which leads me to believe you were not totally innocent yourself in the flirting. Unless you're in an unhealthy relationship with a jealous partner, I think you need to dig deep for the reason why you didn't tell him in the first place."

Guilt. So I was feeling guilty, and according to Ruby Reanne—who clearly doesn't know jack shit—that meant that my body was indicating there was something brewing inside, under the surface. And now... I was pissed again. I yanked my makeup drawer open and slapped the cosmetics on the counter.

I needed to take a break from everything. Working thirty-plus days without a single day off was not doing me any favors. So today, *mostly,* was for me. After getting a beautiful cup of coffee from Connie's place, I'd run to Joe's hardwood store to check if the wood planks for Tommy and Olivia's personalized corn hole stand came in, stop at Julie's glass shop to finalize the couple's glassware, then meet Sam and the kids at the waterfront for the antique festival.

Two hours later, all errands done and belly full of caffeine, I found one of the last remaining parking spots near the waterfront and weaved through the crowd until I found Sam pushing a stroller near the food stands.

"Only the baby today?" I peeked over the stroller canopy at the sleeping, chunky baby. For a moment, I contemplated picking her up and giving her some auntie smooches, but decided the more responsible plan would be to let her sleep.

"Yeah. Lisa took the older ones to a birthday party." He held out a cardboard container. "Cheese curd?"

I popped one into my mouth and chewed on the fried,

salted dough. "God, these are so terrible and greasy." I reached for another one. "I'll take two, thanks."

The festival had the best people watching, from farmers to college students to suburban moms carrying their LV bags, all peering over what seemed like miles-long tables with everything from pickling jars to old stereos to Elvis cookie tins. The scents of hot dogs and mini-doughnuts swirled in the air like a hearty fog, the sounds of kids screaming and haggling of prices and conversation funneled around us.

As I strolled next to Sam, we talked about how our parents were trying to guilt us into going to a family reunion on my dad's side with a hundred people we'd never met and frankly didn't care about. Soon, my shoulders relaxed. I picked up an etched drawing of Marilyn Monroe, trailed my fingers across a standing ashtray from the '30s, and allowed Sam to drag me away from buying a bucket of old buttons (*Seriously, what are you going to do with those*, he'd asked one too many times).

Sam slowed to look at baseball cards and peeked at me from the corner of his eye. "How are things going with Frankie?"

What a loaded question. Work-wise, Frankie was a rockstar. I didn't even understand her stamina—working all day at the barn, then going back to Peaches's house to pack up items. But everything else Frankie-wise made my stomach twist. "She's married."

"Huh." Sam lowered the baseball card. "*That's* how she is to work with?"

I didn't mean it to slip out quite like that, all wrapped up in a truly dejected tone that my brother was doing a terrible job of ignoring. "It just surprised me, that's all. We've been working together all this time, and she never once mentioned a wife, you know?"

Sam tucked the card back in the box and pushed the stroller ahead to the next table. "So, you jealous or what?"

"I'm not *jealous*." *Ugh, I think I'm jealous. Dammit.* I didn't know what the hell I was, but knowing there was some spectacularly chic, ultra-hip, big-city-styled wife out there that Frankie shared her secrets with burrowed under my skin like a parasitic flea. "I just... you know, whatever. Never mind. Anyway, it's fine working with her."

The next table had boxes of brooches: turquoise, bronze, little birds, and butterflies with fake pearls in the middle. I sifted through those and avoided my brother's laser beam gaze. He didn't really want to hear these woes from me, and I didn't have the energy to break it down for myself or him.

"Back then, I thought you and Frankie would be like Lisa and me. Lifers." He pushed the stroller out of the way of a bystander marching their way toward us, juggling multiple canvas bags. "I thought you guys had a really cool connection. It always felt like she was part of the family."

Sam wasn't wrong. Back then, Frankie and I were tight. Closer than girlfriends, different from a family. We had this unbreakable, or what I *thought* was an unbreakable, bond. I swore we knew what each other was thinking, could finish other's sentences, knew every detail about what made the other happy or sad. She was my other half, maybe even my better half.

Until she wasn't. And losing someone so close had really hurt.

"I bet if you dig deep and put aside whatever is going on, you guys could probably be friends again." Sam shrugged and set down his baseball card. "Might make you feel better."

Well, Sam Rose. Who knew? Sometimes, although rarely, I had the urge to hug him. Right now was one of those times. I settled for resting my head on his chest for a quick moment. "You're pretty okay, you know that?"

"I mean..." He laughed and waved to himself. "Besides, God knows you could use a friend. Since you hate cats, I'm worried that soon you're going to be one of those women that talk to their plants and apologize to your couch when you bump into it because you're not getting enough human interaction."

I pinched his arm and refused to tell him I already spoke to my plants, but only because I read an article that it was good for them. "How do you go from nice to dick in zero point five seconds?" I leaned in toward the baby, who was still sleeping, and grinned. "Promise me you will grow up to be like your mom."

The sun reflected off the brass and metal from the objects overflowing the tables. We walked booth to booth and oooh... *What's that?* A steampunk-style clock sat on the edge of the table and it was beautiful. The multiple gears and Roman numerals were detailed, intricate, and sturdy. Maybe I should treat myself. I flipped the price tag... and... maybe not. When I set it back down, a set of old-fashioned milk jugs resting inside a wooden crate caught my eye.

My finger grazed the glass and circled the top. Greenery... cedar... planks... barn. Flowers... glass... centerpieces. I waved to the vendor. "How many more bottles do you have?"

The man checked under the table. "I betcha about another three dozen or so."

My pulse kicked up a notch, the familiar creative adrenaline sparking my cells. This could be perfect. I snapped my head to Sam. "What did you guys do with those extra pallets from the corner of the barn? Did you toss them?"

"No," Sam said, glancing up from digging through a box of silverware. "We added it to the wood pile in the back of the barn. We were thinking about giving it away or burning it."

"Perfect." I dug into my purse and turned to the vendor. "I'll take all the bottles you have."

As the man gathered the items, I panicked at the amount of stuff I needed to carry. I glanced at the baby and back at my brother. "Don't kill me. But I need your stroller. You can have the baby."

"Wow, thanks." He cocked his head. "What are you going to do?"

"I have an idea." I slapped money on the table, my blood pumping with excitement.

First things first, though. I needed to call Frankie.

SEVENTEEN
FRANKIE

My phone vibrated against the dresser, with Morgan's name on the screen. Four days had passed since we last spoke, and I hesitated for a moment and answered.

"Hey, are you free this afternoon to meet at Pete and Patty's?" she asked.

"Yep."

"Great, see you then." *Click*.

Sure, I was glad Morgan called, since she'd all but ignored me since we last talked, but this was all she wanted? I guess I wasn't sure what I was expecting. Maybe an offer to have a talk. Maybe a question about why I never divulged my marriage. Maybe something, literally anything, that had a personal ring. But *nope*.

Being free was irrelevant. Was I sick of refreshing my emails a hundred times a day to check if *Birch & Willow* sent something? Yes. Was I tired of sifting through Peaches's items? Yes. Was I missing Morgan? Also, yes.

Dammit. I shouldn't be *missing* Morgan. Missing human interaction, or someone to chat with, or a working partner, fine. But missing Morgan, *the person*? That wasn't good.

I filled a box with Peaches's old costume jewelry, hats, and scarves, and moved to tape. On second thought... I dug through it and pulled a couple of Peaches's brooches and her obnoxious lavender sun hat with the multicolored peacock feather she wore everywhere. I couldn't part with these. It was like these items were a part of Peaches. I started a new box for "saved" items. At this rate, my two-bedroom apartment in New York was going to overflow with memorabilia if I didn't stop myself, and I'd be no different from Peaches, who stuffed every nook with random shit.

Several hours later, after never wanting to see another cardboard box for the rest of my life, I pulled up to Pete and Patty's farm and slammed the truck door closed. Inside the barn, I scanned the vastly bare floors and shelves. *Damn...* The crew had made a ton of progress in the last few days. Besides a pile of tools, a large table saw, and a few scattered miscellaneous items, the barn was nearly empty. *Outside* of the barn may look like a machinery graveyard, but the inside was good.

I walked the floor, pushing into the planks to check its stability. No matter the filth and cracks, it wasn't actually in as rough of shape as I'd originally thought. Probably a trip hazard here or there, but hopefully decent enough where if we pried up some cracked pieces, slapped on some wood glue, or sourced a few rugs, we could call it good.

"Morgan?" My voice bounced against the empty walls. "Morgan?"

Silence met me until the faint sound of grunting and footsteps crunching over twigs approached. When Morgan appeared in the barn door, her overalls dusty, her cheek stained with a fresh line of dirt, and fumbling carrying a wooden box, I couldn't stop my smile. *God, she's cute.*

"Do you know how to use a table saw?" Morgan asked as she dropped the box on to the ground with a thud.

No "hello." No "sorry, it's been weird for a few days." No "thanks for coming." Just, "can you use a table saw?" I wished I were surprised. But, maybe it was for the best. Was I ready for a deep, heart-to-heart conversation, where we dove into what happened in our past, why I never mentioned Savannah, and more importantly what the hell was this rush taking over me every time I looked at her? No. "A table saw? Um, yes, I do. But it's been a very long time since I've used one and I don't feel like losing a thumb. Why?"

"'Cause... this!" Morgan pointed to the pallets in a corner with a wide grin.

A wide, powerful grin, and it was damn near infectious. In my line of business, I wasn't immune to the power of the pallet. Dressers, tables, sometimes even a bedframe was made with the material. But I saw the beauty *after*... It was hard for me to picture it more than being a pile of dirty wood in its current state.

"Take a look at this." Morgan dug out a dusty glass bottle from a wooden case. "I found this while antiquing with Sam."

I chuckled. "Sam antiques? Not sure if he's leveled up or downgraded in the cool factor. I need to process and let you know."

"I'm sure he'll eagerly await your decision." Morgan tugged on my arm and dropped her hand as quickly as she reached out. I kind of wish she'd put it back. She marched to the back of the barn, her hips swaying with each step. "Anyway, I found these really cool old milk jugs and paired them up with these candles I already had. Then I swung by Delilah's flower shop and grabbed these, and... what do you think?"

What did I think? I thought I could shoot this for a spread for *Birch & Willow*. Among the chaos of clipped flowers, eucalyptus, small rocks, and a *very* splintered chunk of pallet, lay a perfect place setting. Rustic and artsy. Beautiful and simple, yet layered and complex. Earth-colored pebbles filled an old-school milk jug. Lavender, sage, and cream-colored roses tucked in the middle of a few stems of eucalyptus, all nested on a bed of pallets.

"So obviously, the pallet wood needs to be cut, sanded, maybe even stained. And the jar would sit on it just so..." Morgan adjusted the jar resting on the tilted wood and pushed the candle next to it. "Anyway so, that's my idea."

It didn't take a PhD in human emotion to know the blush sweeping Morgan's cheeks and rushed words were a clear indication she was seeking approval. But she must know how talented she was, right? Even if she didn't, Morgan didn't seem like the type to need my approval.

"Morgan." I dipped my head to look into those expectant Caribbean-blue eyes. "This is incredible. Truly. It's perfect. Damn, I wish I would've brought my camera."

Now an even deeper blush and wider smile grew. Morgan grabbed a pair of work gloves and tossed them at me. "Okay, so I think we keep with this whole pallet theme," she said. "We're in a raw, un-remodeled barn and I say we lean into that space. These pallets will hold all the centerpieces, and we can use the same wood to build a side table. Oh! We can also build a pallet wall-shelf-type thing... we'll have small flowerpots with guests' names on it... with phrases about letting love grow, growing with love, something like that. You get the picture. Then, on the side we can..."

As Morgan monologued for the next four million hours, I followed her every direction. I pulled in pallets, dug through the mammoth amount of tools for nails, hammers, and a sander. And even though I really didn't want to lose a limb, one of the crew members showed me how to use the table saw, and I started cutting pieces for the centerpiece. The work was so invigorating, I didn't realize how many hours had passed until my belly rumbled.

Morgan was bent over a table, living fully in the "elbow grease" motto, her ass wiggling as she pushed the sandpaper across the wood. With how grimy Morgan was from today's activities, the action shouldn't have been quite as hot as it was. But damn it, I took way too long of a look at the curved, juicy backside, and when Morgan abruptly stopped and stared, I 100 percent felt like I got caught.

"Was that your stomach?" Morgan wiped her hand on a cloth.

"Yeah, sorry." *Be cool. It was just a damn look.* "I didn't eat much before I got here."

Morgan bit the inside of her lip and glanced at her watch. "God, I didn't realize it was so late. Um... I have a half-bag of mini-doughnuts from the festival today and some Cheetos in the trunk."

I smiled. "Sounds like a perfect dinner."

Outside, the golden sun inched lower as magenta brushed the sky. After hosing our hands down, I flopped next to Morgan against the massive cedar, which was quickly becoming my favorite break spot.

After talking all day, but not saying much, now should be the time. I opened my mouth to broach the inevitable subject but crunched into a Cheeto. Seriously, I just needed to address this, but where to start? *How* to start? "Her name is Savannah."

Morgan squinted and slowed her chewing. "Huh?"

I pulled my legs up to my chest and linked my arms around my shin. "I should've told you I was married."

"Ah." Morgan flicked her gaze to the ground. A solid moment passed before she shrugged. "Like you said, you don't owe me anything."

God, why did I say such a shitty thing? At the time, I didn't mean to snap, but my emotions were all over the place. I took a long drink from the water bottle and used the neck of my T-shirt to wipe my lip. "Anyway, we're no longer married."

Morgan lifted a brow. "That was fast."

I chortled through my nose. "It was a long time coming. And I really mean that. We separated two years ago and lived apart the last year. Honestly, it kind of surprised me that she called."

Morgan flicked at the cap of her water bottle. "Was it... something important?"

The words were lobbed over casually, without Morgan's facial expression changing. But there was something... a pause, a drop in the voice. Something that carried the energy of more intention, and maybe later I'd let myself think about it deeper.

"I guess? Maybe?" I split the last remaining doughnut and held out half to Morgan. "She was letting me know the divorce was final."

"Oh. I'm sorry." Morgan's eyebrows scrunched. "Was it awful? Is she a terrible human?"

"Nah, nothing like that," I said. "We just grew apart. I met her a few years after I moved to New York, probably like twenty-two, twenty-three? We got married too fast."

Morgan dusted the sugar and cinnamon from her fingers. "Tell me about her."

Does she really want to hear this? I wasn't sure who or how much Morgan dated since we last knew each other, and I had absolutely no desire to find out. Maybe Morgan left whatever was between us back on the high school parking lot that day, and I still held a piece. "She was fun, really nice, ambitious. She worked in fashion."

"You hate fashion."

"I'm the most fashionable human you've ever met." I waved to my standard white T-shirt. "She worked as an assistant editor for a high-end magazine, then editor. For a short period there, we traveled to all sorts of runway shows, even Milan."

"Like real runways with the angry models?" Morgan dug

out another Cheeto and popped it in her mouth. "Why don't they smile, by the way?"

I picked up a twig from the ground and picked at the bark. "Not sure if this is true, but I asked Savannah the same thing. She said it'd look unnatural if they smiled the whole time on the runway and it wouldn't sell the clothes the right way. Whatever that means. Honestly, I think it's 'cause they're hangry."

Morgan grinned. "How were the runway shows?"

Oh, those shows. For everything Savannah and I had in common, like music before film, photography before painting, sleeping in before hiking, there were a million other things we didn't—these shows, high-end purses, dancing on tables, calamari (*gross*), the list goes on.

"The runway shows were boring as hell. Truly. Clothes no one would actually wear, most people were stuffy and fake, and really not my scene. Lots of air kisses and talk about getting together." I snapped the twig in half and reached for another one. "Not to me, of course. I was basically invisible, which suited me just fine."

Maybe the runway shows should've indicated that Savannah and I were not meant to be. Sure, a free trip to Italy was nice, but Savannah *lived* for those shows. It made sense for Savannah in her profession, but I started zoning out whenever Savannah talked about the fall fashion lineup.

"So, can I ask what happened with you and... Savannah?" Morgan asked.

My foot tapped against the ground as my cells turned restless. I grabbed two rocks and rolled them in my palm and, after a moment of silence, unleashed. Morgan sat still, as I rambled about how sometimes love wasn't enough and that I let politeness take over. How Savannah had a sister who hated me, a mother who thought she'd settled, and during a hefty argument a few Thanksgivings ago between me and Savannah's mom, Savannah didn't stand up for me and it crushed me.

More time passed, and I talked about the work schedules, and how we made excuses to stay apart, how I started to morph into being more excited to see my sister than my wife. The sun set, and the sky darkened. Morgan asked more questions, and I unloaded about us never addressing our issues, finally going to couples therapy, but when we were too polite to actually address anything, it was like the nail in the coffin.

"Neither of us wanted to fight for us, and it was obvious sitting in those sessions that we had nothing to save," I said, tossing rocks against the earth. "In hindsight, the divorce would've been inevitable, no matter what we did."

The bottom line was, Savannah and I were never soulmates, and I knew that in my heart. There had only been one time in my life I felt like someone was my soulmate. Only one time when I was so deeply in love, I felt the physical pain of my heart breaking when things ended. And only one time where I spent a year wondering if I made the right choice.

I kept this part to myself, however.

My limbs seriously needed to move. Even though I'd been doing physical labor all day, my hands, legs, feet, *everything* needed some circulation. And unless Morgan wanted to offer up her arms as a human fidget toy, I had to get back to work. I stood and dusted off the seat of my pants. "We should head out. The last thing we need is to hit a deer on these pitch-black country roads."

"Good call." Morgan lifted herself and grabbed the Cheetos bag. She looked at me for a moment and paused. "Thank you for sharing your story with me. It's really nice getting to know this side of you."

I moved in and hugged Morgan. Without hesitation, she hugged back. A deep hug, a sturdy hug, one that said so many things without saying anything at all. Morgan's body pushed into me, her chest pressed against mine, and I swore I felt Morgan's heartbeat thud against mine. Even through the sweat and dust, that signature vanilla rose scent filled the air, and I dipped my head to inhale.

Morgan pulled back with a grin and squeezed my shoulders. "Good night."

She got in her car, and I hopped in my truck, but there was so much more to say.

Unfortunately, I had no idea where to begin.

So, Frankie wasn't married anymore. Like *really* not married. No reason to grab a local priest and confess my lusting after another person's wife or bury my face in shame. But also no reason to go to bed thinking of her every night.

Three weeks had passed since we talked at the farm until the moon filled the sky, and a couple of things had happened. One, we made so much progress on the farm that I had solid hope on the horizon. Two, our relationship settled back into the friendship we once had. Three, I was slowly, quietly, heart-breakingly, falling back in love.

Was that stupid? Absolutely. But this time I knew what I was getting myself into. Frankie had been nothing but upfront and honest about moving back to New York, and I couldn't blame her. The opportunity at *Birch & Willow* was beyond all dreams. And even if Frankie didn't get that opportunity, it was clear Frankie had made a life out there.

Last week, she mentioned I should come visit her sometime. She said she'd take me to all the spots, the Twin Towers memorial, Times Square, and Central Park, of course. But then she'd show me the *real* city. Frankie would take me to her favorite place in Spanish Harlem for apparently the best homemade horchata ice cream of my life. We'd go to an Italian restaurant, Louie & Giovanni's, that looked like a hole-in-the-wall with nothing more than red-checkered tablecloths and uncomfortable wooden chairs. But Frankie said the place took at least a month to land a reservation and the rigatoni was the best in the city. Then we'd swing by a queer art gallery in Queens that only had a black door, no signage, and you had to walk up a hidden cement stairway to enter. The first time Frankie visited, she said she thought she was being led to her death. After that, we'd have a tarot card reading in the basement of a cigar shop with a ninety-year-old woman who was so gifted Frankie was sure she could read her soul.

I skipped up the three porch steps to Peaches's house, knocked twice, then cracked open the door. "You decent?"

"Depends on your definition." Frankie rounded the corner, carrying a large box and, *of course*, wearing her signature T-shirt that somehow perfectly accentuated her forearm muscles. Was it normal to have a "thing" for forearms? I couldn't ever remember being attracted to this random body part, and here I was, salivating at the sun-kissed skin, with the deep ridge carving all the way to the elbow.

That's it. No more jokes. I really needed to get laid.

"Dang, you made a ton of progress since yesterday." I looked at the twenty-plus boxes stacked against the wall. "We didn't even leave the barn until after seven last night."

"I know." Frankie plunked the box on top of another, pushed it against the side of the wall, and breathed bangs out of her face. "Got my second wind and packed until midnight. Hyperfocus for the win. Doesn't always happen, but when it does, ya gotta seize onto that shit, baby."

When Frankie had finally opened up about being diagnosed with ADHD, the puzzle pieces had connected. Sure, she was always hyperactive. Honestly, I thought that's what made her such a tremendous athlete since she had an unlimited supply of energy to burn. From study sessions where Frankie couldn't focus and I'd get so pissed, to being late due to "losing track of time," to Frankie constantly interrupting me, making me feel like my opinions didn't matter... it all made sense.

"I texted Olivia last night, and we're going to mark each table with an aged photo." I followed Frankie into the kitchen and helped her roll packing paper around glasses. "Table one will show a picture of each person when they were a year old. Table two, two years old, etc. I think it's going to be really cute."

"That's a good idea." Frankie stretched to reach the top shelf and pulled out the last two glasses. I tried hard not to notice her perfect ass as she did it, but I failed. As per most of our interactions. "Adds something interesting for people to look at while waiting for dinner."

I peeked at the towers of boxes, several of them with the word PHOTOS splashed across in Sharpie. "Dang... I can't believe all these boxes. How many photos did Peaches collect over the years?"

"A gazillion. Funny enough, it took me until now to realize my love of photography was probably inspired by Peaches." Frankie stuffed newspaper into the box. "You can look through them if you want. There's a ton of Quinn and me, but surprisingly a bunch of you."

I snapped my gaze at Frankie. "Me?"

"Yeah. I mean, not solo pics of you, but pics of us. Proms, homecoming, my sports, when we graduated..." Frankie's voice went low.

High school graduation, both a high and a low point in my life. No matter how close me and Frankie had become over these last seven weeks, we'd avoided talking about what actually happened that day. Because clearly I didn't have enough to occupy my time between planning the wedding and getting the barn ready, I spent my downtime reliving my last year with

Frankie. Sure, that night was tattooed on my brain as the greatest devastation I'd ever felt, but it wasn't like everything was perfect until that moment and it snapped. Even though it was easy to look back and think that graduation was when everything collapsed, that wasn't the truth.

Frankie stepped into the hallway and returned with a plastic tote that I swear was large enough to hold a king-size bed. She set it on the floor next to me and returned to sifting through the kitchen cabinet drawers. "Here's another one. She's got more in the basement, but you can get started."

Inside the tote were maybe a half dozen photo albums, and the rest shoe boxes overflowing with hundreds and hundreds of photos. "What are you going to do with these?"

"I'm not sure. I can't throw them, but I don't have the time to sift through them. I was going to ask my parents to hold on to them, but they're as responsible as a pack of ferrets, so I'm not sure I should." Frankie ripped tape across the box and scribbled with a marker. "I might just hire someone to scan them. Dig through and take any that you want."

I sat cross-legged on the floor and shuffled through. God, so many photos. Peaches's small garden, her grandkids, plants, and animals. There seemed no rhyme or reason to the organization, except that the pictures were roughly separated by decades. I opened the FRANKIE AND QUINN box. A smile passed my lips at the dozens of photos. "You were such a cute little kid. What happened?" I grinned and ducked as Frankie balled up a sheet of newspaper and threw it at me.

Photos of Frankie with a chocolate-smeared face, riding a bike with a lopsided helmet, her and Quinn in a strawberry field with gap-toothed smiles holding up red-stained hands. More and more pictures. I smothered myself in the nostalgia.

More pictures, Frankie growing older, skating on the ice rink, running on the field. Frankie with a huge Nike headband on her forehead, soccer ball tucked under her elbow, her arm slung around a teammate.

"Oh my God, I remember this place." I held up the picture of Frankie and Quinn sitting in their hoodies around a firepit. "Did Peaches keep her Brainerd cabin?"

Frankie leaned forward and squinted. "Nah. She got rid of that like twelve, thirteen years ago. Too bad, too. That baby would be worth a fortune by now."

No doubt. I thanked my lucky stars I bought my small townhouse when I did, back when home prices were affordable and interest rates were next to nothing.

I sifted through more pictures when I found *the box*. Maybe it was because they'd grown older and Quinn was doing her own thing, but soon Frankie and *Quinn* pictures morphed into Frankie and *Morgan* pictures. Thickness built in my throat as I flipped through dozens of photos. Frankie and I running through sprinklers, having a sleepover in Peaches's house with a plastic gallon ice-cream bucket filled with buttered popcorn. More photos of sporting events, standing outside the movie theater after Peaches dropped us off. Of course, I distinctly remembered telling our parents we were going to watch some PG movie, then sneaking in to watch an R-rated horror movie. We stuffed ourselves with so many grape pixie sticks that I threw up after I got home. I kept flipping. More pictures of us as we grew older, both of us holding up our driver's licenses with a big thumbs-up, and of course, prom.

The prom photos nearly made my eyes prickle. Frankie had her long hair slicked back in a tight ponytail and wore an oversized suit with a tie. I vaguely remembered Frankie's parents throwing a fit and begging her to wear a dress, which Frankie, always the tomboy, had scoffed at. But I had felt like a princess that night. Floor-length, dark blue, spaghetti-strap, draped dress with a sequined corset top and matching blue heels. I'd spent the two weeks prior learning to walk in heels and had loved being nearly as tall as Frankie that night. As Frankie's shipping tape screeched, adhering another box, I kept sifting.

And then, the picture of high school graduation. My breath froze. The *before* picture was full of hopeful smiles, glowing with the energy of people ready to enter the real world. My pinkie flicked the top corner of the photo, lost in the memory of that day, a swirl of cap throwing, cheering, and sobbing while saying goodbye to friends.

"What are you looking at over there?" Frankie asked as she tossed utensils into a box.

"Oh, um…" I cleared my throat and tossed the photo into the box. "Nothing."

I needed to address our relationship, and soon. The closure we both deserved lingered like a droopy, gray cloud. No matter how much the conversation was digging into the tip of my tongue, I just couldn't release it. I wasn't ready to hear the confirmation that I wasn't good enough for Frankie to have stayed back.

"Hey, you good if we swing by the donation center and drop off a load on the way to Zoey's Bakery?" Frankie asked.

I checked my watch and lifted myself from the floor. "If we don't leave now, we won't get to the bakery a proper ten minutes prior, then we'll be late."

"Heaven forbid." Frankie smirked, then paused. She shifted, her expression serious, and took a quick breath. "So sorry. I didn't mean that. Of course we'll make sure to get there early. That's important for you, so… it's important to me."

Wow. Frankie really had heard me the other week about punctuality. A warmth spread through me.

"Hey, maybe after Zoey's we can…" Frankie started to say but closed her mouth when she heaved a box and moved to the front door. "Oh shit, that's heavy. Can you grab the door?"

I scooted to the door and opened it, being super helpful by following Frankie to the truck, armed and ready to call out if any rogue squirrels ran in her path. After she dropped the box into the bed with a heavy thud, I walked with her back into the house. "What were you saying, about after Zoey's?"

Frankie lifted a box and squinted. "Oh. Sorry. Who knows? I'm like a fish, I swear. If it didn't happen two seconds ago, I have no idea."

Those were her words, but her avoided eye contact conveyed something else. I lifted a smaller box, my insides unsettled, and trailed Frankie back to the truck.

NINETEEN
FRANKIE

Seriously, stop using ADHD as an excuse. I pulled Peaches's truck out of the driveway with Morgan riding shotgun and scolded myself. My therapist would *not* be happy with me right now. Because I knew exactly what I'd been going to say to Morgan back at the house. I was going to ask her out for dinner.

After working together for two months and eating sandwiches or takeout at the barn or Peaches's house, having dinner probably didn't seem like that big of a deal. But I didn't mean *supper*. I meant *dinner*. At a restaurant with wine and a server, eating from a plate with actual silverware, not a box with chopsticks.

But also dinner was a terrible fucking idea. What in God's name was I thinking? If dinner went well, then *after* dinner might go really well, and if all that went well... then it wouldn't be well. *At all.* I'd be repeating history, with full knowledge of how painful everything was last time.

As the truck shook from bumping over a hefty pothole, I looked at Morgan's bouncing body like a horny teenager and gripped the steering wheel to stop myself from doing something stupid. But being in such close quarters with Morgan was doing me no favors, and more than once I lingered over Morgan's shoulders to inhale the signature scent from her neck.

After dropping off a load at the donation center, I steered the truck down Main to Zoey's Bakery. Inside, the air swirled with an intense chocolate and buttered-dough aroma. *This might be the best job ever.* Morgan said earlier she'd never encountered a couple who wanted the coordinator to cake test before but was up for the challenge. Of course, she'd said that with a twinkle in her eye, and invited me along. The combination of spending some non-manual labor time with Morgan while eating sugary desserts sounded like a perfect afternoon.

Zoey popped around the corner. "Hey, friends!" She waved Morgan and me to a small side table in the corner. "You excited for today?"

"Cannot wait. I finally have an excuse to try everything in your shop." Morgan pulled out a chair and sat. "Hey, how is prepping for the Fourth of July event going? I heard from Connie at the coffee shop this morning that it's going to be huge this year."

Morgan should really run for mayor. Or CEO of Spring Harbors. Or *something*. Because I swear to God, she knew everyone and everything that happened around here. At first, it seemed almost creepy, how everyone knew everyone's business. But now it was comforting. I ran into the guy from the auto shop the other day at the grocery store, and he asked me if Morgan's car was still holding up after I fixed it back in May.

Back in May.

"You know the whole gratitude thing, right? Great opportunity, great for business, excited to do it. Blah, blah. I know it hasn't even happened yet, but if I never see another red, white, and blue firework cupcake in my life, it'll be too soon." Zoey leaned back on her heels and tugged on her pink apron string. "But I'm actually really excited for today. We have the usuals, of course, but I just tried a new salted black sesame and pistachio cake that was freaking delicious, if I do say so myself. So, even though that's not a typical wedding cake, I want you to give it shot."

"That actually sounds really good," I said, my mouth already watering. "Can't wait to try."

As Zoey walked away, I eyed the display case next to the table. Behind the glass lay chocolates shaped like miniature gift boxes with edible gold, a small fruit tart that looked like glass, and delicate yet beautiful pink cupcakes, all nestled around pink tulle. Normally, this much pink would give me serious Pepto vibes, but Zoey had it decorated with perfection.

"Does Zoey do this all herself?" I asked.

Morgan unfolded a napkin and placed it on her lap. "She does, at least most of it. I think she has only like two staff members. Rumor on the street is that she practically lives here."

Ah, Mayor Morgan strikes again. "How long has she had this place open?"

"About five years." Morgan tilted her head forward. "Let me tell you, there was some major drama around that."

Dammit. She sucked me in. Now I must know everything. "Spill."

In a hushed voice Morgan talked about how Zoey once worked at a local diner famous for the best coconut cream pie in town. The diner had been around since before I was born, so I knew what place—and pie—Morgan meant. "But after Zoey left and started the bakery, rumors that she stole recipes spread through the town like a bad case of chicken pox in a daycare center. And you know me," Morgan whispered. "I had to know, so I just point-blank asked her."

Dear God. "You didn't."

"Oh, I did." Morgan tucked a piece of hair behind her ear. She scanned the buzzing customers like a spy, then leaned in. "Turns out the owner of that place was a super creeper, and his wife is a total enabler, so they started this whole smear campaign. Went to the church circle and asked everyone to *pray for Zoey.*"

Morgan didn't need to do air quotes around the word *pray* for me to know what she meant. No news travels quicker than the church ladies' "prayer" circle. Sometimes it was done with good intentions, but mostly it was used to gossip with impunity. "I'm not sure if it's impressive or terrifying how you know everything around here. I'm pretty sure you know everyone in this town."

"The city is my home, you know? I like to know people who are in my home." A softness took over Morgan's face. "It feels good. Safe. Like someone will always be there if you need them."

In New York, even though the same guy worked at the corner grocery store for years, and I was a regular at a few restaurants, I didn't know anyone at this level. With a constant rotation of people, I barely even knew my neighbors.

"Okay, friends... ready for this?" Zoey stepped from around the corner holding a large white tray with what must've been fifteen different desserts. My blood sugar rose just looking at it. If for some reason the whole *Birch & Willow* thing didn't work out, I was putting in an application somewhere as a professional taste tester. I refrained from drooling and tried to pay attention to Zoey's words.

"The cards are underneath the place setting, but here we have classic vanilla, chocolate, red velvet, almond, pistachio cream, butter mocha..." As Zoey continued pointing out the flavors, her employee popped out with another tray holding water, milk, and coffee. "To cleanse the palate," Zoey said.

Yeah, yeah. Got it. Drink in between sips. Label underneath. Lots of flavors. My mouth was salivating so much I might need a napkin. When Zoey stepped away, I rubbed my hands together with my eyes cartoon-wide. "Okay, where are we starting? Left top to bottom?" I sliced into the cake with the side of my fork without waiting for answer. The warm vanilla sweetness melted into my mouth. This wasn't any ordinary vanilla, either. It was simple and smooth, but full of flavor, and perfectly accented with a pillowy lavender frosting. "Winner. No need to try any more."

Morgan laughed and dug out her notebook. "We can't declare a winner already. We need a rating system. One to ten."

"Eleven." I dug my fork into the cake but stopped when Morgan touched my wrist.

"No judgment here, but you might want to pace yourself. We have another dozen to try."

"Rude." I looked down at the second bite with a grin. "Okay, *fineeee*. Good call."

The cakes were phenomenal. Truly. When did I turn into a big city snob that thought a town like this couldn't compete with Manhattan bakeries? Although, and I'd never say it to the nice lady, Connie, at the coffee shop, but NYC still had the best bagels.

So many bites and sips of coffee later, I bounced between marveling at a simple chocolate cake with a thin layer of raspberry that was equally as delicious as the complex coffee cake layered with swirls of salted hazelnut and topped with a Kahlúa-and-amaretto-based mousse. I was completely useless at giving recommendations, but thankfully Morgan was taking the job way more seriously.

Morgan slid a small chunk of red velvet in her mouth and swirled the food like she was at a wine-tasting event. "Tell me what New York was like when you first got there."

Hmm. How deep did I want to get, here in the middle of tasting treats at Zoey's Bakery, with the bell dinging above the door anytime new customers entered? "Exhilarating as it was terrifying. That first year, I was *so* homesick, even for my parents, if you can believe it. Terrified to walk at night." And heartsick over Morgan, but I didn't tell her that.

During those first years, though, I was also alive, free, and curious. Feeding my curiosity was all-consuming. As I discovered the city and what made it spark alive, I discovered myself. Getting diagnosed and finally treated for ADHD, learning to drive a motorcycle, going to underground clubs, listening to slam poetry at a small bar in West Village, taking a woman or two home from a speakeasy in SoHo, all contributed to the woman I became.

"Not everything was perfect, but God, it was freeing to just... be, you know?" I said. "I learned who I was. Before Quinn arrived and I met Savannah, let's just say I had some... interesting apartments and even more interesting room-mates. Lived above a Subway shop and my clothes smelled like dough and onions for a year. Which honestly could've been worse."

Oh, the sugar hit. Glaze covered my vision and I slammed back a full glass of water. "I did the most random jobs while developing my client list and skills. Bike messenger, dog walker, server. Oh! I even nannied for six months."

Morgan's eyebrows shot up. "Shut the hell up."

I laughed. "It's true! It was pretty great, if you can believe it. The family was nice and I would've stayed for a few years, but they left for a job overseas. I used to take all sorts of fun photos of the kids, and legitimately thought I would go on a full Annie Leibovitz trajectory and become a famous portrait photographer. But then I got hired to shoot real estate photos, and it just evolved from there."

"I could see you doing the portrait photography. Those ones you took of Olivia and Tommy were amazing." Morgan sipped on coffee, her eyes dipping. A few moments passed when she set her cup down and her gaze bounced between my eyes. "So, are you ready to share how you evolved from Katey to Frankie?"

Sugar high for the win. I dove in, told her something never felt right, whole, inside my heart. I left out the part about how the self-exploration I had to take was also to learn who I was without Morgan. Being co-dependent for so long left with me a debilitating self-identity crisis. Who was I, if I wasn't Morgan's girlfriend?

"It wasn't the name Katey so much as it was what Katey represented, you know? It was the long hair, and my parents, and the need to be known as more than someone who could kick a ball and mess around with teachers." I added a dash of cream into the coffee and stirred. "So, one day I just had this epiphany and shaved off my hair. Which was not the smartest thing to do in the dead of February, but whatever. And that day I decided I wanted to be known as Frankie."

I kept talking, telling Morgan about my therapy and learning everything I could about ADHD, forgiving myself for past mistakes and forgiving my parents for being the way they were. I told her about my fear of never being good enough, always a few steps behind, never taken seriously and how I fought like hell to shed that insecurity.

Morgan's eyes glistened as she plopped her elbows on the table and leaned forward like she didn't want to miss a single word. The plates hadn't been touched, the coffee left un-sipped. After God knows how long, I glanced up, emotionally raw. In the middle of rotating customers and the ringing bell, and half-eaten plates of cake samples, I shared more with Morgan than I had with Savannah.

But also, it was more than Savannah ever asked. No one had ever shown this much interest. Watching Morgan's eyes grow wide, her hanging on my every word was doing something to my insides. I wanted to grab her hand and kiss it and thank her for being so genuinely interested in me, the person.

And now I was completely spent. I didn't want to talk anymore about this. I was taxed and sleepy. But switching the subject back to Morgan felt disingenuous.

As if she could sense me dropping, Morgan pushed herself away from the table. "I can't eat any more sugar. I'm out."

"Wimp." I laughed then groaned, thankful for the reprieve. "My stomach hurts so bad. I seriously feel like I'm drunk."

After Zoey swung by, and Morgan gave her the top three choices she'd recommend to Olivia, she scooted back from the table and grabbed her purse. "Ready?" Outside, before we got into the truck, Morgan stared at me for a moment.

In the sun, Morgan's purple shirt—which was my favorite color on her—highlighted the round cheeks which turned rosy from the sugar. Her eyelids sagged, and I was almost sure that Morgan would fall asleep before we even reached her house.

She paused on my side of the truck and reached for my hand.

What is she doing? My pulse quickened, unsure how to read Morgan's reaction. There was a softness to Morgan, an unsureness, as she softly nibbled on her lower lip. *Holy shit, she's gonna kiss me.* And perhaps it was the sugar talking, but I was ready. So unbelievably ready.

"For whatever it's worth," Morgan started as she gripped my hand, "even with all the good memories of the Katey I once knew, I really like Frankie."

The words warmed me, more than I could have imagined. But when Morgan dropped my hand without a kiss and moved to the other side of the truck, my heart dropped.

TWENTY

MORGAN

"All right, we've got turkey club, or... turkey club." I held out a sandwich to Frankie, who passed back a sparkling raspberry soda. "Oh, raspberry. I feel like you're spoiling me."

"Anything for my girl," Frankie said with a wink and tucked herself deep underneath the shade of the cedar tree.

She was kidding. She was *so obviously kidding*, but that message refused to translate to my heart. Much like every message, every mannerism, every look that Frankie had flashed me since we started taking over this project. Now, with less than four weeks left until the wedding, our time together was coming to an end. And then Frankie would go back to New York, and it would all *really* come to an end. So, damn my heart misunderstanding when Frankie was kidding.

"I'm sweating my tits off." Frankie fanned her face with a flimsy napkin. "Hope to God this heat wave breaks before the wedding."

"I have sweat dripping in places that I didn't even know contained pores. It's disgusting." The lack of air-conditioning was an issue. So far, my only solution for the wedding was to buy a portable air conditioner and create a barrier at the head table to trap the cool air. But at this rate, Tommy and Olivia would absolutely melt into the floor even if I had the portable air conditioner.

"So... did I freak you out last week at Zoey's when I word vomited all over you?" Frankie asked before sinking her teeth into the bread.

I held the cold sparkling can against my moistened neck. Freak me out? No. Make me fall harder, yes. Hearing everything about Frankie, her journey, her time in New York, even learning more about Savannah, filled in so many holes. "Not at all. I loved the story about you finding you in New York. I thought it was gutsy, you know, to share all of that."

Frankie flicked the top of the can. "There's things I want to know about you, too, during that time." Frankie gulped back the raspberry soda and wiped her mouth with the back of her hand. "Like did you end up living in the dorms, or failing chemistry, or... finding a special someone."

I didn't know what to think of this question. Frankie's eyes lowered to the ground as she asked. Was she curious? Shy? Sheepish? It was hard for me to tell. "No. No dorms. After the plans... fell through, I just lived at home and saved money."

After the plans fell through. The humid air turned heavier with the unsaid words. I didn't need to say it. *The plans* were that Frankie and I were going to share a dorm. *The plans* were that Frankie and I were going to go to football games and concerts and study at night. *The plans* were that Frankie would not leave me.

I needed to call it out. This conversation had been lingering in the air for the last two months, but we were both so obviously avoiding it. I took a breath. "Back then... why did you ever say you were going to college with me?"

"Morgan." Frankie's chest lifted and lowered with a heavy exhale, her voice soft. "I didn't say that I was going with you."

What? Of course Frankie said she was going with me.

That's all we talked about our senior year. After Frankie's games, on weekends, I would sit with Frankie at Peaches's house and plan our future. I even bought us matching UMD sweatshirts and took pictures and framed one in a homemade maroon and gold bedazzled 8x10. "What do you mean you never said you were going? You applied. You got accepted. We literally talked about it all the time."

Frankie shifted toward me, taking slow, easy breaths. "I did apply, yeah. But I... you *made* me apply. I never wanted to, but I caved under the pressure. Didn't you even fill the application out for me?" Frankie kicked a twig out of the way. "I told you a million times that I wanted to go to New York. You just never listened."

My chest heated. Was Frankie really putting this on me? "I *did* listen to you. But... people say so many things, you know? Sam was going to get drafted into the NFL. That girl in our class was going to Hollywood. What was that kid's name... Jordan something or other... was going to get a record deal. People say things like that all the time. You saying you were going to New York was just a dream."

"It *was* a dream. My dream. It had always been my dream. And you totally refused to honor it." Frankie's word speed increased. "I swear to God the only person who ever supported me was Quinn. My parents laughed at it. You never believed it. Peaches was in denial, told me I was going to end up living with the rats and freaks on the train. I told you a hundred times, and you refused to respect what I wanted for the future."

Frankie was completely rewriting history to make herself feel better, and I had no interest in playing this little game with her. From the outside, I'd imagine that to people looking at us—two thirty-three-year-old professional women—rehashing the high school days, we probably seemed a little pathetic. Like, how were we *still* talking about this, all these years later?

But our relationship was so much more than our age.

Deeper somehow, and even as an adult, I'd still never had that same connection with anyone.

I crunched into the sandwich, which now tasted flat and dry. Back then, had I thought Frankie was serious about moving to New York, I would've listened more. Clearly, with how blindsided I was at graduation, I'd never thought Frankie truly meant she was leaving.

You know what? Screw her. She was doing that thing again —completely altering our past to fit her narrative—and I was so freaking done. "You were never serious, Frankie. Everything was a joke to you. Why would I have believed you? You always said the most off-the-wall shit." *How can she possibly be putting this on me? That I didn't respect her dreams?* "I couldn't believe half the stuff that left your mouth."

Frankie's mouth dropped and an angry red strip flew up her neck.

Standing in our graduation gowns that day, I remembered the heated pavement soaking into my feet as tears streamed each of our cheeks. Frankie bawling, wiping her nose on her sleeve, her fingers folded as she pleaded, "Please, Morgan, please come with. Just for a year. If we hate it, we can come back. I need to get out of here. Out of this town, out from my parents, I need to go free." Frankie was a caged bird, needing to fly, and I was the net that trapped her in this town.

But I had wanted to go to UMD since I was little. And up until that day, I swore Frankie wanted the same. I stared at Frankie, who leaned back under the cedar tree. "I wanted you to come with me to college." *So bad.* God, I would have done anything to have Frankie go with me to school. Entering a world like that, alone, had terrified me. The plans I had until that point crashed and burned in a snap, and it wasn't fair.

"I never wanted that." Frankie tossed her sandwich to the side. "I didn't even have the grades to get in, and you just wouldn't believe it. You just didn't listen."

That's not true. "But you got in!"

Frankie released a heavy breath. "No, I didn't."

What? No... this is a lie. There could be variations of the truth, different perspectives, different interpretations of a situation for sure. But right now, Frankie was full-on gaslighting me, lying to my face. I specifically remembered celebrating our acceptance. We even splurged and went into Duluth to an Olive Garden. "Why are you even saying this? I *remember* you getting in. I didn't make that up."

Anger filled Frankie's face and she pulled her lips into a tight line. "How the hell did you think I got in? I was pulling a C average *at best*, and even now I'm pretty sure the only reason I got those grades was because Coach went to bat on my behalf."

"But... but you *told* me you did."

Frankie's head dropped. The flex in her forearms softened, and she exhaled. "I know I did. I lied, okay? But... you wouldn't listen. Ever. I finally just told you what you wanted to hear so you'd leave it alone." She lifted her head, narrowing her eyes. "Christ, Morgan. It has always been about you. I told you college life was never for me. Sitting in another classroom for four more years was like a prison sentence. College was *your* dream, had always been your dream. Never mine."

Unbelievable. How dare she continue to put this back on me? Frankie had lied and just admitted it. Which was not the first time she did that in our relationship. Frankie always said some sort of "white lie," something harmless, and she'd later fess up. But over the years it created a distrusting wall. And now she was blaming me. I was *done*. "Well, at least my dream didn't constitute traipsing around a huge city with no money, no family, and no education."

And, well, those words hit down like the hammer I intended. *Shit.*

Frankie pushed herself up, her face on fire. "I think you're just pissed that you stayed here, stuck, and never got out. You're thirty-three fucking years old having the same conversations with the same people, picking through the same women that were available back then. You are so goddamn stubborn, you know that? And for what? Are you actually happy? Because it sure as shit doesn't seem so."

Frankie stormed into the barn and a minute later the screech of the table saw fired to life.

And I sat there, furious. I refused to let her change history.

But I had no idea what I was going to do about it.

TWENTY-ONE

FRANKIE

Did I even fall asleep last night? I blinked at the ceiling, my eyes crusty and on fire. Yesterday, the blowup with Morgan was the very last thing I wanted, and I'd felt sick about it since.

With how heated both Morgan and I were yesterday, the timing was not right to explain the correlation between ADHD and lying. For so many years, I had just thought I was a bad person. I used to hate myself for lying, and every time it happened, a shame spiral sucked me in so deep, I could never dig myself out.

The compulsion to lie was still there, lingering beneath the surface. I was just more medicated, mature, had gone through enough cognitive behavior sessions to learn how to control it. Back then, when I lied, it was like a mosquito landed on my arm and I slapped it. Quick, without thought, without regard. But then, to keep the itch away, I had to keep lying. Even when I knew I was lying, I was so invested, like my brain and body were pedaling, pushing me downhill, and I couldn't slow down.

As I moved into the kitchen, then crunched into my granola cereal, I remembered my therapist saying ADHD could be a gift. I had thought, *Yep, what a scam. This is exactly why I don't do therapy*. But over the years, I understood. My body needed to move, and finding an art that I loved that allowed me to move provided more happiness than I could've dreamed. I needed a job with bite-size pieces, but, man, when those periods of hyperfocus hit, I was invincible.

If the teachers back then would've listened instead of scolding me when I panicked that my limbs were locking up and I needed to get up and sharpen a pencil, go to the bathroom, or grab a Kleenex, who knows what would have happened? Maybe I'd rule the world by now.

But blaming this on Morgan last night? Unforgivable. The knee-jerk reaction was decades of built-up self-loathing, anger of a lifetime of not being listened to, and years of holding guilt that I never really, actually sat Morgan down properly and told her I was leaving for New York.

Sure, I said it a million different ways, a million different times. But did I ever, until graduation night, make Morgan listen? I should've tried harder. And the guilt of leaving Morgan sobbing in the parking lot, even knowing it was the best thing for my own life, prevented me from reaching out.

I drove down Main Street to the floral shop. Although Morgan and I basically avoided each other for the rest of the night, we did leave with a cordial enough "good night." Hopefully today would be less awkward than last night. No matter how hard it was going to be, I *had* to apologize.

And *maybe*, perhaps, if the timing seemed right, tell Morgan the truth—that I was falling back in love with her, moment by moment, day by day. But leaving again would tear me apart, and I couldn't do it to myself, or to her. So, I'd bury my feelings, to protect myself and protect her.

Morgan would never move to New York. I knew this was her home, Sam and his kids were her life, and I couldn't ask her to give it up. Even if I *did* ask her to give it up, she wouldn't. And if *Birch & Willow* didn't offer the job, then maybe options were open. But until that door officially closed, I had to assume I was returning to the city.

Inside the floral shop, a gorgeous gust of lilac-and-rose-filled air wafted to me. I inhaled. *Mmmm.* No one could possibly be sad in a flower shop. The beauty, the smells, the people popping in to grab something for their loved one—this place might be second best next to Zoey's.

Delilah waved from behind the counter, as she stuffed long-stemmed pink and white roses into a vase. "Hey there, Frankie."

"Wow, good memory." Being on a first-name basis, even though I only stopped here a couple of times with Morgan, was something else. Did everyone in Spring Harbors have a photo-genic memory? "Is Morgan in the back?"

"Nope, not here yet." She propped bifocals on her head and continued clipping the bottoms of stems onto a newspaper. "I betcha she's on the way, though. Make yourself at home. Coffee's in the corner."

I couldn't help but smile. Sure, I was fifteen minutes early, not ten, but *ohhh*, it was pretty delicious beating Morgan here. I might add this to my arsenal of things to give her shit about. I crossed the room to grab an idea book off the counter and flipped through the pages.

Olivia and Tommy had come back, finally, with flower color choices: sage and lavender. Today, Morgan and I were going to finalize the arrangements so Delilah could prep everything. The book had so many gorgeous ideas. The simplicity and beauty of calla lilies set next to lavender-colored roses would be beautiful. Or maybe sage roses, and a couple of sprigs of purple eucalyptus? Morgan really was the expert with these types of things.

Speaking of... I checked my watch. Eight minutes early, so two minutes late. I pulled out my phone. No new messages. I scratched the back of my neck and peeked out the window.

When the door rang, I looked up so fast that I nearly got dizzy. A solid moment passed as I stared at the nearly six-foot-tall woman who walked in. The woman's eyes locked with me, and she cocked her head. *No way.* Parker Freaking Johnson.

Parker tucked a piece of her mom-bob haircut behind her ear. "Katey?"

"Parker?" I scooted over to Parker and pulled my former teammate in for a hug. "It's been a million years. Look at you! It's so good to see you. What are you doing these days?"

"You'll probably never believe this," Parker said with a grin. "I'm actually an eighth-grade teacher at our old middle school."

Shut up. Ever since we were little, Parker went from being the kid who was always in the principal's office, to the one who had the connections to show up at a party with a case of beer, to the one who snuck out by the dumpsters with her pack of smokes to light up during her sixth-period nic-fix. "No way? You look so..."

"I look like a mom." She laughed and dug her wallet out from her cross-body bag. "Or a teacher. And both are true. I've got three little ones."

When I left town, I left everyone behind, not just Morgan. The old teammates, classmates, people I hung with, were all stunted in my mind as seventeen- and eighteen-year-olds. Seeing Parker messed with my head a little, but in the best way possible. Like nostalgia and curiosity combined.

We chatted for a bit as Delilah rung up Parker's order. After we chatted about all the differences between eighth-graders then and now and laughed about how we would have possibly navigated social media back then, Parker checked her watch and frowned.

"Darn it. I've got to run to an anniversary party that I'm seriously late to." She scribbled on a piece of paper and handed over her number. "We should grab coffee and catch up. Last I heard is that you were some big hotshot in New York."

I grinned and said I'd reach out. In New York, encounters like this happened every so often. I'd meet someone, run into an acquaintance, exchange numbers, and promise to catch up. No one ever did, though. Or rarely. But here, it seemed like people genuinely would meet for a chat. This authenticity felt pretty damn nice.

The clock on the wall showed three minutes after. Morgan was officially late. I grabbed my phone and broke one of my cardinal rules by cold-calling Morgan. The phone rang, but no answer. An uneasy, sticky sensation swirled in the pit of my belly. Was this because of our talk yesterday? Yes, it was kind of icky, but we also hashed out a lot of things. And we said goodbye at the end of the night. Besides, Morgan was a consummate professional and would never not show up to an appointment because she was pissed at me.

"Hey, Delilah?" I approached the counter. "You haven't heard from Morgan, have you?"

Delilah wiped up the clipped stems from the paper and shook her head. "No, dear. Sorry."

Five more minutes passed, and I sent Morgan a text. Then called again. At the ten-minutes-after mark, the pit in my belly roared. Something was definitely off. I paced the floral shop. It was pointless to stare at the arrangements without Morgan. Should I call Sam and see if he heard from her? It probably seemed alarmist, but now twelve minutes passed, so twenty-two minutes late by Morgan's standards, and everything in the shop dimmed.

When the doorbell rang, a man with a scruffy white beard walked in with a cane. He nodded at me and shuffled to the counter.

"Well, hiya, there, Dave. It's been too long. Getting something for your bride?"

The man leaned against the counter. "Sure am. Our fifty-second anniversary is tomorrow. Make it something real nice. I know Esther likes those purple things."

"The purple carnations. I remember from last year." Delilah

grinned and reached for a vase. "Why don't ya have yourself a seat over there, and I'll whip up something Esther will love."

The man, Dave, shuffled over to the seat and hung his cane from behind the chair. "I sure am running behind. Still need to swing by Zoey's and grab a nice pie, then grab a card from the grocery store. I tell ya, there was a heck of an accident out on Superior Road."

My ears turned hot. The road was near Morgan's place.

"Oh ya?" Delilah said as she tore a long piece of flower paper off the roller and laid it across the counter. "That's too bad. Anyone hurt?"

Dave shrugged. "I couldn't tell ya, but I heard the sirens, so ya know that wasn't good. Truck rolled over, a few other cars. I think I saw that Rose girl out there."

My neck hair leaped straight up. "Did you say *Rose*? As in Morgan Rose?" *Please, please, say it was someone else.*

Dave looked at me, surprised. I didn't have time for introductions, but he probably didn't even know I was here, lurking in the corner.

"Yeah, that might be her name," Dave said. "Mike and Linda's daughter, you know the ones that own the remodeling company? I only recognized her because she has that decal thingy in her window advertising her place and she helped with my son's wedding a few years ago."

My chest flamed. *Oh my God, oh my God. Think, think.* Was she hurt? If something happened to Morgan, and our last interaction was heated words and a fake goodbye, I would never forgive myself. "Did you say that *Morgan* was in the accident?"

"I didn't look too close." Dave tapped his ring finger against the table. "That was her car in the pileup, but I didn't want to be too much of a lookie-loo. But gosh, lots of broken glass, smashed-up cars... I really hope no one was hurt."

My heart leaped into my chest and I bolted to the door. "Where exactly did you say this was?"

Dave barely finished giving me the approximate specs when I burst through the door, yelled an apology at Delilah, and revved my bike. In an instant, my heartbeat pounded in my throat and I became the motorcycle driver that I despised—speeding, weaving in and out of traffic, gunning at the intersection right before the light turned red.

She had to be okay. She *would* be okay, right? Morgan was so stubborn that even if something happened, it probably bounced off her like nothing. She was fine, she was fine. She *had* to be fine.

Oh my God, she *had* to be fine.

I'd been holding back telling her so many things, scared, unsure of her reaction. And now I may have missed the opportunity of a lifetime. My knuckles turned white, cramping, as I seized the handlebar. For the first time since I was a kid, I prayed. I wasn't even sure who to, but to any entity that would listen.

I got there in less than ten minutes. My mouth depleted of all moisture as the scene came into focus.

A tipped-over truck. Hay everywhere. An ambulance, two sheriffs' cars, and a crunched-up truck. My stomach coiled so hard I thought I might pass out. I skidded to a stop and leaped off the bike, tossing my helmet to the ground. Morgan was okay, right? She had to be okay. I scoured the small crowd of onlookers until my breath stopped at what I saw.

Morgan, on the side of the road, in a state I could've never imagined.

Fucking chickens.

I handed the last clucking one back to the grateful farmer and swiped my grimy palms down my capris. *Filthy*. My outfit was probably ruined unless I got home within the next five minutes and dumped a gallon of OxiClean on it. This event might be one of the top ten, maybe even top five, craziest things that have happened to me.

Two arms caught me from the back, whipped me around, and engulfed me in a hug.

"Oh my God, are you okay?"

Whoa. The frantic tone in Frankie's voice caught me off guard. Frankie held my shoulders, her eyes trailing every inch of me as if she was inspecting to confirm that I was, in fact, okay.

"Yes, I'm fine." I looked down at my clothes. I plucked a few feathers off, then gave up completely. "Filthy, though. Gross."

Frankie's eyes folded in concern, her firm grip still holding me. "Your face... your hair. It's so bad... You look so bad..." She nibbled on her lip, her forehead creasing.

"What every woman in the word wants to hear: You look

like shit. Thanks for that." I smiled, even though my body was on active alert.

The tiniest crack of smile teased at Frankie's mouth. "I was at Delilah's shop, and this man Dave came in and said there was an accident on Superior Road and you live here and I was freaking out... and *shit*. Are you sure you're okay? What the hell happened?"

When I left my house an hour ago, which now felt like five days ago, I trailed a trailer-truck as it jerked down the road at the speed of a sloth. *Road-rager* was never a word I would use to describe myself while driving. I was more... road-irritated. But this guy was over the top and I knew I had to get to Delilah's.

On the single-lane road, I would've passed the guy, but it was a no passing zone, and I wasn't going to risk get smooshed in my little sedan. But that didn't stop the guy behind me from doing it. The truck swerved sharply, the trailer tipped over, a car rear-ended the truck, and, well, the chickens broke free.

The panicked farmer and his wife ran around screaming, trying to scoop the chickens back into their cages. After I checked everyone was okay, I grabbed a blanket and chased after the chickens alongside the farmers.

Frankie's hand dropped from my shoulders. *Put them back.* The adrenaline coursing through me had my hands trembling something fierce, and Frankie was just so... *sturdy*. Not that I couldn't handle it, of course...

"You're shaking." Frankie grabbed my hand and escorted me to a patch of grass away from the chaos. "Let's take a seat."

I normally would have thought twice about sitting on the side of the dirty road, but at this point, I had so much muck on me that it didn't matter. I lowered myself to the ground and rubbed my temples. Having Frankie here with me this summer allowed me to do twice as much wedding prep as normal. But that was also cut in half with the unforeseen barn renovations.

We still had so much to do, and moments like this—wasting hours on stuff that had nothing to do with the wedding—cut into the precious moments we had left to execute this day to perfection.

"The *flowers*," I whimpered. The wedding had a ton of important items, of course, but this rated pretty high on the list. "I need to call Delilah and reschedule. Maybe this afternoon or tomorrow? But the electrician is finishing the wiring tomorrow, but maybe Sam can be there? Ugh. I forgot—Sam needs to go to the other job site, but maybe he can stop by first? I don't know, though. The electrician gave us a time-frame, and you know—"

"Hey." Frankie's voice was low, soothing, as her fingertips stroked my arm. "We can figure this out later. Delilah was there when we heard about the accident. I'm sure she'll work with you to reschedule. I took some pics of the flowers and Delilah already had some great ideas. We can manage this. For now, let's head back to your place and get you cleaned up, then figure out next steps."

She was probably right. I wouldn't go into town looking as dirty as I was, and if Delilah was fine with rescheduling, the best thing would be to clean myself up and work on things I could manage from home. "Okay, I'll head home and call you later. Maybe I'll finish up the childhood photo stands and get those packed up."

Frankie shook her head. "If you think I'm leaving your side right now, you're insane."

Damn my insides turning warm at those words.

After I slipped into a pair of cotton shorts and a tank top, I could finally inspect the scratches all over my arms. Thankfully, they were only surface level and no blood, but enough covered me where my skin flamed pink. I slathered anti-bacterial ointment on myself just in case and moved into the living room where Frankie was sitting, focused on her phone.

When Frankie's eyes shifted from her screen to me, her gaze dipped and slowly inched up my body and *dammit*. I *felt* that look. I really needed to ignore that look, but I couldn't. I wasn't an expert at reading body language, but it seemed pretty obvious to me that Frankie, at least physically, wanted the same thing as me. Instead of indulging in the idea, I moved into the kitchen and grabbed a bowl of grapes and two lemonades.

When I returned and scooted next to her, an entirely new look replaced Frankie's face. Knitted brows, a slight frown, and heavy sighs.

"Why are you looking at me like that?" I asked.

"Like what?"

I plucked off a grape and rolled it in my fingers. "Like you're worried I'm going to keel over or something. You know I wasn't *hit* in the accident, right? The scratches and bruises are because I lost a serious fight with some feathered friends." I meant to lighten the mood, but Frankie almost looked like she was going to cry. Sure, terrible joke but *come on*.

Frankie stared at her hands, rubbing each fingertip with her index finger. "I just can't stand the thought of anything happening to you."

"Aww." I crunched on a grape and grinned. "I didn't know you cared so much."

"I never stopped caring."

Wow. Frankie's tone was filled with so much intention and sincerity that I didn't know what the hell I was supposed to do with that. I slowly swallowed the fruit as the silence grew.

Maybe it was the drama of what happened, or the acknowledgment that I had limited time left with Frankie, or a desperate, desperate need to conclude the past. But something in me propelled me to say, "You never cared enough to stay."

I didn't want to hear that I was right. I wanted Frankie to break down and say she regretted leaving and that she had never stopped thinking about me over the years, and if she had to do it over again, she would've never left.

Yes, Frankie leaving destroyed me back then, but I really did get over it. Over the years, I had numerous relationships, built my business, and went months, perhaps years, without thinking of her. But I can't say that it didn't affect me—that my first great love not loving me enough to stay didn't still burn a hole inside my heart.

Frankie's chest lifted and then dropped with a heavy exhale. For a moment, it seemed like Frankie might storm out. Instead, she shifted closer. "That's not true."

I stared out my front window and watched a squirrel run up a tree trunk. Now was the time, but how do you tell someone everything you've kept bottled up for years? How could I put into words how this affected me and get closure from something that happened fifteen years ago? "You broke my heart when you left."

There was a crack in my voice that I didn't appreciate, but the words were true. Frankie gutted me when she left.

"You broke mine when you wouldn't go with me," Frankie said through a sigh.

My heart squeezed, and I blinked back tears.

Frankie propped an elbow on the couch's back and rested her head in her hand. "I thought for sure you would. I thought you would take a chance, for once in your life, and do something spontaneous. College would always be there, but we had a real chance to get out, to make this other life for us, to try something different. And when you wouldn't come with, I just... Everything crashed." Frankie paused, staring into my eyes. "It felt like your life plan was more important than my life plan, and... it just killed me. I never stopped thinking about you. That first year, I picked up the phone a million times to call you. I missed my girlfriend. I missed my friend. It was the hardest thing I've ever done."

Oof. That never occurred to me. I just assumed since Frankie left, she hurt less. She left for this fabulous new life in an amazing city, and I shifted into an afterthought.

So many moments passed, my stomach dropping by the second. "Do you ever regret leaving?"

A soft sad grin tugged at Frankie's mouth. "There's a ton of things I regret. I regret the way I left things with you, that I let my stubbornness take the better of me, and that I never reached out to you." Frankie exhaled. "But no. I don't regret leaving."

Those words were not harsh, but they hit in the realest way possible. Frankie didn't regret leaving me or moving to New York. Which means, given the same opportunity, she'd do it again. My insides burned with the words, but it was also what I needed to hear.

"Do you ever regret not coming with?" Frankie asked, her eyebrows pinched.

Like Frankie, I had a lot of regrets—allowing our friendship to die along with our relationship and letting anger prevent me from reaching out as well. But staying? That was always the right move. I was never meant to live anywhere else. "No. I don't regret staying. This will always be my home."

I lobbed the words softly like a feather and yet they carried the weight of a boulder.

And there it was. Neither of us regretted our decision. And there wasn't much more I could do with that. Did I regret the way things ended with Frankie? Yes. But regrets only take you so far. And Frankie was truthful and honest, and I needed to hear it.

Frankie's gaze focused on the couch cushion between us, and her thumb grazed the material. "It took me years to get over you."

Dammit. God, I didn't want to hear this and I also did, and

it hurt as much as it felt good. There was no use in playing the "what if" game at this point in our life. We both made the best decision for ourselves, and neither of us regretted our choices. "Well, if it's any consolation, I don't think I ever fully got over you."

Frankie stared hard at me, her eyes unmoving and focused. They dropped, slowly, looked at my lips, back to my eyes, then back to my mouth. She inched forward and closed the gap between us. She pressed her mouth into me, softly at first. I jerked only for a moment from the shock of the touch. When Frankie pulled back, I moved in, pressing my lips back into Frankie, the sweetness of the grapes and lemonade dancing across my lips, my tongue. God, this was so familiar and unfamiliar and heavenly.

Frankie cupped my neck, her thumbs swiping my cheeks, firm and sturdy, yet delicate somehow, and my breath hitched. She parted my lips with her tongue. My heartbeat kicked up again, thudded in my chest, in my throat, and my body started tingling. I grabbed Frankie around the waist, held her tight, my mouth moving against hers, when Frankie stopped.

It was like a Band-Aid was ripped off, the worst kind, and I immediately wanted Frankie's mouth back on mine.

"Jesus Christ. I'm so sorry, I don't... I can't believe I did that." Frankie leaped off the couch and dragged her hands down her face. She grabbed her keys from the coffee table and rushed to the door.

Please don't go. "Wait, no, it's fine. It's good." I hopped off the couch and rushed to Frankie. I gripped her forearm before she reached the door handle. When Frankie turned the knob, I squeezed tighter. "Please... I." *God, just do it. Be vulnerable. Tell her how I feel.* I lifted my chin, begging to have Frankie's lips against mine. "I really don't want you to go."

Frankie looked like she was going to break down. Her dark eyes widened, a look of regret washed over her face. The saddest, heartbreaking half smile appeared. She stroked my cheek with her thumb. "I really don't want to go, either. Which is exactly why I need to."

And even though I hated it, I knew Frankie was right. When the motorcycle kicked on, and faded into the distance, I flopped myself on the couch and cried.

TWENTY-THREE
FRANKIE

The tingling sensation of Morgan's mouth on mine lingered long after I returned home. I brushed my fingertip across my lip, picturing her warm mouth on mine. *Fuck.* What in the hell was I thinking? Stupid, stupid, stupid. What an emotional wreck of a day. A month. A summer. I needed to finish this stuff up here, hop on a flight back to New York City, and forget everything about this town.

Or did I? *Ugh.* I taped together yet another box, one of the last in the basement, and lugged it upstairs to the main floor. I'm surprised my body hadn't started rejecting cardboard particles or adhesive and burst a nasty rash across my skin. Once I got Peaches's place packed up, I was never moving again.

The main floor was nearly empty, the bedroom almost completely packed. After I tackled the garage, which I seriously considered just burning because it'd be easier, I'd be done. Finally, I could put the house on the market.

My phone buzzed on the kitchen counter with a message. Morgan? I sprinted across the room. *Nope.* Just a reminder to make a yearly wellness exam. Granted, only a few hours had passed since I kissed her, but I thought she'd reach out. And my

God... what a kiss. Her lips were as sweet as I remembered, but more womanly, more intentional. *I can't believe I did that*. And I wanted to do more. If anyone ever challenges me on my willpower again, I will enter this into exhibit A. It took everything in me to not drag her into the bedroom. But I couldn't. *We* couldn't. The Great Heartbreak Era of fifteen years ago could not be repeated. No matter what my body was screaming at me to do, I wouldn't put myself, or Morgan, through that again.

I flopped down on a barstool and dialed Quinn. Before she even finished saying hello, I blurted, "I kissed Morgan."

"Well, holy shit. Good afternoon to you, too," Quinn said. "So tell me, sailor, what's behind door number two? Happiness or sadness?"

What a loaded question, and I hadn't processed it enough to know the answer. Right now, sad at myself for walking away, but also patting myself on the back for doing the right thing. God, doing the right thing sucked. "You did not just call me 'sailor.' Seriously, are you ninety?" I picked up a marker at the table and tapped it against the laminate top. "Confusion maybe? I don't know. Christ, it was a stupid move, though."

Quinn's heavy breathing showed she was most likely doing a speed walk around the outside of her office building. "Stupid how? Like stupid when I agreed to share a cab with that sketchy dude downtown? Or stupid like you're worried about getting all butt-hurt and broken?"

"No one in the world says 'butt-hurt' anymore. You really need to get out of the office." My limbs needed to move. Tapping my fingers on the counter didn't help alleviate the need to burn energy. I paced the kitchen, then hall, then back to the kitchen. "And yes. I'm worried about getting hurt. You know what a hot mess I was after she and I broke up. I couldn't deal with it. But now I'm doing stuff, what, 'cause I'm horny? 'Cause it's been almost two years since I've had sex with anyone."

"*Two years?* Christ, no wonder you're cranky all the time."

"Quinn," I snapped.

"Okay, okay, sorry. Obviously, I know you haven't dated since Savannah. I just didn't know you were flying the celibate flag." Her breathing slowed and she exhaled. "So, what did you do after you landed a fat one on her?"

I left. As usual. Per my MO. What was wrong with me? Communication avoidance was clearly my drug of choice. With Savannah, with Morgan, with everyone. I'm not even one of those people who are afraid of conflict, and yet I run like a child. My stomach knotted. "Nothing. I just left the house. And before you even say a word, yes, I feel shitty about it, but trust me, had I stayed, I would've felt shittier because I *know* what would've happened." Pacing inside was still not helping. I opened the patio doors to roam the yard. "I just don't know what to do. I swear being around Morgan is like putting on my old basketball jersey. Like so comfortable, so familiar. She *knows* me, you know? Not *photographer* me. Not *New York* me. Just me."

"God, that's appealing. I think of how fake we are in our normal lives, pretending to like people we don't, smiling when we want to scream." The sounds of cars honking faded as Quinn must've stepped inside a building. "It takes forever to get to that comfortable space. Skipping all that and diving directly into the deep end sounds like some kind of wonderful."

I scraped at a tree trunk with my booted toe. Quinn was right. Dating was miserable. When I did it before Savannah, I'd come home exasperated or annoyed. Putting on my best face, watching what I said, tiptoeing around political issues... No wonder when Savannah and I clicked, I jumped in headfirst.

So, was Morgan just a convenience?

No. She was so much more. Deep down, in my core, Morgan had always been something else.

My one true love.

"It's not fun doing all the bullshit pleasantries, that's for sure." I snapped off a dry branch from the tree and twisted it in my hand. "But I'm going to be back in the city in just a few weeks. Maybe I'll push it out until the end of August, but if I don't get the *Birch & Willow* gig, I need to book more jobs." I crossed the yard and pushed the twig against the tire swing. "And then what? I try to maintain some sort of long-distance thing with her? It's not logical, or practical, for me to start things back up with Morgan."

A huff came through the phone. "Since when are you known for your practicality? God love ya, sis, but you are more impulsive than the average bear. You've always trusted your gut. How about you just keep doing that? Stop trying to explain things, justify things, and worry about things. Just go for it. Whatever that looks like. At least this time you both know exactly what you're getting into."

Was Quinn right? Sometimes I questioned her judgment, like staying at her god-awful job over the years. But right now, I was pretty sure she was the voice of reason I needed to get out of my head. I might just jump through the phone and squeeze my sister. "God, I love you."

"Love you, too. Now, I seriously need to drop before I get fired. Although at this point, getting fired sounds as wonderful as going to a day spa."

I frowned. "Still that bad?"

"*Always* that bad." Quinn chuckled. "See ya. Call me later when you figure out the rest of your life."

After I hung up, I hovered my fingers over the screen. Text Morgan, or don't text Morgan? It shouldn't be this hard. Did I want to talk to Morgan? Yes. Then, great, pick up the damn phone. Did I not want to talk to her? Kind of. Cool, then stop thinking about her.

What an emotional roller coaster of a day. It was five million hours ago when I was in Delilah's flower shop wondering why Morgan was late. The hint of losing Morgan when I heard about the accident freaked me out so much that all I wanted to do right now was to wrap Morgan in my arms and keep her safe.

But I had a lifetime of making impulsive decisions, and this could *not* be one of them.

TWENTY-FOUR
MORGAN

Oh, how things change in a twenty-four-hour period. First, I was nearly scratched to death by poultry. Then Frankie flipped my world upside down by kissing me. And then I got a major break in the final missing piece for the wedding. After I threw a wedding-day Hail Mary pass (Frankie would be so proud I know that term) and posted a Facebook message seeking a connection to a DJ who was open for that date, a former classmate DMed me saying he'd been DJing for the last year and was available for the wedding.

A miracle. DJs book up almost as quickly as venues, and I had burned through my entire digital Rolodex last month trying to find one in the state.

I popped bread into the toaster and tugged on my lip, the one that still had the reminiscence of Frankie's mouth on it from yesterday. I thought about calling or texting Frankie last night, and I assumed Frankie was weighing the same pros and cons. Being an adult, and not a starry-eyed teenager, came with a whole different perspective. We each had lives and careers and homes, and whatever was brewing was not as simple as "let's just do this!" Too many consequences were involved, and I needed to take a long moment to think.

Or perhaps, maybe for once in my life I didn't need to think and plan and organize. We were still working together for the rest of the summer, and as of now, Frankie would be in my life. So, maybe we could continue being friends, and I would bury all of this.

Or maybe...

MORGAN:

hey, I know I said we get to take this weekend off...

I held my breath, which was not a smart thing to do as Frankie notoriously never had her phone on her. But before I passed out, the three dots appeared.

FRANKIE:

Yes, you sure did. The only thing I'm doing this weekend is sitting in Peaches's fuzzy pink bathrobe and taking a bath in her seashell-decorated pink bathroom with a box of twenty-year-old Calgon bath salts I found in the closet.

MORGAN:

Wow. That is an oddly specific agenda for a Saturday night.

FRANKIE:

I could be talked into something else. Have something in mind?

Yes, I *very much* had something else in mind. I breathed through the tingles.

MORGAN:

Remember Tag Docksen from our class? He's a DJ, is free for the wedding, and just so happens to be playing a show tonight in a dive bar about five minutes outside of Superior. I wanted to scope him out, and if he doesn't suck, hire him for the wedding.

FRANKIE:

Tag? Really? That guy was such a tool.

Frankie was not wrong. Tag was a star hockey player back in high school, and definitely the guy who liked to brag how many "chicks he banged." Gross. A rumor floated around senior year of some seriously creepy shit he pulled on our classmate Jenny Smith but was never confirmed. Tool or not, he was our very last option. Besides, *hopefully* he'd matured a bit since high school.

FRANKIE:

Didn't he ask you out once?

MORGAN:

Hmmm. Don't remember. I thought I had *lesbian* stamped across my forehead.

FRANKIE:

Haha. That you did.

MORGAN:

Anyway, you interested?

FRANKIE:

Definitely. I can pick you up at eight.

Not a date, not a date. I replayed that mantra all day, but by the time eight rolled around, I'd loofahed my skin until it shone, brushed my teeth twice, and changed my outfit no less than five times. I settled on a cute pale green skirt with a light cream knitted sweater, and wedge sandals, and I had to admit it, my legs and ass were killing it in this outfit.

Since working in the barn all summer, I had nearly forgone my typical hair and makeup routine that was my signature. But tonight, I took extra care in applying eyeliner, gloss, and flat ironing my hair that had finally grown out to a respectable length.

Three knocks landed on my door, and my heart skipped a beat. "Come in!"

When Frankie entered the room, I stopped and stared. Frankie's gaze traveled leisurely from my toes to my head, a thirsty smile tugging at her lips, and damn if that wasn't the look I was hoping to get. "Wow. You look incredible."

I felt my cheeks blush. "So do you."

Frankie grinned. "I'm literally wearing the same thing I do every day."

I know. The jeans, the snug white shirt, the boots. But after a few months of hard work in the barn, Frankie's forearms bronzed in the sun, and her rounded shoulders and deeply defined biceps were even more pronounced than when we first met. If that was even possible.

"Hey, yesterday..." I started when Frankie held up her hand.

"I'm still really sorry." Frankie tapped her thumbs against her upper thigh. "But I'm also not sorry. If that makes sense."

It made so much sense that I felt a small crack in my heart. I didn't want to have this conversation now, but I needed the weirdness between us to stop. "I don't know what will happen. But I want you to know I'm really happy I could spend this summer with you."

There. I said as much as I could say right now. The rest we'd figure out later.

Frankie's dimples appeared. "Same. It's been more than what I could've ever asked for." She held the door open and waved me through. "Ready, my little lady?"

"Ewww." I locked the door and scrunched my nose. "You didn't just call me that."

"Oh, I did." Frankie hopped down the porch steps and held out her hand to me. "Figured if we were going to be hanging with Tag for the evening, I better get my creeper lingo down."

I slid into Frankie's truck and slammed the door. "Come on, maybe he's not that bad."

Tag may or may not be bad, but the bar was the divest of the dives. *My God.* It smelled like stale beer and old fryer grease, and my wedges stuck to the floor. The night was still pretty early. The crowd comprised of day drinkers finishing up, a woman behind blotchy plexiglass selling pull tabs, and a bartender yawning and scrolling through his phone.

"This is one of the saddest places I've ever seen." I kept my arms crossed to prevent myself from touching anything. The room was too dark, the neon bar lights too bright, the hops smell too overwhelming.

"It's not that bad. Kind of the type of place that makes you want to throw down and hustle some dude for pool money, right?" Frankie jutted her head towards the pool tables in the back next to the dart boards. "I think we could take them."

Sure, easy for her to say. Frankie looked like a badass biker bitch with her cropped hair and motorcycle boots. Not to mention she looked like she could bench-press all the guys in this place. "Not even for a second."

"I bet they don't play Britney Spears here, unfortunately for you." Frankie nudged my elbow.

"Why would I care if they played Britney Spears?" I asked.

Frankie lifted a brow. "Do you seriously not remember? You forced me to learn the choreography to '...Baby One More Time.'"

"I did?" I searched back far in my memory bank until... *Oh yeah.* Sophomore year, a local radio station was offering a five-hundred-dollar reward for the best Britney lip-syncing contest. I giggled at the memory of an absolutely irate Frankie having to swap out her gym shorts for a plaid skirt, pigtails, and crop-top button-down shirt. And if memory serves, we did pretty good but failed to earn top spot. "How do you even remember that?"

Frankie glanced down at me. "I remember a lot of things."

Me too. A playful smile tugged at Frankie's lips, but I felt anything but playful. All I wanted was to recreate everything from last night, and then some. Screw consequences, broken hearts, and repeating history. I wanted to take Frankie home, ravage-style.

"Hey, can I get you two something?" the bartender asked, flipping a towel over his shoulder.

"No thanks. I'm here to chat with Tag. Is he around?" I scoured the dozen patrons to see if one of them was what I remembered as Tag.

"Oh yeah, he's in the employee break room." He flicked his finger toward the kitchen doors. "You guys can just head in there. In the back past the kitchen, take a left."

Wasn't there something deeply unsanitary about having two non-employees traipsing through the kitchen? No matter, though. Hopefully I'd be in and out, drop off a contract for the gig, and then hang around for a bit to make sure his DJ equipment worked.

"I'm curious what Tag looks like nowadays," Frankie asked as we weaved past the tables to the kitchen. "Seems like the type of guy who probably peaked in high school."

"Shhh. Small town, remember? Whatever shit you talk will

get back to him, and I need him to DJ the wedding." Although Tag *was* that type of guy. Sort of like the universe giving his peers a parting gift for putting up with his crap for all those years.

Frankie followed me when her phone rang. "Hold up, one sec. It's Quinn." Frankie put the phone up to her ear. "Hey, I'm just about to head in somewhere, can I... Wait, what? Okay, slow down, slow down... Are you sure... Quinn, you gotta breathe... Okay, give me a second."

Oh no. This did not sound good. I searched Frankie's eyes to see if this was a "somebody died" call or a "my boss is an asshole" call.

Frankie pushed the mouth receiver under her chin. "Sorry, I've got to take this. Something happened with Quinn's work. I'll be outside. You good?"

Chivalry for the win. "For sure." I tugged my sweater across my chest. "I'll come find you when I'm done. Shouldn't take more than five or ten minutes."

Frankie lifted the phone back to her mouth. "All right, I'm heading outside so I can hear you better. Start at the beginning..."

As Frankie moved to go outside, I crossed the bar to the kitchen doors and swung them open. A wave of humidity and a cloud of cooked onions funneled out. The two cooks glanced up with a totally uninterested look as I went past the prep station overflowing with plates and burger fixings to the employee break room.

Outside of the closed wooden door with a dangling EMPLOYEES ONLY sign, I knocked. A moment passed before I realized the man who opened was, in fact, my former classmate. Too bad Frankie couldn't witness this—half the hair, twice the size, and already a solid smoker's cough.

"Morgan Rose." He crossed his meaty arms around his *way too snug* short-sleeve, shiny button-down shirt. The top three buttons were opened with tufts of chest hair sticking out, and his fourth was threatening to burst.

Oh, Tag. Already so little has changed.

"Man, you don't look a day over twenty-one." He snapped his can of chewing tobacco. "Did ya get carded when you walked in here?"

Ewww. That whole "you look so young" was never a compliment. The maturity and wisdom I gained with age was a gift. "Good to see you. Thanks so much for messaging me about possibly performing at the wedding. I know the timing is short notice."

He crossed his arms, the movement hitting me with a nauseating wave of spicy cologne.

"Sure, sounds like I saved the day, huh?" He packed his chewing tobacco into his gums and leaned in. "Wouldn't be the first time."

Yep. High school rushed back. Confirmed—Tag was still a tool. Whatever, though. I could handle just about anything for one day. Jerk or not, I was absolutely out of options for DJs at the reception if this didn't pan out.

Tag stepped back and let me into the break room. In the corner, the small TV showed Sports Center. A rickety round table with two folding chairs held a pile of discarded newspapers. A green couch, which looked like it was freshly hauled off the street with a FREE sign attached, lay in the corner. It smelled like nicotine and alcohol, although that could've been seeping from his pores.

The quicker I could get out of this place, the better. I dug out papers from my purse. "Here's the contract for the wedding, with the rate we messaged about." I laid it on the table. "If you could just take a peek, make sure it looks good and—"

"So, whatever happened with you, anyway?" He slumped on a chair and tilted back on the legs, pointing at the adjacent chair. "You stayed back in Spring Harbors, huh?"

This place gave me the creeps, and I didn't love my cute skirt getting nasty with beer residue. Yet, business was business. I reluctantly took a seat. "Yep, sure did."

"Yeah, I split from here and moved to Minneapolis the second I could. I'm only back here doing a favor for my buddy who owns the bar." He swiped the inside of his cheek with his tongue. "Seems like I be doing lots of favors lately."

Cool. We've established you've saved the day. "Seems like it, huh?" I forced a smile. "I'm not sure how large your setup is, but do you know how much electricity or power strips you'll need? The place that's holding the reception—"

"Yeah, I'm so glad I jetted from this place. But there were some good times, huh?" He lowered the chair and leaned onto his elbows. "All the keg parties at the Hank family farm. Epic, right? Gotta admit, those were the days. After we won the hockey tourney junior year, that was the best party I've ever gone to. You were there. You remember."

If he weren't so off-putting, I'd think that was the saddest thing I'd heard in a long time—that the best party this adult man went to was when he was sixteen. But instead, the sentiment was tiptoeing on pathetic, although I didn't want to be that mean. "No, I don't think I was there." I inched the paperwork towards him.

He didn't even glance down and instead stroked his thick goatee. "Nah, you were definitely there. I remember 'cause you were with *Katey.*"

A line of hairs stood up on my neck, with the way he said *Katey.* I quickly scanned the room. Exit door behind me, fire door in the left side. I exhaled through my nose. *How do I even respond to something like that?* "Ah, um." I swallowed. "Maybe I was there, then. Such a long time ago, I guess I don't remember."

"Honestly, I never really got what you saw in her." The chair squeaked under him as he leaned back. A shadow crossed his eyes, and his gaze bored into me. "Katey wasn't all that, but everyone thought she was."

"Her name is Frankie," I said through gritted teeth, then breathed it out. He probably didn't know she'd changed her name.

"See? Can't keep it straight. What a flake." He chuckled, his bloodshot red eyes narrowing. "Who changes their name like that?"

Too many moments passed where I opened my mouth to defend Frankie but paused. Every lesson I'd learned about dealing with guys like this tumbled forward—from my mother saying to turn the other cheek, or treating every interaction as a business interaction, or keeping quiet to keep safe. I needed to get him to sign this contract and leave, as quickly as humanly possible. "You, ah, probably have to take the stage soon. Will it just be you at the reception, or do you have a team? I just need to make sure that the subcontractors are listed in the paperwork and—"

"Remember when I asked you to homecoming freshman year? You were hot as fuck, but like, what the hell was I thinking?" A sinister chuckle escaped. "You were so stuck-up. Always thought you were better than everyone else."

The room narrowed and black spots reached my peripherals. God, it was so hot in here. I pushed the chair back and stood, cold sweat reaching the back of my neck. I fumbled, reaching for my papers. "You know, I think this isn't going to work out. I'm sorry..." *Stop apologizing. You did nothing wrong.* "I'm really sorry. I think maybe this wasn't the best idea."

He stood, disgust on his face. "Dick tease. You were back then, and you still are."

What in the hell is happening?

He stepped closer, all friendliness gone. My hands shook, and I stuffed the papers into my purse to distract myself. I tried to swallow, but my mouth was dry. I wanted to tell him to screw himself, that he was the last person in the world I would ever work with, but words twisted at the rate of my gut, and my heartbeat thudded in my throat.

"*You're* the one that needs me, not the other way around," he seethed.

How in the hell did I get in this position? *Where's the door?* I stumbled, just a bit. Stupid effing heels, and before I knew it, I was nearly up against the wall. Whatever lifelong anger this entitled prick held was directed at me, full speed. Screaming would be dramatic. I just needed to move, but I was frozen as he continued ranting about high school and *chicks like you* never keeping our word and so many other things that I couldn't think straight.

The door flew open and Frankie stepped in with a grin. "Sorry 'bout that—" She took one look at me, one look at Tag, and the grin dropped. Frankie's eyes turned dark and she crossed the room in two strides, putting herself directly in between me and Tag. "You all good in here?"

Relief flushed every part of me. My sputtered heartbeat clicked back into a normal rhythm. "Yeah, I'm good."

"Katey fucking Lee." Tag chuckled and refused to step back. He licked his teeth back and forth with a sneer. "Rescuing your girlfriend, as usual. Nothing changes, does it?"

Frankie pushed me behind her with steady hands and turned her body to face Tag directly. "There a problem here?"

A vein strained from Frankie's neck, and her back muscles firmed. I peeked from behind Frankie's shoulder at Tag, whose eyes flicked between Frankie and me. Who knew what the hell he was thinking? But he took a menacing step toward Frankie, and I held my breath.

Frankie didn't even flinch. "*Trust me.* We don't want to do this. I promise it won't end well for you."

I melted under the fire in Frankie's voice and, for the first time since I was a kid, felt truly supported. I wasn't sure if

Frankie was itching for a fight, but I had no doubt that if Tag would make even a hint of a move, the night would end with the guy on the floor and Frankie in handcuffs.

When Tag finally laughed and stood back with his hands up, Frankie clutched my hand with a vise grip and led me out of the bar.

Inside Frankie's truck, I breathed through the knots in my stomach. Why didn't I tell Tag to shove it up his ass the moment something felt off? I froze, lost control, clammed up, and dammit! I fiddled with the sleeves of my sweater, trying to shake the ickiness.

"You okay?" Frankie placed a warm hand on my leg as she navigated up the freeway back to my place.

A warmth seeped into my leg from Frankie's palm and fluttered up to my belly. I sighed. The only thing that was okay about this situation was how Frankie stepped in to help me. "I'm just so... I don't know." I twisted the ring on my finger. "I'm so pissed at myself for letting him do that. So mad at him for thinking he had the right." *And so freaking turned on right now that you came to my rescue.*

I would never, ever consider myself the damsel-in-distress type, but this ran deeper than watching a hot-as-hell Frankie blaze alive in that room. For the first time in forever, someone was whole-heartedly, unequivocally, in my corner. But seeing Frankie's eyes go dark, having her step in front of me, watching that dickhead cower because of Frankie's presence, that fire reached my core. *Oof.* Never before had there been quite the aphrodisiac.

"Do not be mad at yourself for acting the way you did. Men like that... they're unpredictable. You have no idea how much it would've escalated. You did exactly what was right for you at that time. Don't second-guess yourself." Frankie slowed to a stop at a light and glanced at me through her peripherals. Her knuckles turned white on the steering wheel. "I should've never left you."

"No, you don't get to do that, either. Your sister needed you, I'm a grown-ass woman, and you couldn't have known he'd try anything." I laid a hand on Frankie's thigh. I meant it as a reassuring squeeze, but it didn't stop the tingles from flying up my arm. "Thank you for standing up for me. I can't believe I froze. I don't know what I would've done if you weren't there."

The light changed and Frankie turned back towards the road. "I have no doubt you would've handled it." Frankie tugged her bottom lip between her teeth. Several silent moments stretched between us before she inhaled a sharp breath. "You're killing me, you know that?"

I searched Frankie's eyes, but they remained fixed on the road. "What do you mean?"

Frankie just shook her head, but her pained face spoke volumes. I didn't want to force anything. But would it kill Frankie to open up, just a little, and tell me what was going through her head? Talk to me. *Something.*

When we pulled into my place, Frankie cut the engine and gripped the wheel. Long, heavy sighs left Frankie, but I remained silent. I reached for the door handle, but Frankie pulled me back. "I *can't* have anything happen to you."

Those words reached inside, to my toes and back up. I wanted to say a million things, do a million things, but ugh, this all hurt so hard and felt so good, and I was stuck in the middle of past, present, and future. "Thanks for coming with tonight." I needed to get out of here, get air, stop being in the same place as Frankie. I couldn't do it anymore. The fresh air hit my face as soon as I hopped out of the truck. I stepped to the porch when the truck door behind me slammed.

Frankie crossed towards me, her eyes fierce and determined. I waited. *Please, please say something. Tell me you're thinking about me the same way I'm thinking about you.* My heart was cracking and filling, and the confusing messages messed with my mind. "God, I hate you sometimes," I finally said.

And maybe it wasn't exactly what I wanted to say at the moment, but I was raw and emotionally drained and tired, and it needed to be out. Frankie, for her credit, only scrunched her eyes at my random comment.

"I..." I didn't want to cry, but my chest was tight, and my eyes were hot and Frankie was just right there, being so... Frankie. Hands in pockets. Unaffected. Gorgeous. I stared at the sky and blinked back the stinging tears. "God, I loved you so much. It's stupid, right? We were kids. It shouldn't still affect me like this, and it does. God damn you, Frankie, it affects me every single moment and I want it to stop."

Frankie's gaze burned a hole into me. She shook her head. "It's not stupid. It took me years to get over you. And honestly, there was a part of me that wasn't sure I ever did."

The stars flickered above us, as the quiet neighborhood stayed asleep. The porch light shone, highlighting Frankie, accentuating the shadows and angular cut of her jaw. She really was so beautiful, always had been. I dipped my head, and Frankie hooked a finger around my hair and tucked it behind my ear.

"Don't," I whispered, and Frankie dropped her hands. But it wasn't what I meant. I didn't mean *don't touch me.* I meant... *don't leave me. Don't go back to New York. Don't hurt me.* The words gripped at my heart, but I stayed silent. At the same time, everything was sparking and, God, I just wanted to touch her, to taste her mouth again, to feel her next to me. The body tingles collided with the pragmatic thinking, and I was at a loss. I was an adult, for God's sake. I could have sex and not be all in my feels, right?

I ran my hand across Frankie's forearm and tugged Frankie close to me. Even under the rough exterior, her skin was smooth and silky, and my fingers immediately wanted more.

"I thought you said 'don't,'" Frankie whispered, her breath heating my neck.

My heartbeat steadily rose. I slid my fingers across Frankie's hip, tugged her even tighter, and melted in the sensation of Frankie's body pressed against mine. "Don't make me fall in love with you again."

But it was too late. I already knew I had fallen back in love. Every feeling, sensation, the same as when I was a kid. And yet, it was stronger, more mature, *scarier*.

Frankie put her mouth to my ear, her hand gripping my waist. "I make no promises."

I lifted my mouth to Frankie's, brushing my lips against hers. Frankie's mouth was so soft, so full, so ready. I pulled back, my eyes reading hers, needing confirmation we were on the same page. But what page was that? This, now, forever, temporary? I didn't know. But the fire in Frankie's gaze showed me that Frankie wanted me just as much as I wanted her.

Frankie grasped me from behind the neck and pressed her mouth into mine. My knees nearly buckled with the sensation. Frankie's lips were firm, controlled, *heavenly*, and moved against mine. Frankie circled her velvety tongue, separated my lips, and slid into my mouth.

When I stepped back, the porch creaked under my foot. I stared at Frankie, terrified I broke the spell.

"Are we good?" Frankie asked as she pulled away, breathless.

I nodded and trailed my finger up Frankie's forearm.

Frankie was always strong, an athlete, but now she was a woman, with rippling muscles and dips in her forearms, and I wanted to kiss every part of her. Enough thinking. No more second-guessing anything. "How do you feel about moving this inside?" My heartbeat kicked in, thudding against my chest. What if she said no?

What if she said *yes*?

Without a word, Frankie interlocked my fingers in hers and tugged me inside. Each footstep felt heavy and light at the same time, filled with intention and promise. Purse dropped, shoes kicked off, and I surrendered all control. Frankie didn't even stop at the couch. She clasped my hand and tugged me down the hall.

Oh damn. This is actually happening.

Inside my bedroom, I thought for sure Frankie would tear my clothes off. Instead, she sat on the edge of the bed and patted the comforter. Too many moments of silence followed with Frankie staring at her hands and my libido shrunk. Maybe this wasn't the right time, and I misread the signals. "Are *you* okay?"

"Yeah, for sure." Frankie focused on her hands, squeezing the tips of each finger. "I... um... It's been a *long* time. Like not since Savannah. And I want this. Like holy shit, woman, I want this so bad. But I'm a little freaked out."

Oh, this rush of honesty was a hit of endorphins. Libido officially returned. I shifted closer until our thighs touched. I'd always been the practical one, the analytical one, the pragmatic one. Frankie was the spontaneous, fly-by-the-seat-of-her-pants dreamer. And now Frankie was questioning everything and I didn't know what to do with that uncertainty.

Frankie skimmed her fingertips across my bare thigh, her thumbs caressing above the knee. "I mean, there's a lot on the line. So much has changed... You, me, we're totally different people, you know?" She swallowed. "And, I, uh, don't have casual sex. Ever. I'm not trying to overthink this, but I just wanted you to know that this is a really big deal. It's not just a fling for me, which is why I'm tripping out."

Not casual. So... serious? Which meant what? But honestly, I didn't care at this point. All I wanted to do was feel Frankie's body, touch her skin, not worry about anything until morning. I stood and nestled myself in between Frankie's legs. I tucked my fingers under Frankie's chin and lifted it so I could read her thoughts. The warm, deep, bourbon-brown eyes stared back into my soul.

I licked my lips, my hunger growing stronger. "How about, just for tonight, we let go? Let's not think about the past or the future, or anything except the right now."

Frankie grasped my arms and kissed the inside of my wrist, her mouth leaving a soft imprint on the skin. "Just for tonight. I can do that."

I lifted a leg to set my knee on the outside of Frankie's thigh, then climbed on top. Straddling her, I pulled Frankie into my chest and held her. Strong hands fanned across my back, holding me upright, providing the balance, the support and safety, I desperately needed. Frankie stayed there, her head pressed against me, being held, holding. *Breathing.*

Fingertips moved, shifting from my back, my ass, down my legs. Frankie slid her hands up my skirt and gripped my hips. The touch on bare skin made me nearly collapse. Frankie ran a trail of kisses up my neck to behind my ear, and I felt like I'd submerged myself in a warm bath.

"Mmmmm." A muffled sound released from me. Oh, this all felt so good. Familiar and totally different at once. I pushed my mouth against Frankie's, tasting her lips, moving, swirling. My arms wrapped Frankie, tugging her tight against me. I needed to be closer. Every part of me wanted to be closer.

Frankie moved her hands now, lifting my shirt just a bit, her fingertips whispering against my bare back. *More. Take it off.*

Take everything off. The hands crept higher, past my rib cage, bra strap, up until she clasped the base of my neck. My pulse thudded in my ear.

"Is this all... okay?" Frankie breathed into the crook of my neck.

When Frankie swept her lips across my jaw line and back to my mouth, I could barely manage a whisper. Goosebumps skittered across my skin and I deepened the kiss. "Yes... everything's perfect..."

Everything was too tight. The shirt, the bra, the skirt constricted at my skin, and I wanted to rip it off. But Frankie's hands moved slowly underneath my shirt, taking her sweet-ass time like she was worried if she moved any quicker, she'd miss some of my skin. But I needed more, quicker. This shirt had to go. I whipped it off and threw it into the wall.

"Shit. You're so beautiful." Frankie buried her face in my cleavage.

Soon, warm breaths moved over my bra. *Strip it off, latch on, move against me,* something. *Please.* The wet breaths were so intoxicating, fogging my skin, making me quiver. I pulled on Frankie's shirt. "Can I take this off?"

"Yes." Before I could assist, Frankie gripped the shirt behind her neck and ripped it off and... *damn.* The black racerback sports bra was sexy and fierce, everything Frankie was. I hooked my finger under the strap, ran my tongue up Frankie's collarbone and into her lower neck. Her skin tasted so good, clean and salty, and I wanted all of Frankie in my mouth. Frankie moaned, filling my ear with delicious sounds.

Frankie leaned into the kisses, then cupped my ass, tight, and lowered us both to lying. *Jesus,* she was so strong. So fully in control. *Confident.* I sat up, still straddling a lying-down Frankie. I needed to see more of her. My flattened palm moved down her sternum and over the ridges in her stomach. Okay, seriously, the ab muscles were ridiculous. For a fleeting moment, a brush of insecurity moved through me for my much curvier frame, but the way Frankie moved her hands, squeezing me, like she was desperate for more, silenced that voice.

Frankie hooked a finger under my bra strap and lowered it just an inch. "Is this okay—"

"Take it off. Now." The commanding voice that slipped out almost surprised me, but I ached to feel Frankie's mouth on me, savoring me, *owning* me. In one snap, cool air-conditioned air hit me, and I shivered. Frankie held firm and steady with one arm, as her other hand cupped my breast. A thumb grazed my nipple and my breath hitched.

"You're so beautiful, Morgan. You're perfect..."

Frankie's mouth hovered and I swore if Frankie didn't put her mouth on me, I was going to lose it. The anticipation was making my limbs weak and... *Oh. Right there.* Frankie swirled her tongue, long, leisurely on my nipple, her soft moans matching mine. But when she pulled me into her mouth, sucking and licking, I couldn't breathe. If I died right now, this was exactly how I'd want to go out. The mouth alternated firm and steady, hands and fingers pinching and rolling, and a heated deliciousness filled me. The moment was hypnotic, my eyes turning glassy and unfocused.

I need friction. I moved from straddling Frankie's entire body, to just one jeaned leg, needing more pressure on my center. Rocking and swirling my hips didn't provide enough relief, and dammit, I needed more. *So much more.* I should slow down and savor, but I wanted everything *so bad*, right now.

"Can I?" My thumbs grazed under Frankie's bra. When Frankie nodded, I tugged and Frankie peeled, both of us all fumbling hands and arms. "Why are these so freaking tight?"

"Ugh, I got it, wait, no, here, *ouch*, no I'm good, I'm good, don't give up now." Frankie chuckled and finally got the sports bra over her head and chucked it to the floor.

And I stopped all movements. I didn't want to stare, but I

really wanted to stare, to absorb everything about this moment. I remembered this body—the trio of angel kisses resting to the left of Frankie's heart, the color of the pale skin, the scar on the lower right ribcage from a childhood bike accident.

But I also didn't remember. Not like this. She was *perfect.* "I, you, agh... You're... God, you're so freaking hot." Every part of me wanted to taste Frankie, to fill my mouth with Frankie's skin, to inhale her scent.

The movements quickened. Fingers unclasping buckles, jeans hitting the floor, skirt and underwear and every article of clothing, gone, until it was just us. Heartbeats pounded so loudly I didn't know which body they belonged to. I moved to the side, pushed my thigh in between Frankie's legs. Hungry mouths and breaths and lips moved, tongues grazed and lingered. Frankie's wet mouth met my breasts again, and I dug my fingers into Frankie's neck. I wanted more. I wanted all of Frankie.

Hands gripped me and flipped me on my back. "*Ohhh.*" This was real. For right now, everything was real and hot, and intense, and perfect. Maybe we could be like this forever. Pretend that New York and jobs and stress didn't exist.

When Frankie's palm slid down my chest, to my belly, and lowered, she hovered. "Can I touch you?"

The needy huskiness in Frankie's voice was almost too much. I couldn't speak. There was not enough air, and anticipation seized my lungs. My heartbeat pounded in my chest, so loud, so hard, and I knew Frankie could hear it. I grabbed Frankie's hand and guided her to my center. "*Please touch me,*" I finally moaned.

Frankie dipped a finger inside me and my breath hitched. Circles and swirling and movement, and *my God, how does she know the right spot?* Then another finger, and I was blinking away the stars. The way Frankie moved, slow at first, then increasing pressure and *shit.* I gripped Frankie's shoulder, needing more... needing less... no, definitely more... and Frankie read me perfectly. History or intuitiveness, it didn't matter. Frankie knew when and where and how much.

My legs quivered under the touches. But when Frankie lowered herself, stopping at my chest, then my belly, then lower, warm misted breath and kisses traveling with her, I hovered on exploding. Right here and now, and Frankie hadn't even reached the spot yet. "Please..." I whimpered as Frankie, who was clearly enjoying making me wait, slowed the kisses. I was so close. "Put your mouth on me, please, so close... *Yes. Right there...*"

My eyes fluttered. I wanted to touch Frankie back, needed to feel Frankie in my hands, in my mouth, but I was powerless as a skilled strong tongue and mouth worked my body. My limbs trembled already, my brain shutting off completely, as the air in the room heated and I melted.

Oh my... What was that? Something new and delicious and it felt *so effing good.* Frankie combined a palm, and circling thumbs and tongue and the pressure. Oh God, the pressure was perfection. My pulse increased, higher, more, clouding my vision. "Oh, yes, there, *so close... ummmmm,* please don't stop..."

And Frankie kept the rhythm the same, rocking and tasting. Gliding and circling. So, so, so close. My fingers gripped the sheets. Almost there. I bit my lip, my legs trembling, quivering, and..."Ahhh!"

I was loud and I didn't care. My body clenched, tight, as the waves ripped through me, euphoric and releasing. My heart thudded, hard in my chest, and I shivered against Frankie's body.

As Frankie slowly removed her touch, I lazed my fingers through Frankie's hair. I didn't want to move. I was sleepy, yet didn't want to sleep. My body was warm, listless, my limbs immobile on the bed. Soon, my heartbeat slowed, my trembles evened. Frankie shifted herself higher and planted soft kisses on my shoulder.

Neither of us spoke. For so long, I didn't want to even think. I just wanted to be here, lying with Frankie as she stroked my hair, her chest lifting and lowering against mine. Nothing else but this moment mattered.

Recovering at a record rate, I rolled over. I nestled up to Frankie's neck, the sweet smell of Frankie's body fired my cells, igniting the tingles I just released. I put my mouth to Frankie's ear, my mouth watering in anticipation. "My turn."

TWENTY-SIX
FRANKIE

"A little higher. No, wait, tighter." Morgan propped her hands on her hips. "No, definitely higher. Wait... definitely tighter."

I dropped my arms and stared at Morgan as if that would make Morgan's instructions any clearer. I'd been up and down the ladder a dozen times today, stringing lights across the barn ceiling, and my arms burned. Although that was probably less about stringing the lights, and more about the marathon sex sessions Morgan and I had been engaging in for the last two weeks. I glanced down at Morgan's pouty lips and grinned. The stamina on that one, though. And I thought *I* was the athletic one in the relationship.

"Morgan," I said, waiting for confirmation of life. "*Morgan.*"

Morgan's head snapped toward me. "What?"

"The lights are fine. Everything is fine. They look great. This place looks great." I stepped off the ladder and swooped her into my arms. "Okay?"

Morgan leaned her head against my chest. "But I want it to be perfect."

"It *is* perfect."

The venue was incredible. Against all odds, we had transformed this barn into a pretty spectacular wedding venue. Of course, provided no one looked in the machine shed or three acres down the property, which turned into a busting-at-the-seams junkyard. Hard to think just a few short months ago it was overflowing with tools, junk, and dirt. And today, it damn near sparkled. The broken window was replaced, the floor sanded and stained, and the electrical and plumbing in full working order. Even the inspector signed off. Now, two days before the wedding, we just needed to add the final touches.

The tables and chairs that were delivered this morning needed to be set up, the centerpieces placed, and the table settings set. Delilah would deliver all the flowers the evening before the wedding. Of course, there was no DJ. My blood boiled thinking about that Tag asshole and how close I had been to letting him meet my right hook. I breathed it out, though, not needing any negative thoughts to send me down a rabbit hole. Besides, Olivia's cousin stepped up and said she'd manage a loudspeaker and a solid playlist from her phone. Not ideal, but Tommy and Olivia were surprisingly cool about the situation—not that they had a lot of choice.

Not only was the venue perfect... so was Morgan. *Dammit.* So fucking perfect. I watched Morgan as she moved to the side wall and was doing some sort of wedding-day sorcery by revamping the old window we replaced, with some greenery and white chalk paint. Everything she touched morphed into something beautiful and special, and I was truly astounded. Which made my stomach turn.

After our first night together, we made a pact to not talk about the future. Just not mention it at all and bask in the moment. We were taking everything day by day. It was a huge leap of faith for both of us. Morgan always had a plan, and this meant living without one. Although I'm spontaneous in my daily life, I'm absolutely not when it comes to relationships. And now, my time was coming to an end, and I still had no idea what the hell I was going to do.

I started unloading the folding chairs from the cart and set them up near the tables, stealing as many glances at Morgan as I could. What would life look like if I stayed here? The town was so much kinder and lovelier than I remembered. With how often I frequented Connie's Coffee and chatted with her niece Megan in the morning, we were damn near a second family at this point. When I saw Joe from the hardware store at the gas station, we talked for ten minutes about the Vikings' season. I visited Zoey's more often than I'd like to admit, because Zoey made the best salted caramel macaroons I had ever tasted. On my last visit, I ended up staying for twenty minutes, discussing the upcoming back-to-school events in the fall.

I even talked to the neighbors—which I definitely didn't do in New York—who stopped by multiple times, checking in on the progress on Peaches's house. Last week, after being burnt out beyond capacity from clearing out Peaches's place, I told the neighbors to come through the garage and take anything they wanted. In fact, I begged them to. Thank God they seemed to be of a similar hoarding nature as Peaches because they took a ton. When they offered me money and I declined, a few days later they showed up with a homemade pecan pie, a beautiful crocheted scarf, and a tater-tot hot dish. Somehow, I'd reattached myself to this town and it had started to feel like home again.

And I'd fallen, 100 percent, head over heels, back in love with Morgan.

But moving back here meant starting back at the beginning. In New York, I'd built a reputation and clientele. I had an apartment I loved and lived in the city of my dreams. NYC had been my home nearly as long as Spring Harbors. Quinn was there.

Friends, and memories, and a city that welcomed me with open arms as a scared eighteen-year-old, and I couldn't just leave it.

Metal chairs fell from the cart, and the sharp piercing *clank* echoed against the hallow room. "Damn, sorry."

Morgan looked over her shoulder. "You okay? Need me?"

I will always, always need you. "No, I'm good." I unfolded the chairs and pushed them under the table.

A long-distance thing might work temporarily until we really figured out what to do. But, ultimately, that was never a way I wanted to live. I deserved more, and so did Morgan. And I had to be realistic, Morgan was never leaving Sam and the kids. Her home, family, community, the niece and nephews she loved as her own children, her business... Morgan was here to stay. So I was at a total loss. The idea of leaving Morgan gutted me. I wanted her folded into me at night, to taste her and kiss her and have her hold on to me during scary movies.

"Hey, do you have that extra box of tulle in your truck?" Morgan called out from behind the bar as she unpacked wine glasses.

"Yeah, I think so. Want me to grab it for you?" I asked.

"Yes please. And if you could bring in a soda and maybe those chips from my trunk, that'd be awesome." Morgan looked back at me with a grin. "You're the best, you know that?"

"Sure do." I smirked. "It's going to be a minute. I need to call Quinn back when I'm out there."

Morgan hovered a box cutter over the next wine case and slit it open. "Is she still dealing with the work drama?"

"Always." Poor Quinn. She was never *not* dealing with work drama. The night of the fiasco with that dickweed Tag, Quinn apparently had a major blowup with her manager because she didn't properly index something on an email—whatever the hell that even meant—and he laid into her in front of everyone. I could never work with someone like Quinn's boss, but for whatever reason, she held on for dear life.

Outside, I squinted into the sun. Thank God the heat broke. Even though the barn would be warm for the reception, with all the shade, fans, and a single portable air conditioner at the head table, we'd make it through without our skin melting off.

When Quinn didn't answer the phone, I grabbed the tulle and started heading back inside when my brain flickered. *What else, what else?* Oh yeah. Food and drink. I spun on my heels to go back to the car when my phone vibrated.

An unknown number flashed across my screen, and I almost didn't answer it. But it was a New York City area code, and God knows if it was Quinn calling from an office landline because something happened with her phone.

"Hi, I'm looking for Frankie," the voice on the other end of the line said.

Suspicious. Probably trying to sell me something. "That's me..."

"Hi, Frankie! This is Lorena from *Birch & Willow*. Is this an okay time to talk?"

I froze. *Birch & Willow. Holy shit.* A pinprick of nerves needled my neck. "Yes, of course, now's a great time." I glanced behind my shoulder, then rushed onto the lawn out of earshot.

"I just want to say thank you so much for your patience as our team worked through all the portfolios," Lorena said. "This took much longer than we expected, and we in no way wanted the applicants to think the delay was a reflection on their talents."

My pulse thudded in my neck. Was this the nicest rejection in the world, or a job offer? As Lorena continued talking about the grueling decision-making process, the top-tier talent, and a delay in the decision-making process due to a small department reorganization, Morgan peeked her head out of the barn. The sun beamed down, her blonde hair even paler under the rays, her golden sun-kissed cheeks, and she was glowing. Sure, sweaty and messy, but perfect. Morgan was everything that was missing in my life, everything I needed.

Morgan made the phone gesture with her pinkie and thumb and rolled her eyes with a wink. She grabbed the broom on the outside of the porch and went back inside.

"Anyway, I promise I'm not normally this wordy, but I really wanted you to have the full context so you know we didn't take this decision lightly," Lorena said. "The team here at *Birch & Willow* would love to offer you the position."

My heart stopped beating. *I cannot believe I did it.* All the years of work, sacrifices, honing my craft, learning to believe in myself, trust myself, everything paid off. I was *good* enough. I, alone, earned my spot.

"Frankie? You still with me?"

I paced in a circle with my hand held to the back of my neck. "Yes, of course. I... Wow. Thank you so much. Truly. I've been such a huge fan of your brand for years. As an artist, this offer is an absolute dream come true." *Oh God, oh God.* This was actually happening.

"If you're interested, we'd love to get you onboarded within two weeks. Sorry about the short turnaround time. But with the delays, we need to get working right away on the holiday campaign. HR will reach out with paperwork, exact timing, and begin salary negotiations."

Salary. Benefits. A 401K, real health insurance, and paid time off. Being a freelancer for my entire career, this was completely unheard of. I scratched at my neck, the words swirling as Lorena chatted about next steps, coming into the office for onboarding, and something about sending an offer letter, but my brain short-circuited with all the information.

"Do you have questions for me?"

"Oh, uh, no. I don't think so." Heat filled my chest. My dream was right here, within touching distance. And Morgan was right in there, a few yards away.

A pause followed. "So... do you accept?"

This was the opportunity of a lifetime. And, without a doubt, Morgan was the love of my life. This was one of the single greatest moments of my life, and the most gut-wrenching. *Birch & Fucking Willow* wanted *me*. The decision weighed on top of me and I held my breath for so long, I became dizzy.

"Thank you so much for the offer." I exhaled. "I accept."

TWENTY-SEVEN
MORGAN

My belly fluttered. *Today's the day!* The wedding day had finally arrived. Sure, it wasn't *my* wedding, but my insides didn't know that. In my wedding coordinator role, I could be such a jerk leading up to the wedding day. Anxious, snappy, and maybe a little (*a lot*) overbearing. But the day of, I was typically freakishly calm. Being hyper-prepared meant during the event, as long as things went according to plan—which they usually did—I enjoyed the wedding as much as any guest.

Last night, Frankie and I completed the final touches on the venue. The pallet centerpieces looked even better than I imagined. If Olivia and Tommy didn't want them, I was going to see if I could keep them for a future event. We were totally drained, working until midnight. But the effort was worth it. Although Frankie had clearly been exhausted as she insisted on sleeping at her own place for the past two nights. I tried not to think too much into it, but I missed Frankie's warm body at night.

As I fastened studs in my ear, I heard the faint sound of Frankie's truck rolling up the driveway. One quick spritz of perfume, another plop of lip balm, and I was ready. I grabbed a phone charger and stuffed heels into a bag. Until any guests arrived, I was sticking to sandals.

The door creaked open. "Morgan?" Frankie called out.

"Coming!" I tossed the tote bag over my shoulder and scooted to the living room and stopped. Well, holy hell. God, Frankie was *hot*. I would never, ever tire looking at this woman. After only seeing Frankie either naked, or in jeans and a T-shirt, this version of her was a delicious treat. A crisp, fitted black button-down with a couple of buttons open on top, a gold necklace, and black slacks.

"Hey, beautiful," Frankie said with a smile, her deep-set dimples popping up. She held my hand and twirled me. "That dress... Oof. Killing me."

"Yeah, um, I was about to say the same thing. You look amazing." I swiped my tongue against my lips. "How about we just skip this whole wedding thing and go straight to the bedroom?" I was only half kidding. Was it an age thing, a Frankie thing, or the fact that I was truly in love, that made me damn near insatiable? I pressed my lips into Frankie's, but my heart quickly dropped.

Frankie kissed me back, but it wasn't with passion, it wasn't with longing. It was with... I couldn't put my finger on it. Sadness? Trepidation, maybe? Whatever it was didn't feel great. I stepped back and searched her eyes. "Are you okay?"

Frankie's long eyelashes swept the top of her cheek. She reached for my hand and kissed the top. "Yes, I'm good." She inhaled and released a slow, unsteady breath. "Big day, though, huh?"

Of course. Frankie might be a very skilled photographer, but she'd never actually shot a wedding before. Ultra-confident, ripped-biker-babe Frankie was nervous. It was kind of cute. "Yes, it's a big day, but it's going to be great. The only thing we need to do is put flowers in the vases this morning after Delilah leaves, keep the wedding party calm, and direct the caterers where to set up. We got this."

"And, you know, shoot pictures for eight hours." Frankie grinned and grabbed the tote from me to carry.

"Oh yeah, that." She gave me one more kiss and led me to the car.

Of course, I was teasing about the minimal work I had to do today. Being the hub of information for the entire day took a ton of energy. From the officiant's microphone, to keeping the flower girl's dress clean, to the processional, I was responsible for everything.

I let it go that Frankie was quiet on the ride out, even though Frankie took multiple opportunities to stroke my leg or cheek. Would I ever stop melting at the touch? Probably not. I pushed it out of my mind that at some point, we'd need to discuss the future. But for now, I'd greedily lean into every touch Frankie gave me.

At the farm, I shifted into business mode. "I'm going to set up for the first shot. Need anything from me?" Frankie asked as she tossed the camera bag over her shoulder and grabbed the tripod.

"No, I'm good." I checked my watch. "Delilah will be here in about thirty minutes and the wedding party will trickle in around ten, ten thirty. I have plenty of time."

"Cool." Frankie creased her eyebrows, patted her pant legs, and reached back in the truck for an item with a frown.

When she slammed the door, I held Frankie's hand. "We got this, okay? I got you. If you need help, I'll be the best damn assistant you've ever had."

Frankie's stern face formed into a smile. "God, I..."

I love you? Was Frankie planning on saying that? I felt it to the deepest part of me, and I was sure Frankie felt the same. But she hadn't said it, and I didn't want to be the one to say it first. I hated that my traitorous face was probably wide-eyed and starry with anticipation.

"I'm so unbelievably lucky to have you here with me." Frankie tapped her equipment. "You're right. You make the best assistant ever."

Not *exactly* what I was hoping to hear. I brushed off the slight uneasiness in my belly and got to work.

"Oh my gosh... this place. Everything... It's absolutely stunning." Olivia, clad in a white bathrobe and rollers in her hair, covered her mouth with her hand. "Morgan, you're a miracle worker! I don't even understand how you transformed this place." Olivia's gaze slowed, scanning the white linen-covered tables with the farmhouse chic centerpieces, flowers, and Martha Stewart-worthy dinner-table settings. The strung white lights beautifully accented the barn's high beams, while the tulle, greenery, candles, and candy jars made the former bare wooden bar area warm and inviting.

"Thank you." I was damn near beaming. This was the most difficult project I'd taken on to date, and I was so proud of the outcome. But having a happy, approving bride... well, that meant everything. "I'm really happy with how it turned out. And thank God for Frankie. I definitely couldn't have done this without her."

Olivia grinned. "She is really something, isn't she?"

More than Olivia could possibly know. These last three months with Frankie had been more than I could've ever dreamed. My gratitude bucket overflowed, having Frankie by my side this entire time. "Is Tommy in the RV with the guys?"

Another item for the gratitude bucket? That Pete and Patty had a huge, modern, and fully functioning RV parked on their property. Keeping the bridal party apart until the women finished getting ready was always a challenge, but as long as the men had a spot for taking shots from a flask and playing a poker game, they were fine.

"Yes, he is." Olivia shifted her tote bag to her other shoulder. "My sister will be here pretty soon. Can you show me where I'm going to get ready, then send the women back when they arrive?"

After I escorted Olivia to the "bridal suite," which was essentially a corner section with added mirrors, chairs, and a room divider for privacy, I grabbed Frankie to let her know Olivia was ready for the "getting ready" photos.

During the next few hours, I developed a deep appreciation for Frankie and her work. Frankie was an absolute master in her domain, even if she'd never shot a wedding before. Candid photos, posed photos, outdoor, indoor, everything looked effortlessly thought-out and organized. She had a way about her, a kind but in-control demeanor that calmed everyone. Phrases like "you're beautiful, you're doing fantastic" rolled off her tongue a hundred times, but each time it sounded authentic and genuine. She even coaxed the flower girl down from a pretty hefty tantrum and snapped a few photos until the little girl crashed again.

I escorted the last guest in and stepped outside to where the bridal party stood. "You ready?" I asked Olivia, who nodded enthusiastically while gripping her bouquet. Through the years, I had seen it all... the nerves, brides shaking, crying, some excited and some with that *oh shit, what am I doing* look. But Olivia was calm, settled, and stunning.

The music started, and I motioned the wedding party forward. As the flower girl waddled down the makeshift aisle, tossing flower petals from her basket onto the hardwood floors, I took a quick peek inside as the guests turned their heads to the entrance. Was sitting guests in the same place where dinner would be served to watch the wedding march unconventional? Most definitely. And I probably wouldn't do it again. But, for today, it worked.

Olivia gripped her stepfather's arm as he shuffled next to her. "Ready, Papa?"

Her stepfather nodded, steadied himself with his wooden cane, and dabbed at his eyes with his handkerchief. Once they stepped into the barn, I circled outside and slipped into a side door to make sure the rest of the ceremony went off without a hitch.

No matter how many weddings I attended, watching the bride or groom walk down the aisle always gave me flutters. Olivia's cousin had pulled through on makeshift DJ duties, and the speakers blasted the wedding song without feedback. I assumed that Olivia and Tommy would choose "Wedding March" or "Canon in D," or something similar to walk down the aisle. Instead, they chose a country song that would normally not be my style, but the lyrics about stars aligning and fate bringing them together struck me and I blinked back tears. I peeked at Frankie—her cheeks dewy, her expression serious and determined while capturing photos—and thanked the stars for realigning us again.

After the ceremony, I guided the guests outside for a quick cleanup of the scattered flowers and so the caterers could get set up. "This way please. Wine, lemonade, hors d'oeuvres behind the barn." I really hoped people didn't wander too much, because if they stepped fifty feet farther than they were supposed to, they'd see piles of junk.

Soon, the property sprung alive. Guests tossed bean bags into the "Mr. and Mrs." corn hole game, kids chased each other while screeching, and a long line of folks lined up to congratulate the bride and groom.

I stretched my neck, looking behind the guests and caught Frankie's eye. *God, she's spectacular.* Frankie pointed the camera at me and snapped a few pics, and when she lowered the camera, she gave me a wink. Yep, flutters yet again. This entire day my stomach was ready to take off in flight.

The chicken Kiev and grilled asparagus dinner looked as good as it smelled, and without question, Zoey's chocolate and raspberry cake made my mouth water. Really, would anyone know if I took a little slice before the couple? As the guests returned, the space warmed again. A few people fanned themselves with wedding programs, but overall the shade and fans staved off most of the heat. With the guests happily munching on their dinner, I slipped behind the bar area and took a few bites of food.

Frankie stepped behind me and rested her chin on my shoulder. "Can I have a quick bite?" She grabbed my fork without waiting for a response, swallowed back some chicken, and give me a quick love pat on the side of my leg.

Melting. I'm positively melting.

The maid of honor, best man, and parent speeches were beautiful. Everyone, including me, teared up when the stepfather spoke about being at peace after watching Olivia find her happiness with Tommy. The guests raised their glasses in cheers and the couple kissed under a round of hoots and hollers.

Then the maid of honor/designated party starter/definite former sorority sister grabbed the microphone and said, "Let's dance!" and dragged a couple of very reluctant groomsmen on the floor with her. Laughter, chatting, and clapping soon filled the space along with the music.

Among the clicking of glasses and silverware tapping the plates, and good old '80s pop rock playing in the background, I floated around the room checking tables, answering questions from the caterers, and pointing people to the bathrooms outside. I lifted a water bottle to my mouth when a woman approached me from the side.

"Hey, there. I'm one of Olivia's classmates." She shook my

hand. "You did amazing here and Olivia damn near sung your praises from the rooftop. Not sure what your schedule looks like, but I just got engaged last month and I'd love to talk to you next week about hiring you for my wedding next summer."

Relief washed over me. I handed the woman a business card and said I'd be thrilled to help. More time passed. With music thumping in the background, the caterers silently cleared dishes, the bartender kept busy with filling glasses with wine, and Frankie continued working the crowd like a pro. I took a moment of reprieve, stepped out behind the building, and kicked off my heels. The sun warmed my chest, the grass cooled my feet, and the evening filled my heart.

Back inside, the mother of the bride crossed the room toward me, her perfectly smooth bob not moving while she walked. "This was *stunning*. I cannot begin to imagine what you had to go through to get this place ready with such short notice." She laid a hand across her pearl necklace. "Now is not the time for details, but could we have lunch maybe Wednesday or Thursday? We're planning a major spring event for a charity auction in Minneapolis. The company I hired have been incompetent and uncommunicative, and I would love to bring you on instead."

Swear to God, I almost turned around to make sure she wasn't talking to someone behind me. I nodded way too vigorously and pushed my arms into my sides to refrain from hugging her. "I would love to!" were the only words I could form.

By the end of the evening, three things happened. I had given out at least twenty business cards, booked three appointments, and for the first time in two years, felt that my company —and myself—would be okay.

Yawns from some, drunken laughter from others, and hefty whines from a very, very cranky flower girl filled the room as the crowd trickled down. The music shifted from all the "YMCA,"

"You Shook Me All Night Long," and "Bye Bye Bye" songs, into a ballad.

Frankie lowered her camera and crossed the room to me. "May I have this dance?" She bowed and held out her hand.

"Such a gentleman." I grinned and set my palm in Frankie's. "Don't you need to capture this on film?"

Frankie swung the camera hanging from her neck to her side and tucked it under her arm. "I'm on break."

Her hands gripped the small of my waist and she tugged me into her chest. *Oh, wow, guess so.* I rested my head against Frankie and felt her heartbeat pulse against my ear. I exhaled, breathing out the chaotic day, the even more chaotic summer, and softened into Frankie's touch.

Now that the wedding was over, and the summer's end approached, I knew Frankie and I would have to address all the unknowns. Living in a fantasy world was pretty amazing, but reality was going to set in soon. But for this moment, with the hardwood squeaking under my heels, the room warm and steamy, I closed my eyes and melted into Frankie's arms.

When the next song started, Frankie kissed the top of my head and the warmth spread to my toes. Frankie's head buried into my shoulder, and I snugged her tighter. Whatever would happen, we'd figure it out. I let Frankie go once. I wasn't sure I could do it again.

Moisture hit my neck. *What was... Oh.* Frankie's tears glided down me. I sighed and pulled her tighter. Whatever was happening inside her, I wanted to take it away, to squeeze it from her. Maybe if I held her long enough, reality wouldn't set it, and we could live in this moment forever. I stroked her neck as the tears from her continued. All the unspoken words were loud now. Frankie was as scared of the future as me.

I lifted my head and swiped her cheeks with my thumbs. My heart ached. I lifted my mouth to Frankie's ear. "I love you."

I didn't need to hear it back, but I needed to say it, get it out in the open, and whatever happened after this was meant to be.

Frankie didn't move her head but squeezed me a little tighter. Moments passed, the end of the song nearing, the swaying almost complete. Finally, Frankie leaned into my ear. "I never stopped loving you."

TWENTY-EIGHT
FRANKIE

I slithered out of bed and tiptoed from the room. Morgan was still sleeping, exhausted after the wedding the previous evening. Thankfully, last week she finally listened to reason and hired a cleanup crew so we could leave at a decent time, but we were still there until after midnight. At the door, I took another helping of bliss... A naked, pink-cheeked Morgan lying on her stomach, her back rising with each soft breath, her blonde hair matted against the pillowcase.

Needing the comfort of the familiar home, I brought us to Peaches's house last night. The days left here were limited, and I wanted to suck up every last moment. I flicked the realtor card against the countertop as the coffee pot brewed to life. I'd been avoiding calling, making every excuse I could. Home renovations, wedding stuff, storage nightmares. Sure, I had some of my typical decision paralysis, but even this was to the extreme.

I tossed back my medication, then grabbed one of the two coffee mugs still left in the bare cabinets. Minus the heavy furniture, a couple of bowls, silverware, and some towels, I packed everything. My lip trembled, but I bit it to stop. *I can't believe I'm leaving this place.*

How did I not appreciate it this much when I was in New York? When I'd come back and visit home, I'd spend time with Peaches, obviously, but it was maybe a day or two, tops. I was always so itchy to leave and go back to the city that I never let it fill me the way I needed. But now the idea of leaving it for good tore me apart.

Okay, okay, I needed to call the realtor today. No more excuses. I had to leave on a flight in less than a week to head back home. And honestly, the money from the sale would be a nice nest egg if I were ever out of work—which right now seemed unlikely. I wasn't as worried about finances as maybe I would've been in the past. The job offer and compensation package from *Birch & Willow* was extremely generous—signing bonus, yearly bonus, and the ability to earn commissions on work outside of my normal scope. But this house was Quinn's, too, and would provide Quinn enough of a security blanket to quit her terrible high-stress job.

I flung the card back on the counter. Maybe tomorrow I'd call. Today, I didn't want to have conversations with anyone except Morgan. Time was slipping through my fingers, and I wanted to savor every single moment. How the hell was I supposed to leave Morgan again? I dragged my hands down my face. This job was what I wanted more than almost anything. I hit a professional high, and it'd be insane to give that up now.

But I also wanted Morgan. More than anything. Life repeated itself in almost the cruelest way possible. Two spectacular gifts, but I could only have one. God, what was I going to do? I'd bring it up to Morgan about coming with, but I already knew the answer. This town was part of Morgan's soul. Even if she did come to New York, she wouldn't be happy. She needed expansive land, to know everyone's name at the store, to have the same neighbors for twenty years and be around Sam, Lisa, and the kids. In New York, she wouldn't have any of that.

The coffee pot beeped. I filled the mug, stepped out onto

the patio, and sat on the swing. My legs pushed into the floor, and I squeaked back and forth. Yet another thing I wasn't quite ready to let go of—the swing. This house had too many memories. How would the new family be that moved here? Would they respect the space or strip everything that made it unique? Would they fill the cellar with jars of fruit and veggies, or remodel it into a sauna to fight off those long winter nights?

The coffee warmed my body, and I closed my eyes against the morning sun. My nose filled with the scent of fresh cut grass. My brain slowly settled, allowing me to take in the morning's stillness. When the patio door slid open, I blinked at Morgan—a beautiful, tousled-hair, plump-lipped, fresh-faced Morgan in a rumpled T-shirt and cotton shorts. I loved her in almost any way, but Morning Morgan was my favorite.

"Hey, you. Did I wake you?" I shifted and patted the seat.

"No, but the coffee did, in the best way possible." She grinned through a yawn, her eyes crinkled with sleep. She lifted the mug to her nose and sniffed. "It's like those Folgers commercials about the best part of waking up. I need to buy myself one of those coffee pots with automatic timers so I can wake up to the smell of coffee beans instead of my alarm clock blaring." She slid in next to me and rested her head against my shoulder.

When I kissed the top of Morgan's head, I nearly burst into tears. *I have to tell her.* "Can you believe the wedding's all done?"

"I know. It's pretty surreal. So much work for an eight-hour period in someone's life." Morgan sipped the coffee. "I have three meetings set already for next week, but then I'm taking some time off. This one really did me in."

I stared at the trees. "I bet." *I bet? That's all I have to offer?* I had so many things to say. I wanted to tell Morgan I thought she was the most incredible person I'd ever met. That she pulled off something that very few people could, simply because of her resilience and work ethic. I wanted to tell her that she was amazing, and beautiful, and smart as hell, and that my heart was ripping from my chest with the thought of not spending every day with her. And even if it was a rocky start, these past three months had been some of the happiest of my life.

Several moments of quiet passed when Morgan lifted herself. "Hey, are you okay?" She seemed to search my eyes for an answer as she remained silent. "I'm sure you're as tired as me, but am I in my head? You seem so quiet."

I looked at Morgan. Really, really looked at her. Not the eighteen-year-old I left all those years ago. But as the thirty-three-year-old woman who had always held a piece of my heart. I struggled to find words as the graduation night flooded my mind. My stomach knotted. *This conversation might be what ends us for good.* No matter how much more honest and mature we both might be, I wasn't sure of either of our reactions if things got heated.

I gnawed on the side of my cheek, then let out a slow exhale. "I need to tell you something."

Morgan lowered her mug and shifted a few inches back, her eyes folding.

"I got the job offer from *Birch & Willow*."

Morgan's face mirrored my insides. At first, raised eyebrows and a mega-watt smile. Then the smile dropped. Tears brimmed in the corner of her eyes. "I'm so... I'm so happy for you." Her lower lip trembled. She swiped her eye with a pinkie. "This is a dream come true."

It really is.

"Are you..." Morgan cleared her throat. "Are you going to take it?"

I felt like shit. Did I have an obligation to tell Morgan immediately when I got the offer? Probably not. It had all happened so fast. They offered me the job, I didn't have time to fully process, and I made an impulsive decision. Okay, maybe not *that* impulsive as I had wanted this job for as long as I could remember. But I could have told the hiring manager that I needed twenty-four hours. "I already did."

Morgan flinched like a pound of bricks landed on her chest. "You did?" Creases lined her forehead. "And you didn't tell me?"

The voice was more hurt than accusatory, which was a harder emotion to process. I didn't want to hurt Morgan. The thought of hurting Morgan made me sick. But I was an adult and made an adult decision. And... *and!...* we had only been a few days away from the wedding and I hadn't wanted to derail Morgan for something inevitable.

At least, that's what I'd told myself that day. But truth was, I also didn't want to break our spell. Being back with Morgan was heaven, and I wasn't ready to let that go. However, if offered again, I'd still take the job. "I'm so sorry I didn't tell you. I wanted to, the second they offered, I was going to tell you." I took a breath and reached for Morgan's hand, which remained stiff. *Shit.* "But I thought it was selfish to burden you when you were trying to finish everything for the wedding."

Morgan stared at the yard, her feet pushing against the porch to swing the bench. She swiped at tears and remained silent.

Say something. Do something. Christ, was I making the right decision? I thought so. I hoped so. But my heart was crushed. I wanted to touch Morgan, to hold her, but I didn't want Morgan to run away. If I moved, Morgan might move, then this would be the last moment we'd spend together.

More time passed, maybe five, ten minutes, I wasn't even sure, when Morgan buried her face in her hands and cried. A sob that came from so deep in her gut that I wanted to do anything to take it away. I pulled her into my chest, her vanilla-scented shampoo wafting to my nose, remembering what it really felt like to be in love. God dammit. I didn't want to leave, either. My heart was breaking, healing, breaking, in split seconds, like ice cracking and refreezing in the dead of winter. "I don't know what to do."

That was the truth. Maybe we could make a life here. Maybe Morgan would come with. Which choice was I willing to live with? Sure, I accepted the job, but maybe I could push out the start date. Or reject it altogether?

That thought also made my stomach coil. Morgan lay against my chest until her tears stopped. She was so silent I thought she fell asleep. After an eternity, Morgan lifted herself and grabbed my hand. She ran her fingertips across the top and kissed my knuckles. "I think you should go." Morgan's voice cracked. Her gaze shifted between my eyes, her eyebrows knitting. "I don't want you to leave. More than anything, I want you to stay. But you need to go."

Panic seized me. No, this was a bad idea. Maybe I could stay and we'd set up a house, and adopt some dogs, and plant a vegetable garden in the backyard and everything would be okay. Morgan could have her business and I could.... Ugh. What could I do? Hang on her coattails like the last time we were together? I knew I couldn't give this opportunity up. I'd regret it for the rest of my life.

But I couldn't give up Morgan. *Shit, shit, shit.* The urge to pound my fists into the ground overtook me. God, why was this so hard? This should be the highlight of my career, and I wanted to throw up. "I don't want to go without you." I kneeled on the ground in front of Morgan, gripping her hands so hard I was sure I'd break her fingers. "Come with me. *Please.* We gave up those chances all those years ago, and I don't want to do that again. I don't want to regret leaving you, leaving us."

Morgan's hands cupped my cheeks. "I can't," she said, barely above a whisper.

"Please, Morgan. *Please.* I think you'd be okay there. You don't have to work for a while if you don't want to. And if you do, there are so many event places... and tons of wedding venues... and maybe you could come on location with me... I saw everything you did for the wedding and you'd be a perfect stylist for *Birch & Willow* and maybe—"

"I'm not coming with," Morgan said with so much regret in her voice that I crumbled. "This is my home. My family is here. I won't ever leave it."

The tears burst from me. I cried in Morgan's lap until I couldn't breathe, until I was limp with fatigue. Morgan ran her fingers through my hair until my tears stopped. I knew I was grasping, but maybe if I said the right thing, Morgan would change her mind. "Maybe... maybe I should turn down the job. Tell them I made a mistake when I accepted."

Tears slid down Morgan's cheeks. She swiped the top of her hand under her chin to catch the drops. "An opportunity like this is life-changing. Take it, Frankie. You would regret it forever if you didn't."

I knew this was true, but I hoped Morgan would say something different. Force me to stay so the decision didn't rest on my shoulders. "But what happens with us?" I had to ask but already knew the answer. Long-distance relationships were nothing I ever wanted, and I couldn't imagine Morgan wanted that, either. We each deserved more.

Morgan grinned. A sad, terrible, heart-crushing grin. "We'll stay friends. I'll call you without texting first. I'll send you random messages on all your electronic devices, and I'll stalk you on social media." She squeezed my shoulder, her bloodshot eyes making the blue even more intense. "And I'm going to be your biggest cheerleader ever. You deserve this. You *earned* it. And you are going to absolutely kill it."

When Morgan shifted, I released my grip. I didn't want to stop touching Morgan, ever. But there was nowhere to go from here. The Band-Aid was ripped. And my heart was broken.

"I'm going to head out, okay? I need to shower at my own

place, finish sleeping in my own bed." Morgan crossed the patio to the door. "Thanks for the coffee."

The unspoken words amplified the heaviness in the air. I knew what Morgan meant. It wasn't a shower. It wasn't her own bed. It was Morgan, leaving, shutting down, and protecting herself.

What have I done?

TWENTY-NINE
MORGAN

I made it all the way home, all the way into my driveway, and just about into my house when I broke down again. I kicked the door closed behind me, collapsed to my knees, and bawled into my hands.

I wanted to beg Frankie not to leave. To tell her I thought we really had a shot this time, to convince her to stay and try, and build a life together. But last time I did that, I nearly destroyed Frankie's chances at what turned out to be a better life. And as much as it killed me, Frankie never regretted her decision back then to leave, and neither did I regret staying. Even at eighteen, we knew what was right for us.

When I said we could be friends, I meant it. Sort of. But eventually, Frankie would find someone. And when that happened, I would not be able to watch the love of my life be with someone else. People who can do that type of thing are much stronger than me. The idea of another woman holding Frankie at night made me want to throw up. But until that inevitable day came, we could try and maintain a friendship, even with my heart breaking. I didn't want Frankie out of my life, I knew that for sure. But friendship would never be enough.

The next several hours drifted by in a daze. Minutes flew by like hours, and yet I couldn't believe it was the afternoon before I finally dragged myself out of bed and stepped into the shower. The water did little to relieve the tension in my body. I wasn't sure if it was from the months working in the barn, the wedding last night, or the physical pain of my heart splitting, but I almost felt worse when I stepped out.

Cozied up in my robe, I tried to read a book—something I didn't normally have the luxury to do—but the words blurred. I slammed it shut and pulled open my laptop instead.

Emails from the last few days piled up, but I didn't have the energy to respond. I flipped on the TV, but the images were too much for my eyes. All I wanted to do was to go back into the bed and cry it out. But even dragging myself down back to my bed felt exhausting, and I wasn't even sure if I had tears left. I was dehydrated and dizzy with fatigue, but when I closed my eyes, I couldn't sleep.

When my phone buzzed and I saw a message from Frankie, I couldn't read it. Contact with her right now would just reinforce that my heartache was real. Besides, nothing she—or I— could say would change the situation. Frankie was leaving, and we would never be together.

I lifted my phone to call Sam and get some solid sibling advice, but depending upon if it was before nap time for the kids, or a rare nap time for himself, his emotional response might not be what I needed. So, I lay back in bed and put on the *Love 'Em or Leave 'Em* podcast.

Different callers left various messages for Ruby. One was a burnt-out mom crushing on the nanny, one a dad who asked how wrong it was to pretend to be in the garage working to avoid dishes, and one a wife supporting her spouse on a new work adventure. The question "do I clip their wings or let them fly" resonated with me. As much as it was killing me right now, at least I would never clip Frankie's wings again. She deserved to fly.

"So, everyone, I'm doing something a little different today." Ruby's voice shifted, and something in the change made me crack my eyes open. "A caller left a message last week but wasn't asking for any advice and instead offering some of their own. For whoever needs to hear this, here's Laurie from Iowa."

I tapped up the volume and wrapped my arms around a fuzzy pillow.

"Hi, Ruby. I'm not sure why I'm calling you, but I really needed to talk to someone. Which I understand is strange since I'm not really talking to you, just leaving a message," the woman with a worn, tired voice started. "Last month, I lost my husband of forty-two years. He was the love of my life, the father of my children, and as the grandkids like to say, my partner in crime—although we were always pretty outstanding citizens and never even got so much as a speeding ticket."

I smiled at the sweet woman and threaded my fingers on the pillow frays.

"We worked hard our whole life and saved for retirement. Felt like we made a lot of sacrifices for this magical retirement number, and we'd always say, 'When we retire, let's take the cruise,' or 'When we retire, let's buy that fancy bottle of wine,' or 'When we retire, let's do date nights on Wednesdays.'"

Her voice cracked and my ears perked.

"And, well, I never quite did feel like we were living in our moment. We got by, day to day, and waited for our time to come. Well, George and I both retired in May. Had a big cake, said goodbye to his job, and was ready to get to the good stuff. We started having date nights on Wednesdays, and we booked a cruise for September."

Her voice cracked again. I didn't know this woman, but my heart tugged for her.

"Well, all that to say is, my George died last month. Was there having supper with me, and the next morning, gone." A sniffle sounded through the speakers. "So I guess, I just really like listening to your podcast but never had a need to write in because George and I had such a good marriage. For forty-two years we talked about all the things we would do. But ya know, we didn't do none of them. And by God, if I could have a do-over, I would not wait for retirement. I would not wait until the kids got older or until the grandkids were born, or until the house was paid off. I'd take that trip, drink that wine, have that date night. So, not sure if your listeners will need this at all, but if you could just tell them, do the things that make you happy *in the moment*. You can figure out the rest later."

I flipped onto my back and stared at the ceiling. *I* was the listener that needed to hear that message, and someday I'd write Ruby Reanne and tell her that. Even in the short term, I deserved happiness. Frankie was leaving regardless, and it was going to hurt like hell no matter if I spent the last days with her or sobbing into my body pillow. At least now, I could spend the time loving the hell out of Frankie, not crying over her departure.

I bolted from the bed and grabbed the phone. When I dialed Frankie, she answered within two rings. "I have an idea."

"Oh yeah?" Frankie said, a smiling hesitation in her voice. "What's that?"

I stuffed my legs into a pair of jeans and grinned into the receiver. "Can you pick me up on your motorcycle in an hour? I need to take you somewhere."

THIRTY
FRANKIE

For four glorious days, I never mentioned New York or dreams or jobs or plans with Morgan. We were living on borrowed time, and we both treated it as such. After Morgan called on Sunday to pick her up on the motorcycle—which in and of itself shocked the hell out of me—we flipped a switch and treated this time like a vacation.

Sunday afternoon, we went for a long motorcycle ride across country roads and ended up at Lake Superior to watch the sun set. On Monday, we took the truck up to Grand Marais, strolled through an art fair, ate a ridiculous amount of cheese curds, and spent the night in the cutest cottage while listening to the frogs outside the window.

After I gave my dad back the motorcycle, and gifted him Peaches's truck, Morgan took over as chauffer. Tuesday and Wednesday were a mirror image. Marathon movies, marathon bedroom time, and more takeout than should be legal. The only time I even left Morgan's side was to pack my suitcase to go back to New York. And now, lying naked in my bed, I absent-mindedly twirled a silky strand of Morgan's hair around my finger as she slept on my chest.

The alarm went off and I choked up while turning it off. *I can't believe this is over.* I slid back into bed. Maybe if I just lay here and didn't move, time would stop. Give us just a few more borrowed moments that I'd pay back when I was older. Morgan stirred against me and I kissed the top of her head. "Sorry, did I wake you?" I was pretty sure she'd been awake as long as me, however, staring at the same spot on the popcorn ceiling.

"No," Morgan whispered.

After our shower, I stuffed my toothbrush in my toiletry bag and zipped it up. My heart was heavy, beating a slow, groggy thump. Leaving felt so different this time. So much more final. Back then, when I left, I knew I could return if I needed. But now, I was selling Peaches's house, accepting my dream job, and leaving the love of my life. Nothing about this felt temporary.

I rolled the suitcases to the door and handed the house keys to Morgan. "Are you sure—"

"Stop." Morgan palmed the key. "Of course I am."

Over our week of bliss, Morgan had said she felt like she owed me for everything I did for the wedding. Even though I'd scoffed, Morgan had insisted and offered to finish getting Peaches's house ready for sale. "It's nothing," she'd said. "I'll get a few guys to move the furniture, give it a good scrubbing, and meet the realtor. We can even FaceTime a walk-through if needed. This will take an afternoon, tops."

Of course, it would take more like a week, but I encouraged her to hire out for anything she needed, and Morgan could just supervise.

I turned to look one last time at the nearly bare house. My gaze traveled the raggedy orange carpet, the faded wallpaper, the scuffed-up floor, and my chest tightened. "Hey, I need a minute by myself," I said to Morgan. I needed a final, solo walk-through and to say goodbye to give me the closure I craved. "Meet you in the car, okay?"

"For sure. No rush." Morgan grabbed a suitcase and opened

the front door. "We still have plenty of time to get to the airport."

Of course we did. When Morgan offered to drive, she calculated an arrival of a solid two and a half hours before departure —even though the Duluth airport only had three airlines, and I had never waited longer than twenty minutes in TSA. But I learned by now, never, ever to question Morgan's punctuality.

The sewing room is where I started my goodbyes. I stared at the faded yellow wallpaper, the bleach stain in the carpet, and the crack on the closet door. "Thank you for the memories," I whispered.

I moved to the pink bathroom with the seashell soap dish and tile and said the same. Through the guest bedroom, Peaches's room, basement, the kitchen, I repeated this statement, each time my heart sealing. The patio was the hardest, though. Scanning the lush green backyard with the huge maples and evergreens, the tire hanging from the rope, and the old shed, my chest ached. No more tears existed in me, otherwise I'm pretty sure I would have bawled. I took one last seat on the swinging bench and breathed. This home would no longer be my comfort space but a lockbox holding my childhood memories. I patted the frame. "Goodbye."

The ride to the airport was almost totally silent. There was nothing more to say. Words about regrets, love, and missing each other didn't need to fill the space. This was an ending. A heartbreaking, gut-wrenching ending of something that could've been, but wasn't.

Much-needed rain started. Good for the town, but the gray and clouds mirrored the dreary sentiments in the car. Morgan turned for the exit to the airport and my breath seized. *I can't do this. I can't let Morgan go again.* My neck pricked with sweat. I swiped my wet palms down my thighs, then gripped the seatbelt that was cutting off circulation. *This* cannot *be the end.*

When Morgan eased the car up to the curb, I clutched her

hand to my chest. "Come with me." I cupped her face, my gaze dashing between her eyes, praying that she'd change her mind. "Please, Morgan. *Please*. I'll do anything. I don't want this to end. I want to do this with you, together. We lost each other before, and we found each other, and this cannot be the end of us." A sob choked in my throat. "I *know* we can make this work. We can do *anything*. Morgan and Frankie against the world, just like old times. You're stubborn, and I'm a fighter, and please..."

Morgan's eyes drooped. She kissed my palm and pressed it to her heart. Tears brimmed in her eyes, a look of sadness and regret contrasting hard with my desperation. "I can't."

"*Please*." My voice cracked and I swiped a tear dripping down my cheek. "I know we can make this work. I've regretted for a lifetime leaving you here, not begging hard enough, not telling you everything. So I'm telling you now. *I love you*. I love you so much that it is killing me inside, the thought of not being around you. I want to be with you. I want you in my life, forever. Please come with me. I can't... I can't do this without you."

Morgan cupped my face back. "You're going to be amazing, you know that? And you're going to be amazing *on your own*." Her lips trembled, but she grinned through it. "You can do anything you set your mind to. Look at what you've done! You made it. You are the top of the top in your profession."

"But—"

"I can't live in your shadows, Frankie. I can't leave Sam and the kids, and my home, my community. I just can't. They've pulled me up when I was at my lowest. They've rallied and carried me. But I believe in you *so fucking hard*. I have *always* believed in you. Don't hold back, okay? Follow your dreams. I promise I will google everything you do." She pressed her forehead into mine and closed her eyes. "I love you. I love you so much that it hurts. Watching you give this up for a life you never wanted, to be trapped in a box that was never meant to hold you, will kill me. I won't do that to you."

I kissed Morgan, hard. There was no sweetness to it, no love, just desperation, pleading. "I love you, too." I opened the door without another word and totally understood when Morgan did nothing else but pop the trunk and look straight ahead until I slammed the trunk shut.

I was doing the right thing. I knew this. But I had no idea it would hurt so fucking much.

THIRTY-ONE
MORGAN

My shaky hands couldn't grip the steering wheel. I clutched it, tried to control the tremors, then pounded against it with my fists. "Why!" I screamed, my heart ripping from my chest. Why did the universe bring Frankie back to my life just to rip her away? What sort of cruel, effed-up joke was this? The back of my throat stung, an unreleased sob tearing into me, as I traveled down the road back to my place.

No, no. I couldn't go home. Frankie's scent would be lingering in the sheets, and I couldn't deal with that now. Maybe never. Maybe I'd have to burn my goddamn house down so I never had to think of her again.

The wipers squeaked against the windshield, leaving streaks of rain. I pressed my palm into my eye socket to wipe the tears. If I didn't get off the road, I was going to get in an accident. My stomach clenched, holding in the guttural cry, burning my insides. I didn't want to talk to Sam, I didn't want to eat, I didn't want to think. But I needed to do *something*.

I jerked the car to the left lane. "Go!" I yelled at a vehicle in front of me. My insides were boiling, a dam about to burst. On autopilot, the car led me to the shore. I screeched to a stop, slammed the doors, and ran to the beach.

The soggy sand squished beneath my feet and I collapsed to my knees, sobbing into my hands. This wasn't real. It couldn't be real. How was Frankie gone again? I cried so long that I didn't know what was rain and what was my tears. Trickles dripped down my chin into my palms, my hair matted to my cheeks.

When there were no more tears left to shed, I plopped down on the wet sand and pulled my knees to my chest. The seizing in my lungs slowed until finally my shoulders slumped.

The rain pelted at the lake and danced on the surface, the tiny ripples the only movement on the otherwise still water. My eyes focused so hard that the water morphed into a mirage. Lake Superior had always been like a big warm mug filled with hot cocoa on a frosty night. I celebrated there, cried there, slept with Frankie for the first time there. Did New York even have freaking lakes? Logically, I knew it did, but that state was as foreign to me as a different country. What did it matter, though? This area was my home, and I'd never give it up.

Digging my fingertips into the sand, I sighed. I gathered a fistful of rocks and tossed them in one by one. Letting Frankie go so she could follow her dreams was absolutely the right thing to do. A no-brainer decision that I'd make a million times over again.

But, God, it hurt. It hurt so much that I knew I'd never recover. The ache in my heart might fade, but it would never leave. Why did this have to be so hard? Life was unfair and cruel, and I was just so goddamn sick of it. Of everything. I hurled a rock with so much force I felt my shoulder pop.

The rock plopped into the water and was quickly swallowed to the bottom. I tossed another, and another. My breaths evened out and my heartbeat slowed. So, Frankie was following her dreams. *What's my dream?* For so long it was building my own business. Then for the last several years, it was keeping that business afloat. The dream shifted into survival, and less about the actual dream. But now, with four new events booked this week, my business would be fine. Everything was looking up.

So, then, what was my *new* dream? I tossed another rock, hoping it would give me clarity. My dream was to be in love, have my own fabulous wedding, and a wife, and maybe a sweet senior rescue dog that we'd nestle between us on lazy afternoons.

But I was *already* in love. So madly, deeply, painfully in love, and I wasn't sure I'd have that same love with anyone else. "GOD!" My scream was muffled against the rain.

Frankie was my dream. Frankie had *always* been my dream.

Was my dream to be with Frankie? And if that was my dream, was I really ready to let that go? I stared at the dock. Almost twenty years ago, I was at a fork-in-the-road decision, and I chose the more practical one. My entire life, I'd been nothing *but* practical. Was I really ready to give this all up? For love? *That's completely asinine. Who throws away everything for love?*

Or! Or, should I give it a shot? Sacrifice one type of life for another. *No... I can't... right?* What the hell was happening here? I could not be considering what I was considering. The emotions of this day, this week, this summer were messing with my head. That was the only explanation for this nagging sensation in my gut. The rain tickled my face, and I blinked off the drops from my eyelashes. *Think clearly.* Now was *not* the time to make a rash decision.

I palmed the rocks and breathed in. My entire life, I used logic to drive my decisions. Ruled by my brain and never my heart. And it fared well for me, for the most part. I was happy, I was loved, I had a great family.

But wasn't I thriving? Did I *need* to be in a relationship to soar? No.

But did I *want* to be in a relationship, a secure one, with someone I knew to my core? Yes. Unequivocally, overwhelmingly, without a damn doubt in my mind, yes. My heart started to pound. *Oh my God... am I actually going to do this?* What would my world look like if I took a chance, a real chance, and chose *love* first?

Fifteen years ago, I made the decision that was best for me at the time. Now I needed to do the exact same thing.

I dropped the rocks and sprinted back to the car, wiping the wet sand from my butt. I squealed out of the parking lot. Yes, the adrenaline was talking, and yes, none of this made sense, and God dammit, maybe this time things didn't need to make sense. Maybe practicality and organization and following clear perfect lines was not my life plan. Maybe I needed more. Deserved more.

"Move!" I yelled at a driver in the passing lane who slogged two miles above the speed limit. I swerved into the middle lane, then back to the left lane, and accelerated.

What was I thinking? This was crazy, right? I'd never been spontaneous, never done something like this, and maybe I could just try. For once, I could do something completely out of the norm and what was expected.

I grabbed my phone. "Dammit." Frankie's phone kept sending me to voicemail, but I tried one more time and finally gave up.

In the airport parking lot, I screeched to a stop. Never before would I have rushed through a place looking like I did, wet clothes, matted hair, beach sand stuck to my backside, but I didn't care. The only thing I cared about was stopping Frankie before she got on that flight. I wrapped a sweatshirt around my waist and sprinted inside. I had exactly twenty-five minutes before the flight left. Just enough to buy a ticket, catch her, and see her reaction in person. Who needed a suitcase and clothes and toiletries when I had *this*?

Thank God the security lines weren't terrible, but my forehead beading with sweat probably put me on the TSA daily watchlist. Five minutes left until boarding, and I ran like I'd never run before, nearly plowing into a toddler who rushed into my line of fire. "Sorry, sorry," I said to the mom, who whipped me a hell of a death stare.

My heartbeat pulsed in my veins. The air in my lungs was almost gone, but who needed air? Who need anything? I had love, for God's sake!

I weaved through people lugging suitcases and strollers and saw Frankie's gate. Finally! Breathless, my eyes scanned the area. The chairs were almost vacant minus a few stragglers, but the line of people holding their boarding tickets was long. Hope burst from my chest. Frankie didn't board yet. I was *sure* of it. The stars aligned, the universe was playing a fate game, the lesbian gods were smiling upon us. I stopped to catch my breath, my body tingling, on fire, and filled with so much joy I could scream. *Where is she?* Maybe the bathroom or grabbing a quick snack?

As the minutes ticked by, my breath evened out. I scanned the crowd. Over and over, I watched the passengers until there were none. When the attendant grabbed the microphone and announced the doors would close, I slunk into a chair. My breath caught in my throat, the intoxicating, thrilling chasing sensation seeped from my body until I was forced back into reality. The finality of it all broke me. It was a beautiful moment, a burst of childlike wonderment, rare impulsivity, and every romance movie I'd ever seen. Somehow, I naively thought I'd just show up at the airport and get on the plane with Frankie, and we'd lead out our merry lives.

But that didn't happen. My heart sank into my stomach.

Frankie was gone.

I propped my elbows on my knees and sunk my head into my hands. Sure, I could get a flight on a different day, actually think through this terribly thought-out plan, but the moment was over. The adrenaline rush subsided. I was never meant to go with Frankie, and I needed this to bring me back down to earth.

Out the window the airplane ascended, taking my dreams with it.

An hour later, I pulled into my garage and shut the door. I dragged myself into a hot shower, then pulled on my pajamas. Despite the intense and swirling emotions of the last few hours, now that I was back home, I knew my actions were a momentary blip. I'd never leave my home.

So now what? I'd get Peaches's house together for Frankie, check in with her about her new job, and then slowly ease myself away until Frankie was a beautiful memory. As much as that killed me, there was no other option.

Even though it was the dead of summer, I dug through my cabinet for tea. The teapot started rattling to life when I heard a car door slam. *Must be the neighbors.* Then, a few footsteps sounded on my porch. My ears perked.

Then, a knock.

I squinted and moved to the door. My heart leaped into my throat. It *couldn't* be. I looked again.

It was.

I dropped my carry-on bag onto Morgan's front steps and gazed at a pajama-clad Morgan standing in her doorway with a dropped mouth and wide eyes.

"I ... No... What are you doing here?" she asked, her hand not leaving her mouth.

A few hours ago, I had the same thought. Although I was asking myself that question as I stared at the gate numbers at the airport. For two hours, I paced that tiny airport, and two thoughts came to mind:

One, I was *so* excited about the job at *Birch & Willow*.

Two, that excitement paled next to the heartbreak of leaving Morgan.

And as much as I didn't want to admit it, I was also not quite ready to leave this town for the New York City hustle. From Zoey's Bakery to the guy who owned the sub shop to Delilah at the flower store, this place had grown on me this summer. It filled a void in me I didn't fully realize I had, made me realize I had been equating this town to my subpar parents and thought they were the same. They were definitely not.

Morgan always said this place was like family, but it took coming back as an adult to experience it myself.

The rain had turned into a soft mist, but I was still getting soaked. Morgan hadn't so much as blinked. "Can I come in?"

"Oh my God. Yes, yes." Morgan snapped out of her trance and tugged me inside. "I just made tea. Want tea? You look cold. I know it's warm outside, though. I've got chamomile and mint and probably some lemon in the back."

Morgan's words were rushed, her eyes darting back and forth like she was daring herself to snap out of a dream.

"No, I'm good." I pushed my bag to the wall with the side of my foot and closed the door.

"Where's the rest of your luggage?" she asked, still unblinking.

"Halfway to New York by now." What a draining day. The last few hours felt like some of the longest of my life. Decisions and methodical thinking were never my specialty. I'd always trusted my gut, and my gut never let me down. Logically, going to New York made sense. Professionally, it made sense. Economically, it made sense. But when my gut kept nipping at me, I had to listen.

After pacing the airport before my flight, I had gone down to baggage claim and watched the luggage carousal spin for two hours. I weighed my options, prayed for clarity, pictured what my life might look like if I stayed here, pictured what it would look like back in New York. Something about going to New York didn't feel right. But *nothing* about leaving Morgan felt right.

Morgan reached for my hand. Her soft touches swiping across my skin snapped me back into focus. "Are you okay?" she asked.

"No," I whispered. It was the truth. My head was pounding, my mouth was dry, my body fatigued. The only thing I wanted to do was to curl up onto Morgan and have Morgan tell me everything would be okay.

Morgan dragged me to the couch and sat down. I hesitated. I was emotionally drained, wanted to rest, but also needed movement. My limbs were bursting with energy, even though my brain was tired. When Morgan crisscrossed her legs and pulled her overstuffed fuzzy pillow into her chest, I exhaled and slid in next to her.

"What happened?" Morgan asked, her voice soft.

Where do I even begin? How do I explain that I took a mental inventory of my entire life from when I was the happiest, to the saddest, from the most fulfilled to the most restless? Or talk about the ping-ponging thoughts, my brain bouncing from past to current to future in no random order, making me dizzy? How my entire life I'd been running and searching, not knowing what it was that gave me the fulfillment I needed.

And I was still chasing. I could feel the tug in me, which swirled the thoughts, but when I was around Morgan, everything quieted. Stilled. I could breathe in a way that I hadn't been able to breathe before. "When I left last time, I knew it was the right decision," I finally said, tugging at my jeans. "It hurt like hell, but there was no doubt in my mind I was making the right decision."

Morgan's eyebrows knitted. We both knew this was the truth, but saying it out loud like this probably didn't feel good for her to hear. But she needed to hear everything, to understand, to be onboard with what I knew was best.

"But this time, it felt so different." I shifted to face Morgan. Oh, those sweet eyes, that soft mouth looking at me like that. Expectant, holding her breath, waiting on my words. I was both so nervous and so calm, and the confusing messages flickered in my brain. "This time, I had so much doubt about what I'm doing, what's best for me, what's best for you... and leaving now is not the right decision."

Morgan's breath hitched. She bit the corner of her lip and shook her head. "It is, though, right? Isn't accepting this incredible job and moving back to New York the best thing for you? You've worked for years for this. A lifetime, really. This chance will not come around again."

Three months ago, I thought that same thing. When the *Birch & Willow* opportunity came up, I even did some of the foo-foo manifesting stuff that Quinn was into. I wanted the job *so bad* I could taste it. Images had flashed of myself on location, hunkered down in front of a massive computer screen to edit, sitting in the ultra-trendy corporate office with other creatives storyboarding about a new campaign. I just knew this was where I was meant to be. But now... I couldn't picture any of it without Morgan. Everything was clouded and dimmed without her there to share this with.

Could I do this alone? Yes. But I didn't want to. I knew what I wanted, who I wanted, and a job was secondary. "If it was the right decision, then why am I so sick over it?" I asked. "Why is the thought of leaving here, leaving you, tearing me up so much?"

"But this opportunity..."

God, I could look into those Caribbean-blue eyes all day. I could watch Morgan iron her clothes and eat her turkey sandwiches, feel her body next to me at night and soak in her feistiness for eternity. I could read Morgan's emails and texts, and follow her color-coded calendar, and take her to get daily ice cream, and dance with her in the kitchen in the morning.

"It's a dream job. It really is. Everything I've worked for my whole adult life." I rested my head on the back of the couch. Quivers started in my chin. I stared at the ceiling and filled my lungs to stop the tremors. When Morgan touched my hand, holding me, the shakes slowed. "But *you*, you are my dream partner." I swiped my thumb on Morgan's silky cheek. "You are the person I want to be with forever. Not taking this job makes me sad, kinda nervous, a little unsure about what my next plan is. But not having you in my life... that's breaking my heart. The idea of not waking up next to you makes me feel like my soul is being ripped from my body and trampled on the floor."

Morgan's eyes welled with tears. Her mouth parted with an *oh*, but no words came out.

"You are my anchor, my sanity, Morgan," I continued. "I can't lose you. I *won't* lose you."

Morgan held my hand pressed against her cheek, her chest flushing with pink. "You can't give up your dreams for me, Frankie. You just can't. I love you too much to let you do that."

Morgan didn't hear the intention in my voice, didn't fully understand. But sitting here, my gut settled, the nagging, biting sensation eased. My heart filled, my spirits lifted, my mind cleared. *This* was where I was meant to be. I had a lifetime to show Morgan I wasn't giving up my dream of working at *Birch & Willow for* Morgan. I was giving them up for myself.

"I *didn't* give up my dreams for you. I swapped them for something better." I cupped Morgan's face, held her with all the intention and promise in the world, and pressed my lips to Morgan. "I traded them for a life with you."

EPILOGUE
FOUR MONTHS LATER

I tapped out the last email for the day, letting Zoey know to increase the cupcake count by another three dozen for an investment firm's holiday event I was coordinating. *Oof.* What a day. Who knew that Olivia's family had such an endless amount of connections? Once Olivia's mom saw the magic we pulled off in such a short amount of time, she tossed my name out to everyone. For the first time in years, I had to turn down a job.

A steaming cup of tea and a plate of cookies were calling my name. I dug through the cupboard to find a mug when my phone rang. I raced back to the desk and my heart skipped a beat at Frankie's name on the other line.

Almost four months had passed since Frankie showed up at my place. Time fluctuated between slogging when Frankie was gone to racing at the speed of light when she was home. Even though Frankie had been traveling for less than a week this past week, I was aching for her to return.

"You know only true sociopaths call first without texting," I said as I lowered onto a barstool.

"Tell me we're past that stage." Frankie laughed. "Just letting you know I'm coming home tomorrow instead of Friday."

"No way!" I didn't know my voice could squeak that loud. "Really? What happened?"

Frankie told me about finishing a shoot early and being able to work late last night with the editorial team to finish a creative review. She barely took a breath while no doubt scrambling to stuff anything she could into her multiple suitcases. Each trip out to New York, Frankie brought an extra set of empty luggage with her to pack more and more of her stuff to bring back home.

Home. In Spring Harbors. Sometimes, I wanted to pinch myself.

"Do not touch the Christmas tree," Frankie said when she finally paused. "I want to be there to put it up."

Oops. But Frankie couldn't be serious, right? Thanksgiving was almost a week ago. I had that baby up the second I polished off the last bite of turkey at Sam's house. "Umm..."

"*You didn't.*" Frankie chuckled. "Just at your place, though, right? Not mine?"

It was still hard for both of us to think of Peaches's place as Frankie's, and it took Frankie until late October to call it "hers." So many changes in such a short amount of time, but I wouldn't have it any other way. Being reunited with my love, my best friend, my partner, completed me.

Against all the protests from me, Frankie called *Birch & Willow* to turn down the job. Although the company ideally wanted Frankie living in New York for in-person creative sessions, turned out they wanted Frankie so much they were willing to work with her to find a solution. They told her to come up with a plan.

Frankie and I worked around the clock, coming up with a pitch that *Birch & Willow* agreed to—an entire series based in small-town Midwest America. Everything from diners to art galleries, from the Boundary Waters to the sun-streaked corn fields in Iowa.

There'd still be a lot of travel, we knew, especially over the holiday season when Frankie was needed in the office for collaborative sessions. So far, this ended up being perfect for Frankie, who missed Quinn and the city, and was one of those weirdos who loved flying. But really, it was a small sacrifice, at least on my end. I'd been single for so long that having Frankie here a little over half the time was just right. And right now, even though Frankie had her house, and I had mine, we already talked about selling my place and me moving into Frankie's. I had no emotional tie to my townhome, but plenty to Frankie's.

Besides, Frankie's house was begging for a remodel. And I itched to take on a project like that again with my love.

I filled the pot with water and fired up the stove. "Is Quinn coming early with you, then? Or taking the original flight?"

"No." An exasperated breath left Frankie. "Seriously, she needs to quit her job, but she'll never listen to me. Her manager revoked her time off. Can you believe that? I don't even understand how that's legal."

"Oh no! Poor Quinn. That's got to be so rough. Can't we just kidnap her or something to get her out of that place?" I tore into a chamomile package. "Someday maybe she'll follow in our footsteps and open her own business."

"I hope so. She's going to come home the following weekend for a few days. I'm going to do everything to convince her to stay and never return to New York." The sound of a zipper rang through the receiver. "A cross-country road trip in a U-Haul with my sis would be so freaking fun. I'm gonna get her drunk tonight and make her sign a contract."

God, I loved Frankie. In every fiber of my being, I knew Frankie was the one. She'd *always* been the one. "That sounds fun and totally illegal. I'll pretend I never heard you say it."

"You know... if we were married, you can't be forced to testify against me in court."

Frankie was teasing, of course. Kind of. We'd talked about it, many times. I knew it was a matter of when and not if. Already a lifetime of wasted moments had passed and neither of us wanted to lose any more. At the same time, we had all the time in the world.

"And you have way better benefits through your company than I do on my own." I grinned and poured the steaming water over the bag. "This is kind of sounding like a win-win situation."

"Definitely." Frankie laughed. "Okay, I've got to go. When I get home, though, can we do that thing we like so much?"

My chest flushed. *I cannot wait until Frankie is home.* "The one thing, or *the one thing?*"

"Definitely that one."

A smile filled me, with more than anticipating a recently found sweet spot we'd been exploring. *Tomorrow, I get to see my person.* My one true love.

I pulled the phone to my mouth. "Done."

A LETTER FROM THE AUTHOR

Hey there!

Thanks so much for reading *The Ex Effect*. I loved introducing you to Morgan, Frankie, Quinn, Zoey, and Ruby Reanne, who will all be characters in the series. I had so much fun writing this book and creating this fictional town in Northern Minnesota, which is heavily influenced by some of my favorite areas in this state—Two Harbors, Duluth, and Grand Marais.

This concept for this book came to me in two ways. One, after listening to some of the hilarious (and sometimes frustrating) stories my niece Megan shared with me about planning her wedding. And two, after living for twenty years in Seattle, I moved my family back to a smallish town in Minnesota and rediscovered the joy of a less rushed, quiet life, low traffic, and sounds of nature. I'm so glad I was able to put this experience into my story.

As I continue to write my sparkly, upbeat romances celebrating queer joy, I'd love to keep you posted about my new releases and bonus content. Please sign up for my newsletter, below. I promise I won't spam you or sell your info.

www.stormpublishing.co/dana-hawkins

I'd be so grateful if you liked this book and wouldn't mind leaving a review. Even a short review can make all the difference in encouraging a reader to discover my books for the first time. Thank you so much!

I consciously choose to write stories where coming out is not an "issue" and being queer is nothing to "overcome." Creating a world where my characters live in a safe, affirming, celebratory space while navigating their relationships and real-life issues fills my heart. I am keenly aware the queer community continues to live in fear and is subject to discrimination, violence, anti-inclusive legislation, and more. I write novels that create a reality I want to be a part of—a hate-free world.

Thanks again for being part of this amazing journey with me! I'd love if you could follow me on Instagram @d.hawkinsauthor and my website www.danahawkins.com Please stay in touch—I have so many more stories and can't wait to share them with you.

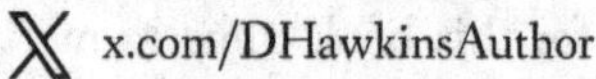

ACKNOWLEDGEMENTS

First and foremost, as always, I need to thank my spouse for continuing to put up with me after all these years and, unequivocally, enthusiastically supporting me and my writing journey. You've taken on extra parent duties, given up date nights so I could write, and given me quiet time when I know you'd rather be doing a fun activity, all to support my dream. There is no way I could ever do this without you.

To my kids, as always, for celebrating and cheering me on. Tanner, Kianna, and Joseph—I love you so much!

To my mom, Esther Dusha, for always being there for me, supporting me in everything I do, and for ignoring when I use the f-word in my books.

To my fabulous critique partner, Jennifer Gatewood, for your constant support, thoughts, pointing out things that both work and don't work, giving me tough love when I need it, and shoulder-shimmying with me during our calls. I appreciate you so much!

To S.E. Reed, my writing confidant. Your friendship means so much to me. Thank you always for supporting me, celebrating with me, and being along every step of this journey. Also, your GIF game is spot on. Thank God for Will Ferrell ;-)

To Megan Kelly, thank you for giving me so much detail about your wedding, and for always answering me, even on my gazillion butt dials. Seriously—I don't know what it is!

To Erica Dusha, thank you for being the best beta reader

ever. I love that you are so honest, so supportive, and that you scream, hug, and celebrate right along with me.

To Hannah Gustafson and Alex Dusha, thank you for all the intel and details you gave me about Duluth and the surrounding areas. Your descriptions and reminders were everything I needed to bring this city to life.

To Emily Gowers, editor extraordinaire. Thank you for jumping on brainstorming calls with me and for being so thorough and kind in your feedback. I've been so proud to be part of the Storm family, and your celebration and thoughtfulness of me as a human and author has been the most wonderful experience.

To "Team Jenna." You all are so freaking amazing. Thank you for the behind-the-scenes support.

And finally, to my agent, Jenna Satterthwaite. Honestly, I pinch myself constantly that out of all the people who want to work with you, you chose me to be on your team. You are an absolute dream to work with, the biggest cheerleader, the fiercest advocate, and the kindest human. Cheers to our first official book together, and many more to come! I cannot wait to see what our future holds.